'I had no right to kiss you,

Cole said, shattering Elise's foolish little fantasy into a million pieces. 'Because nothing can ever come of it... I have nothing to offer a woman—any woman. And you deserve better than that... That's the reason I decided to come clean with you. And the reason you should be honest with *me*, too.'

You may be awfully smart, Cole Hardesty, Elise thought. *But you're dead wrong about one thing. You've got plenty to offer some lucky woman.*

Any woman but me.

Dear Reader,

Welcome! Emilie Richards starts off July's books with her latest HEARTBREAKER title, *Woman Without a Name*. There are so many twists and turns in this that you won't be disappointed by this award-winning writer, no matter how high your expectations!

Next there's a classic on-the-run mother and child story from Kayla Daniels. They find safety and a renewed sense of family thanks to the intrigued and very sexy local sheriff. There's another lawman in Beverly Bird's first Sensation™. John Gunner is irresistible all right—and he knows it! But he doesn't think he's *The Marrying Kind*.

Finally, a completely new author to Silhouette®: please welcome Margaret Watson, who's sent her macho hero off to South America to rescue his woman and his baby. It's the most important mission of his career.

Happy reading,

The Editors

Wanted: Mum and Me

KAYLA DANIELS

First published in Great Britain 1997
Silhouette Books, Eton House, 18-24 Paradise Road,
Richmond, Surrey TW9 1SR

© Karin Hofland 1997

ISBN 0 373 07760 2

18-9707

Printed and bound in Great Britain
by Mackays of Chatham PLC, Chatham

KAYLA DANIELS

is a former computer programmer who enjoys travel, ballroom dancing and playing with her nieces and nephews. She grew up in Southern California and has lived in Alaska, Norway, Minnesota, Alabama and Louisiana. Currently she makes her home in Grass Valley, California.

Other novels by Kayla Daniels

Silhouette Special Edition®

Spitting Image
Father Knows Best
Hot Prospect
Rebel to the Rescue
From Father to Son
Heiress Apparent
Miracle Child
Marrige Minded

To Doris Nuese,
a great aunt in every sense of the word

Chapter 1

"*Mom, look out!*"

Her daughter's warning cry registered on Elise's consciousness the same instant she spotted the long-eared, short-legged puppy come bounding out into the road directly ahead of them.

In the space of an adrenaline-speeded heartbeat, Elise stomped on the brake, wrenched the steering wheel to the right and sent up an urgent prayer that by some miracle she could avoid hitting the poor animal.

The screech of rubber against asphalt filled the air as the rear end of the car slewed sideways. All the rules she'd ever read about controlling a skid raced frantically through Elise's brain, but everything happened so fast, it was all over before she had a chance to put them into practice.

The car veered off the pavement, skidded across the gravel shoulder and launched itself headfirst into the ditch. At the last second, Elise flung out her arm to shield Kelsey from the impact—a purely instinctive reaction, since her daughter was safely buckled into the passenger seat.

The car came to an abrupt bone-jarring, teeth-rattling halt. The engine coughed and sputtered bravely for a few seconds, then stalled. As the dust settled, an eerie silence descended. The only sounds Elise could hear were the tick of cooling metal and the wild thumping of her own heart.

She scrambled sideways in her crazily canted seat. "Peach, are you okay?" she managed to croak out. Her throat felt parched with anxiety and shock.

"Wow, Mom." Kelsey's sage green eyes were as wide as the surrounding desert. "You wrecked the car."

Elise skimmed her hands over Kelsey's body, searching for bumps, bruises or broken bones. The relief that flooded her when she found no sign of injury was indescribable.

Kelsey unbuckled her seat belt and twisted around to peer back over the top of her seat. "What about the puppy? Do you think we hit the puppy?"

"I...don't know. I don't think so." Elise's voice was starting to return to normal. Now that her fear was receding, annoyance was creeping in to take its place. Annoyance at people who let their pets run loose where they could get hurt or killed.

Or cause accidents.

And as soon as she located the dog's owner, she intended to give him a good piece of her—

Darn it.

Elise struggled futilely with the door handle, but the force of the impact had wedged the door shut somehow. She blew an exasperated stream of air through her bangs. Sliding as far away from the door as possible, she proceeded to hurl herself against it with as much momentum as she could muster.

"Ow!" She rubbed her sore shoulder. "Looks like we'll both have to crawl out your side, Peach."

Kelsey was still gazing back toward the road. "I'm pretty sure that dog was a basset hound, don't you think so, Mom?"

"I'm afraid I didn't have much of a chance to identify—"

"If we hit him, can we take him to the vet?"

"Of course, but the first thing we need to do is get out of this—"

"That's what I want to be when I grow up. A veterinarian."

"Yes, I know. Could you please try opening your door?"

"Okay." Due to the vehicle's cockeyed angle, Kelsey had to strain a little to push open the door. "I hope we didn't hit him. But if he's hurt, maybe I could tie a turkey net on him."

"I think you mean tourniquet. And it's not safe to get close to an injured animal. If he's scared or hurt, he might bite." Elise wriggled past the gearshift, crawled on hands and knees over the upward-tilting passenger seat and jumped down to the ground next to her daughter.

"He wouldn't bite *me*," Kelsey said with that unshakable confidence only an eight-year-old is capable of.

"Yes, well, you're not going to have the chance to find out." Elise gnawed her lower lip in dismay as she inspected the damage to their car.

"I don't see him," Kelsey said, scrambling up the side of the ditch. "Maybe we didn't hit him after all."

"Kelsey!" Elise called sharply. "You stay right here by the car!"

"Aw, Mom..." But she obviously recognized the no-nonsense tone in her mother's voice, even though Elise rarely had occasion to use it. Kelsey spread her arms like the wings of an airplane and came zooming back down the sandy slope, golden braids streaming out behind her like twin contrails. She braked to a halt at her mother's side. "Boy, the front of the car's sure smashed in, huh?"

Elise nodded bleakly, absently stroking the top of Kelsey's head. Fixing such extensive damage was going to take a sizable chomp out of her dwindling savings. To make matters worse, she needed the car to get to work.

Despair made her shoulders sag. Just when it had seemed like things were going smoothly at last . . .

"Yoo-hoo! Are you all right?" A heavyset, gray-haired woman came bustling toward them from the house across the road.

"We're fine, thank you," Elise called.

The woman waited for a car to pass before she hurried across the pavement, her apron flapping in the breeze. "I was right in the middle of watching 'Oprah' when I heard this *awful* screech," she said. "Then I peeked out my living room window and saw your car in the ditch." She paused on the gravel shoulder to push her dislodged spectacles back up the bridge of her nose. "Oh, dear," she said, frowning as she got a better look at the situation. "You're most likely going to need a tow truck, aren't you?"

Elise sighed. "'Fraid so."

"Well, just as long as you and your little girl aren't hurt, that's the important thing."

"Or the puppy, either," Kelsey piped up.

"Puppy?" Bewilderment etched a few new lines across the elderly woman's forehead.

Elise's eyes narrowed with the first stirrings of suspicion. "You don't by any chance own a dog, do you?"

"A basset hound," Kelsey chimed in helpfully.

"Dear me, no." The woman shook her tightly permed curls emphatically. "Why, my Chester would *never* put up with having a dog around."

"I see." Chester sounded like a real Prince Charming. "Well, do you and your husband know anyone in the neighborhood who *does* own a dog?"

"Husband?" The woman blinked in confusion.

"Chester," Elise said patiently, wondering if perhaps the woman wasn't a few pegs shy of a cribbage game.

Sudden laughter burbled from her throat. "Oh, Chester's not my husband, dear. I'm a widow."

"Then . . ."

"Chester's my cat."

"Oh." Embarrassed, Elise summoned a weak smile.

Chester's owner beamed back at her and extended a quavering hand. "Dear me, I haven't even introduced myself. I'm Doris Applegate."

Elise clasped the aged fingers gently. "My name is Elise Grant, and this is my daughter, Kelsey. We were just on our way home from school, when . . ." She gestured unhappily at her car. Now she saw that the driver's door was wedged right next to the side of the ditch, which explained why she hadn't been able to open it.

Mrs. Applegate's eyes twinkled with curiosity. "You live out on Saguaro Road, isn't that right?"

It no longer surprised Elise that a complete stranger would know where she lived. Since moving to Tumbleweed, Arizona, six months ago, she'd discovered there were very few secrets in a town of four thousand people. And anyone new in the community was bound to be the focus of much speculation and gossip.

Still, this reminder of how closely people took notice of Kelsey and her came as a nasty jolt. "That's right," Elise replied, injecting a false note of cheerfulness into her voice.

"Well, I'm delighted to meet both of you, although *not*, of course, under these particular circumstances." Mrs. Applegate pursed her lips sympathetically and tsk-tsked at the sight of Elise's car.

"Can I see your cat?" Kelsey asked.

"Kelsey!" Elise shrugged helplessly. "I'm sorry. She's nuts about animals."

Mrs. Applegate chuckled. "That's quite all right, dear." She folded her hands over her apron and bent down to address Kelsey. "Of course you can meet Chester, although I can't promise he'll come when he's called. He's quite the wanderer, that one, and he only comes home when he's good and ready."

"Mom? Can I go see him?"

Elise dreaded having to say no. She knew she was overprotective where Kelsey was concerned, that this instinct never to let her daughter out of her sight was unhealthy.

Having nearly lost Kelsey once, how could she take even the tiniest risk of endangering her child again?

Elise decided to stall. "Mrs. Applegate, would it be too much of an imposition if I asked to use your phone to call a tow truck?"

"Oh, there's no need to do that. The sheriff can radio for one."

Alarm touched Elise with one icy fingertip. "The sheriff?"

"Or one of his deputies, whoever shows up."

Elise fought to keep her voice steady. "But how would—"

"Didn't I mention it? I dialed 911 to report the accident as soon as I saw your car in the ditch."

Icy fingers tiptoed up Elise's spine.

"If we were within city limits," Mrs. Applegate explained, "the police would handle it. But here on the outskirts of town, we come under the county's jurisdiction. The sheriff's department said they'd send someone right away." She craned her neck to peer up and down the highway. "I can't imagine what's taking them so long."

Now icy dread spread its arms, threatening to seize Elise in its clutches. Dear Lord, this was turning into a worse disaster by the minute!

Stay calm, she warned herself. *Think clearly. Get a grip.*

After all, this was only a minor traffic accident. Purely routine. No reason for anyone to get suspicious.

Still, no reason to take chances, either.

"Peach, why don't you go with Mrs. Applegate to see her cat?" Elise suggested, hoping her uneasiness wasn't audible in her voice. "I'll wait here for the sheriff."

Oh, God, please let it be some young, inexperienced deputy, some dumb kid just out of high school....

The thin wail of a distant siren reached Elise's ears.

Apparently Mrs. Applegate hadn't heard it yet. "Thank you so much for taking Kelsey to see your cat," Elise said quickly. "She adores animals—in fact, she wants to be a veterinarian when she grows up. I know she really appreciates your taking the trouble to show her your cat, don't you, Kelsey?" The siren grew louder. Elise's babbling grew a little more frantic. "Go on, Peach. Go see the cat. And take your time."

Please, please, let this be one of those occasions when good old wandering Chester doesn't feel like coming home just yet....

Kelsey cocked her head to one side, tugging doubtfully on a braid and staring at Elise as if she suspected her mother had taken leave of her senses.

"Go on. Have fun!" Elise was sending a furious stream of telepathic messages in her daughter's direction, but obviously they weren't reaching their intended destination.

"I think I'll just stay here with you, Mom," Kelsey said slowly.

Mrs. Applegate perked up her ears. "Oh, I think I hear the sheriff coming."

"Don't you want to see the cat?" Elise practically shoved her precious daughter up out of the ditch and onto the shoulder of the road.

"Yeah, but—"

"Oh, come on. Five seconds ago you couldn't wait to see the cat. Mrs. Applegate's waiting to take you. For heaven's sake, Kelsey, *go . . . see . . . the cat.*"

Finally, one of those unspoken messages must have gotten through. Kelsey hesitated. She was only eight years old, but she was bright enough to know that sending her off alone with a total stranger was definitely aberrant behavior on her mother's part.

She studied Elise's face for a moment, and whatever she saw there finally made her decide. "Well . . . okay. If you're sure it's all right."

"I'm sure." Now Elise could see lights flashing on the sheriff's car as it cruised toward them down the road, cutting arrow-straight through cactus-studded landscape. It was perhaps half a mile away.

Elise grasped Kelsey's shoulders, turned her around and gave her bottom an affectionate, urgent swat. "Scoot!"

Mrs. Applegate took Kelsey's hand as they prepared to cross the road. "We won't be long," she called cheerfully back over her shoulder.

"No hurry," Elise shouted after them, blessing the existence of Chester the Cat. Now, if only he could keep Kelsey occupied and out of sight until this rapidly approaching representative of local law enforcement was gone.

Elise's worried gaze followed her daughter up Mrs. Applegate's front walk. Kelsey had shot up like a weed during the last six months, until she was almost the tallest girl in her third-grade class. Watching her now, Elise felt as if she were seeing her daughter through someone else's eyes. She noted wistfully how all traces of baby fat had vanished, and marveled at the strength and vitality coursing through those long, lanky, constantly moving limbs.

Kelsey's braids danced up and down her back as she skipped alongside Mrs. Applegate—bombarding her with questions, no doubt. Elise's heart contracted in a spasm of love so powerful it made her dizzy. There was nothing on earth she wouldn't do to protect her child.

Nothing.

With mingled anxiety and relief, she watched Mrs. Applegate's front door close behind them just as a white sedan sporting the green emblem of the Creosote County Sheriff's Department pulled up.

The driver veered over to park facing traffic on the shoulder where Elise waited. Gravel scrunched beneath his tires. The siren lowered in pitch, faded, died. Elise's heart began to pound.

Just act natural, she commanded herself. *For heaven's sake, he's not about to fax your description to the FBI over some minor fender bender!*

Not unless you act like you have something to hide, that is.

The emergency lights continued to flash as the driver climbed out of the cruiser, settling his official hat on his head. Despite her nervousness, Elise managed to absorb an amazing number of details about his appearance.

He was tall—six foot one or two, probably. Jet black hair, neatly trimmed. Square jaw, cleanly shaven. Broad shoulders that tested the seams of his tan uniform, and a flat stomach smoothly belted into trousers with perfectly ironed, knife-blade creases.

His dark, metal-rimmed sunglasses concealed his eyes, making him seem even more ominous to Elise in her current jittery state. He angled a brief glance down at her wrecked vehicle as he touched the brim of his hat by way of greeting. His first words were, "You okay?"

"Yes. Thank you. Sir. Officer." *Good going, Elise. Make him suspect you must have crashed while driving the getaway car from a liquor-store heist or something.*

She took a deep breath, but it didn't help. Only made her feel even more light-headed, in fact.

He glanced up from the spiral notebook where he'd apparently been jotting down her license plate number. "I'm Sheriff Cole Hardesty," he said. "And your name is . . . ?" He held his pen poised above a page in his notebook.

Terrific. Just her luck that none other than the sheriff himself would respond to the call about her accident.

"Elise Grant." God, she sounded as breathless as if she'd just run a marathon!

He tipped his hat again. "Pleasure to meet you, ma'am. Address?" He sounded all business.

Elise watched him write down her name and address. His fingernails were blunt, close-cropped, clean. He had big, tanned hands with a light sprinkling of dark hair on the backs. Strong hands. Capable hands. Elise wondered what it might be like to feel those hands . . .

Snapping handcuffs around her wrists.

For God's sake, try to keep your wits about you, she scolded herself. *Remember what's at stake here.*

At the thought of potential danger to Kelsey, Elise's protective maternal instincts took over, restoring some measure of outward calm to her frazzled demeanor. She was able to answer the sheriff's questions about the accident without sounding like some unstable escapee from a lunatic asylum.

"So, you say you swerved to miss hitting a dog, is that correct?"

"Yes."

"See any sign of the dog after the accident?"

"No."

Scribble, scribble went his pen. Elise couldn't help noticing the man was really rather good-looking. Sort of a young Clint Eastwood type. Handsome, terse, impassive. He'd probably be a downright dreamboat, in fact, if he ever smiled. Which didn't seem likely.

"Now, you said this dog might have been a basset hound—is that right?"

"That's what my da— I mean, I think so. I only got a brief glimpse of it when it first darted into the road." Elise swallowed. She'd been so careful to avoid mentioning Kelsey's existence, and here she'd just come close to blowing it.

The sheriff made a three-hundred-sixty-degree survey of their surroundings, as if to confirm for himself that the canine perpetrator was no longer in the vicinity. Elise took the opportunity to secretly study her adversary a little further.

His profile could have been carved out of desert sandstone. His features were rugged, strong, all hard angles and flat planes. His skin had had more than a passing acquaintance with the intense sunlight and dry wind of southern Arizona. From the side, Elise could see behind his sunglasses a little. Judging by the crinkles gathered at the corners of his eyes, she put his age at three or four years older than her own thirty-two.

He projected an air of self-assurance, of patience, of a man confident of his ability to do the job and willing to take the time to do it right. As he scanned the scene of Elise's accident, he came across as observant, thorough, intelligent. And much too good at his job for Elise's comfort.

There wasn't much for him to observe at the moment, however. The houses were few and far between out here on the edge of town. The only thing there was a lot of was prickly pear cactus, which didn't provide much of a hiding place for a wayward pooch.

The sheriff had obviously come to the same conclusion. With a resigned shrug, he turned back to Elise. "Well, maybe I can send someone out to track him down. Be nice if I could have a word with the owners about letting their dog run loose." He aimed his pen at Elise's car. "Could be they might feel a bit inclined afterward to help you out with the repair bill."

"Oh, no, that's not necessary, I assure you. Really." The last thing Elise wanted right now was any more complications from this stupid accident.

The sheriff regarded her thoughtfully for a moment before continuing. "You've got plenty of insurance, then?"

"Er..." Oh, God, what if he somehow took a look at her policy for some reason? Better tell the truth. "I've got to pay a five-hundred-dollar deductible before the insurance kicks in," she admitted.

"Hmm." The sheriff massaged the nape of his neck. He had a disconcerting habit of pausing before he spoke, as if to give Elise a chance to play out a little more verbal rope with which to hang herself. "Seems to me the folks who own that dog have kind of a moral obligation to chip in on that five-hundred-dollar deductible, wouldn't you say?"

"Well, I—"

"At the very least, they owe you an apology."

"Really, it's not neces—" Elise gulped. Just over the sheriff's muscular shoulder, she'd caught a glimpse of Kelsey and Mrs. Applegate coming out of the house. "I mean, it was only a teeny little accident, after all. Not something to make a federal case out of." She gave a nervous chirp of laughter.

Kelsey was sauntering down Mrs. Applegate's front walk, grinning from ear to ear and carrying an enormous marmalade cat that was nearly as big as she was.

"I'm sorry you even had to come out here for such a silly little thing," Elise rushed on, "and I'd hate for you to waste any more of your time trying to track down that puppy." She started backpedaling toward her car. "So I'll just be on my way now, and you can get back to what I'm sure are far more important duties."

The sheriff probed his cheek with his tongue and regarded her silently for few seconds. Then he nodded at her car. "You won't get very far in *that* thing."

"What?" Elise whirled around. "Oh." She'd almost forgotten that she was stranded here with no quick means of escape. One painful glance was enough to remind her. Her poor, crumpled car wasn't going anywhere for the time being, except behind a tow truck.

Kelsey and Mrs. Applegate were about to cross the street. Elise couldn't shoo them back with hand signals or wild facial contortions without alerting the sheriff to their presence.

A moment later, it didn't matter, anyway.

"Yoo-hoo! Hello, Sheriff!" Mrs. Applegate sang out as they started across the road.

The sheriff turned. Elise closed her eyes in dismay. "Mom, lookit Chester!" Kelsey called happily.

The sheriff swung slowly back around to peer at Elise. She offered him a feeble smile. *"Mom?"* he echoed in a stern voice.

Draped across Kelsey's arms, the cat yawned.

The sheriff drew his sunglasses down his nose so he could stare accusingly at Elise over the tops of them. "You didn't mention anything about your daughter being with you, as I recall."

Elise arched her brows in surprise. "Didn't I?"

"Slipped your mind, is that it?"

"No, of course not." Elise gave a little dismissive flip of her hand. "I didn't figure it was important, I guess. After all, it's not as if she had anything to do with the accident."

"Hmm." The sheriff continued to study Elise with a speculative expression that made her squirm. What she wouldn't give right now for a nice, urgent, bank robbery call to come over his radio!

"Sheriff, how nice to see you!"

Elise mentally blessed Mrs. Applegate for providing at least a momentary distraction.

The sheriff tucked his sunglasses into the breast pocket of his uniform and dipped his head in her direction. "How're you today, Miz Applegate?"

"Why, I'm just fine, thank you." She patted her hair. "I was a bit surprised to see *you* pull up. I assumed the dispatcher would send one of your deputies."

"Well, I was close by, so I responded to the call myself." He shifted his attention to Kelsey. "That's some cat you've got there, miss."

Kelsey beamed at him. "His name's Chester. He belongs to Mrs. Applegate, but she said I can come play with him whenever I want."

"That so? Well, Miz Applegate's a real nice lady." He scratched Chester behind the ears. "My name's Sheriff Hardesty. What's yours?"

Elise held her breath.

"Kelsey Grant."

Elise's knees went weak with relief.

"Well, Kelsey, I hear you and your mom had a little accident this afternoon."

"Boy, did we ever! A dog ran out in front of us, and then we drove off the road, and then *bam!* All my schoolbooks went flying." Her braids swirled as she shook her head in amazement. "It was pretty neat."

Sheriff Hardesty chuckled.

Wonder of wonders, thought Elise, *the man can actually smile!*

Amusement mellowed his entire face, from the sexy crinkles around his eyes to the stalwart slope of his jaw. For some reason, Elise found it unsettling to discover that his smile made him even more handsome than she'd predicted.

Chester the Cat apparently hadn't appreciated Kelsey's vigorous narration of the accident as much as the sheriff had. He started to wriggle in Kelsey's embrace and, despite her best efforts to hang on to him, performed a twisting jackknife dive out of her arms.

"Just let him go, dear," Mrs. Applegate advised as Chester beat a hasty retreat into the protective tangle of some nearby creosote bushes. "He'll be all right. I'm amazed he let you hold him for as long as he did."

"My mom says I have a way with animals," Kelsey said, gazing regretfully at the bushes where Chester had disappeared.

"I'd say your mom's right." The sheriff winked at Kelsey and clicked his tongue in admiration. "I've known old Chester a long time, and you're the first person besides Miz Applegate he's ever let hold him that way, far as I've ever seen."

"Really?" Kelsey's chest puffed out with pride. "I'm going to be a veterinarian when I grow up, you know."

"Yeah? Well, I bet you'll be a darn good one." His eyes twinkled as he glanced at Elise over the top of Kelsey's head. "I'll send you a copy of the accident report for you to submit to your insurance company."

"Thank you." Elise looked directly at him for the first time since he'd removed his sunglasses. The vibrant intensity of his blue eyes was astonishing, as if the brilliant color of the cloudless sky above had somehow been collected and distilled into a deeper, richer hue.

There was something compelling about those eyes, about the way he kept looking at her. Elise was surprised to find herself drawn to him, to feel the first faint stirrings of a connection between them.

He was undeniably attractive, of course. And he'd petted the cat and been nice to her daughter. But it was something more fundamental that called to her, an intriguing undercurrent Elise didn't understand.

She forced herself to break eye contact, to sever that momentary, mysterious connection between them. She couldn't risk any mutual attraction, couldn't afford to become even casually involved with a man.

Especially not a cop.

"I'll call in for a tow truck," he said.

Elise nodded, avoiding his glance.

But her gaze trailed him irresistibly as he strode back to his car. At all costs, she had to steer clear of this tall, handsome sheriff from now on. He might be a man of few words, but Elise had the feeling he saw way too much.

The more contact she had with him, the greater the chance he might casually start picking at some loose thread in her life, keep on tugging at it, and eventually unravel her secret.

And just what would this dedicated, no-nonsense cop do if he ever discovered that Elise and her eight-year-old daughter were fugitives from the law?

Chapter 2

Cole guided the sheriff's cruiser onto Saguaro Road and wondered why in blue blazes he was going out of his way. Not that Creosote County was exactly what you'd call a hotbed of criminal activity, but surely he could have found a more productive use of his time and the taxpayers' dollars than running a delivery service.

He scanned the addresses on the mailboxes until he found the one he was looking for. The house, a small, neat, Spanish-style stucco with a red-tiled roof, was set a couple of hundred feet back from the road. Cole followed the curving gravel driveway past the usual hodgepodge of desert plant life—mesquite, agave, prickly pear, several varieties of cholla cactus. In the wake of last week's thunderstorm, a lot of the short-blooming spring wildflowers had made an appearance, so tiny blobs of orange and yellow and blue dotted the otherwise drab landscape.

Behind the house, a low ridge of hills was outlined in red and gold neon, courtesy of the setting sun.

After Cole switched off the engine, his was the only vehicle parked near the house. The carport to one side was empty. The tow truck driver or someone from the garage would have given Elise and her daughter a ride home.

Cole wondered how long it would take them to fix her car. Kind of tough being stranded way out here without one. How would Kelsey get to school in the morning? The budget of the small Tumbleweed school district didn't include money for a bus.

What about Elise? Did she have a job to get to? Cole assumed she worked, since she hadn't mentioned a husband this afternoon. Of course, she hadn't mentioned a daughter, either, until one unexpectedly popped up.

Kind of peculiar, that.

Then he decided that neither Elise Grant's peculiarities nor her transportation problems were any of his business.

So why was he here?

With a grimace of impatience, Cole grabbed the file folder off the passenger seat and jammed his hat onto his head. After a second's hesitation, he took it off and tossed it into the car. Smoothing his hand over his hair, he strode up two broad flagstone steps and came eye to eye with a bronze door knocker shaped like an eagle.

He used it.

Ceramic wind chimes dangling from a beam near the door tinkled faintly as a listless breeze stirred them. Cole crossed his arms over his chest, then uncrossed them again. He shifted his weight from foot to foot. He strained his ears for the sound of footsteps, but it was hard to hear anything on the other side of the sturdy oak door.

From the corner of his eye, he spotted a vaguely face-shaped blur at the window. It ducked out of sight before he had a chance to identify it.

Then he heard the metallic rasp of a dead-bolt lock being slid back. Another rasp. *Two* dead bolts. Most people around here hardly bothered locking their doors even when they went to bed at night.

The door swung open slowly, reluctantly. Elise Grant appeared in the narrow gap she allowed between the door and its frame. "Sheriff Hardesty," she said, her eyes focusing somewhere past his shoulder. "What brings you out this way? Something about the accident?"

She wore a red sweatshirt over jeans, and her feet were bare. Her shoulder-length blond hair had been tied back into a ponytail, making her look more like a college coed than a woman the age listed on her driver's license.

Cole managed to take in all those details without acting like he was giving her the once-over. Or so he hoped, anyway.

He handed her the slim folder. "I figured since I was in the neighborhood, I'd bring by that copy of the accident report for your insurance company. Maybe speed things up a little."

"Why... thank you." She accepted it from him as if he were one of those street hustlers who stick a useless item into your hand and then expect a donation. "You, er, shouldn't have gone to the trouble."

"No trouble," Cole said, even though he'd never bothered to hand-deliver any of the *other* traffic reports he'd written up during his career. "Like I said, I was patrolling out this way, anyway." Which wasn't strictly true.

"You were?" Surprise feathered her brows upward. "I mean, you were on duty this afternoon, and I just figured by now you'd be... off." Her cheeks bloomed a delicate pink. It took Cole a second to realize that she was embarrassed to admit she'd been thinking about him.

Maybe it hadn't been such a waste of time coming out here, after all.

"I generally put in a few extra hours a day. Not at tax-payers' expense, of course," he hastened to add. "Just on my own."

"You must be...very devoted to your job." She sounded a bit disappointed. No, more like worried. Concerned that a workaholic might not have time for a social life?

Naw, he was probably reading way too much into her re-action, wanting her to be interested in him.

Cole didn't bother explaining the reasons for working those long hours. That burying himself in his work was a way of holding unhappy memories at bay. That it was a way, perhaps, to someday atone for his tragic failure.

That it was a way for Cole to avoid spending his evenings alone, in a house empty of everything but a few pieces of thrift-shop furniture and the inevitable guilt that rose up to haunt him whenever he had nothing to do but sit and stare at the four walls.

"Well," he said, clearing his throat. "I guess I should be..."

A pair of inquisitive green eyes peeped over Elise's left shoulder. Elise jumped as if someone had snuck up behind her and yelled "Boo!"

She flicked an uneasy glance at Cole before stepping aside. "Peach, I thought you were doing your homework."

"Finished it." The little girl clasped her hands behind her and rocked back and forth on her heels. "Hi, Sheriff!"

"Hello, Kelsey."

"Didja find that puppy yet?"

One side of Cole's mouth tugged up in a grin. "Nope, not yet. Don't you worry, though." He cocked an imaginary pistol at her. "I've got my best man working on it."

Kelsey tilted her head to one side. "Who's that?"

Cole clapped his hand to his heart and looked wounded. "Why, *me,* of course."

Kelsey giggled. The sound tickled his ears.

Elise nibbled a frown. "You're not serious, are you? I hope you're not wasting any more of your time looking for that dog."

"Well, I must admit, I'm kind of a stickler about not leaving any loose ends lying around." Cole stroked his jaw. "Or, in this case, any loose dogs running around." Okay, okay, maybe that was a pretty lame joke, but she could at least have given him a polite smile.

Instead, the furrows creasing her forehead only deepened.

"I wish *we* had a dog," Kelsey announced. "Then I could feed him, and take him for walks, and play with him after school."

"And what would the poor thing do all by himself during the day while you're at school and I'm at work?" Elise propped a hand on one slim hip and cocked an eyebrow at her daughter.

"Umm..." Kelsey chewed the end of one of her braids. After some consideration, she said, "He could watch TV!"

Elise rolled her eyes and swatted her daughter lightly on top of her head with the file folder. Cole got the impression this was a familiar routine the two of them had down pat. Obviously, the subject of getting a pet had come up before.

Despite their differing viewpoints on the matter, mother and daughter stood there grinning at each other with such fond affection, Cole started to feel like an intruder.

An odd restlessness stirred in his chest. Cole examined it, sifted through possibilities, and was surprised to identify it as envy. It had been a long time since he'd shared that kind of intimate relationship with someone—the kind where two people know each other so well they practically share their own secret language.

It had been a long time since he'd cared about another human being with the kind of deep, unswerving devotion Elise and Kelsey obviously had for each other.

Cole had told himself it was better that way, better to shield himself from any messy emotional attachments that could only end in grief and suffering.

Why, then, did he suddenly feel like a little kid with his nose pressed against the candy-store window, observing the love between mother and daughter with an envious longing that practically made his mouth water?

Maybe he was just getting sentimental in his old age. And after what Cole had been through, some days he felt positively ancient.

He coughed into his fist. "Ah, guess I'll be going."

When Elise and Kelsey turned to look at him, Cole was struck by the strong resemblance between them. Both had the same fine bone structure, the same pert nose, the same green eyes. Kelsey's hair was slightly darker, the color of summer wheat, in contrast to her mother's paler corn silk shade.

They could have been sisters, instead of mother and daughter. It was plain they were friends, as well.

The teasing affection on Elise's face evaporated, replaced by something that might be relief. Hard to get a handle on what exactly she was feeling . . . or why.

"Thank you for bringing the accident report by," she said, already moving to close the door. "I sure appreciate your going to so much trouble." She didn't really *look* much like she appreciated it, though.

"Like I said, it was no trouble." Cole raised a hand to tip his hat in farewell, then remembered he'd left it in the cruiser. He changed direction at the last second and scratched his head instead, feeling about as clumsy and self-conscious as a teenage kid on his first date.

"I hope you find the puppy," Kelsey called after him as he backed down the steps.

"I'll give it my best shot," Cole replied. He climbed back into the cruiser, feeling vaguely dissatisfied by the whole encounter. Like someone had whetted his appetite by setting a delicious-looking meal in front of him, but once he dug in, he discovered it tasted like sawdust.

Well, what had he expected, anyway? An invitation to come on inside, watch a movie and share a big bowl of popcorn with them?

By the time he'd swung the car around in a U-turn to head back down the driveway, the front door was already closed. Cole was willing to bet those two big dead-bolt locks were firmly slammed back into place, too.

Elise leaned back against the door, knees sagging with relief. Her heart was pumping as if she'd just finished an aerobics class. She fanned her face with the copy of the accident report. Whew! She certainly hoped she'd seen the last of Sheriff Cole Hardesty.

Mr. Overtime. Mr. No-Loose-Ends. The last thing she needed was to arouse his suspicions and get *him* nosing around in her past.

Still, it *had* been rather thoughtful of him to bring the report out to her in person. Even though *his* person was almost the last one Elise had wanted to find waiting on her doorstep.

She should have invited him in. Maybe it looked funny that she hadn't. People around here were a lot friendlier than they were in the big city. Probably the normal response would have been to offer him coffee or lemonade or something.

She should have acted a bit more sociable. But she didn't want to encourage his interest in the slightest.

If he had any interest in her, that is. Which he probably didn't.

Feeling a bit calmer, Elise deposited the file folder on the counter that separated the dining room from the kitchen. She tapped her nails on the earth-toned ceramic tiles. She was going to have to have a talk with Kelsey.

To fortify herself for the dreaded ordeal, she got a diet soda from the refrigerator and padded into the living room, where Kelsey was sprawled across the floor on her stomach, watching a nature documentary on TV.

"You *did* finish your homework, I presume?" Elise asked in a stern tone.

Kelsey's thin legs scissored in the air behind her. "Mom, I already *told* you I finished it, remember? When the sheriff was here." Her eyes remained glued to the screen, which was currently showing some sort of acrobatic insect-mating ritual.

"Oh, that's right," Elise mumbled. She'd been so disconcerted when Kelsey had popped up at her shoulder, it was no wonder she'd forgotten what her daughter had said.

Which brought her to the matter they needed to discuss now.

She lowered herself onto the couch, reached for the remote control on the coffee table and switched off the TV.

Kelsey's braids whipped through the air as she spun her head around. "Hey!"

Elise set the remote back on the table. "Peach, I'm sorry, but I need to have your undivided attention for a few minutes."

Instantly, Kelsey's face darkened like an ominous thundercloud. "Uh-oh. What'd I do now?"

Elise hid a smile behind her soft-drink can. She rarely had to discipline Kelsey for any reason. But judging by Kelsey's expression, an observer would guess that Elise regularly locked her in her room and sentenced her to a diet of stale bread crusts and water.

Then Elise's smile faded. During the last few months, their lives had settled into a blessedly normal routine. Kelsey had her school and her new friends, Elise had her job at the café. They'd found a house to rent that they both loved, and for the first time in two years, Elise had dared to hope that maybe, just maybe, they'd finally found a permanent place to call home.

No more frantic flights in the middle of the night, leaving behind all the unnecessary possessions accumulated since their last move.

No more trails of short-term neighbors and acquaintances left wondering what had ever happened to that nice Elise Grant and her daughter. *Kept to herself, she did, but her daughter was awful cute and friendly. Just packed up and left one day, without a word.*

Elise sighed. She hated to churn up the serene sea of the last six months by bringing up any reminder that their lives *weren't* normal.

But it had to be done.

"Come sit up here beside me," she said, patting the cushion.

Kelsey scrambled to her feet and warily approached the couch. Elise's heart constricted in a painful spasm. She *hated* having to live like this, like criminals. But they had no other choice.

She draped an arm around her daughter's shoulders and gave her a reassuring hug. "Peach, remember what I've said to you before about not answering the door? About not following me to the door when *I* answer it?"

Kelsey twirled a braid around her finger and avoided her mother's eyes. "Uh-huh."

"But this evening, after I answered the door, you came to the door, too."

Kelsey's lower lip pushed out a little. "It was only the sheriff. *He* won't hurt us. Sheriffs are s'posed to be the good guys, aren't they?"

"Yes, they are." Once again, Elise found herself walking the uneasy tightrope of explaining to Kelsey why they sometimes had to follow rules that didn't make sense. How you could be on the wrong side of the law, but still be doing the right thing.

She didn't want to alarm Kelsey needlessly by cautioning her that the sheriff, though certainly one of the good guys, could also create some very bad problems for them.

"The point isn't who was at the door," Elise said, setting her soda can on the coffee table. "The point is that you broke the rule about not ever following me to the door when I answer it."

Kelsey kicked her dangling heels against the couch. "I knew it was the sheriff," she muttered. "I reco'nized his voice."

Elise stroked her daughter's rigid back. "This time it was the sheriff at the door," she said soothingly. "But next time it might be somebody else."

Kelsey stopped banging her heels and looked over her shoulder at Elise. "You mean that man who's trying to kill me?" she asked matter-of-factly.

Elise gasped as if someone had punched her in the stomach. "How did you—what makes you—I mean, where on earth did you ever get that idea?" Dear God, she'd always done her best to shield Kelsey from the ugly, awful truth of their situation by implying that *both* of them were in hiding from some vague, unnamed person with vague, unnamed motives.

Kelsey shrugged. "I figured it out." Like she was talking about a multiplication problem in school.

Elise made a heroic effort to conceal her distress. "When?" she asked, sounding as if she had a lump of clay lodged in her throat.

Kelsey shrugged again, reminding Elise how fragile her narrow young shoulders were. Too fragile to be forced to carry the terrible burden that unlucky circumstance had laid upon them. "After I started third grade," Kelsey said. "I just figured it out. Like a puzzle."

Some puzzle. A terrible, dangerous, unfair nightmare of a puzzle.

"It's that man I saw in the woods, isn't it?" Kelsey asked. "The one I saw dragging that other man."

Elise nodded. "Yes," she said through lips that felt icy-numb.

They'd been living in a rural suburb of Boston, in the house Elise and her late husband, Tom, had purchased as newlyweds. Kelsey had been six years old. She'd spotted a bunny hopping across their backyard and had followed it into the woods. She wasn't supposed to go there alone, but her enchantment with the rabbit had made her completely forget her mother's warnings.

She'd finally lost sight of the bunny, but through the leafy trees, had caught sight of something else.

"That man he was dragging," Kelsey said. "He was dead, wasn't he?"

Elise swallowed. "Yes, he was, Peach." Obviously, the time had come to tell Kelsey the whole truth. If she was old enough to figure most of it out by herself, she was old enough to handle the unpleasant details.

Or so Elise hoped. But she wasn't going to lie to Kelsey. If she asked for answers, Elise would provide them. Maybe it would even be better in the long run, if Kelsey understood the full nature of the danger she was in.

"I guess that big man with the beard killed him, huh?"

Victor Dominick. Boston's most powerful, ruthless gambling boss. He'd just murdered his underworld rival, Eddie Buchanan, stuffed the body in the trunk of his car and driven to a secluded, wooded area outside the city.

The perfect place to dispose of the evidence. Except that, unbeknownst to Dominick at the time, a little girl had watched him bury the body.

"That's what the police think," Elise said. "That's why they wanted you to testify at his trial. Because you saw him clearly enough to identify him."

After Kelsey had found her way home and her frantic mother had calmed down enough to listen to her story, Kelsey had told her about seeing a big man in a suit burying something in the woods. Elise had thought it odd enough to investigate, so Kelsey had led her mother by the hand back through the trees.

The minute Elise had spotted what looked like a recent grave, she'd called the police. And she'd regretted that phone call ever since.

"You were the only person who could connect the man to the murder," Elise explained. The Boston district attorney's office hadn't exactly been thrilled that convicting their longtime nemesis depended on the testimony of a six-year-old witness. But they'd been after the slippery Dominick for years. They would do whatever it took to nail him.

"That's why we had to move to that new apartment right away," Elise said. "The police were trying to hide us, so that Dominick wouldn't try to hurt you, to stop you from testifying against him."

"Dominick," Kelsey said thoughtfully, as if another piece of the puzzle had slipped into place.

"Victor Dominick." Elise had the urge to spit, as a foul taste filled her mouth. "That's his name."

Kelsey drew her legs up on the couch and sat cross-legged, as if Elise were telling her a story around a camp fire. "So how come I never got to test—tes-ti-fy?"

Elise brushed Kelsey's bangs out of her eyes, noticing as she did so that her fingers were trembling. "Do you remember that day, out in front of your new school, when that car almost hit us?"

"Uh-huh."

The policeman assigned to escort Kelsey to and from school every day had left them for just a moment when he spotted a disturbance halfway down the block involving fists and lots of screaming.

A diversion, as it turned out. Because fifteen seconds after he left, a big black car with rusted paint and thick, sooty smoke pouring from its exhaust pipe had come roaring around the corner.

Thank God that Elise had always insisted on accompanying the cop whenever he picked up Kelsey. As the engine noise grew louder, Elise had whirled around in time to see the car heading straight for them.

At the last second, as the car had jumped the curb and the full horror of what was happening had struck her, Elise had managed to whisk her daughter safely out of its path, with a mere six inches to spare.

She would never forget the sight of that huge black monster filling her vision, its ferocious roar nearly deafening her, its noxious fumes assaulting her nostrils.

"Was that Dominick in the car?" Kelsey asked, yanking Elise back to the present.

"Probably not," she answered, dabbing a film of sweat from her brow. "But it was someone he paid to hurt us. Just like he paid those men to have a fistfight up the block, so the policeman who was guarding us would leave us unprotected for a little while."

"Oooh," Kelsey said in a knowing voice. "I get it. Dominick was trying to kill me so I couldn't be a witness at his trial, and maybe send him to jail."

The way she said it, as if she'd just figured out the plot of a TV cops-and-robbers show, nearly broke Elise's heart. As it had so many times in the past, a bitter brew of outraged injustice boiled up inside her.

It was so horribly unfair, that her brave little girl should have to face up to such grim realities, when all she should have to be worrying about were things like spelling tests and hopscotch!

Elise hauled Kelsey onto her lap and wrapped her arms around her tight. "That's when I knew that the police just couldn't protect you, Peach. That's why we had to run away."

Kelsey plucked at her mother's sleeve. "What about all those other times we had to move?"

Elise envisioned all the places they'd lived during the last two years as a blurred procession of city limits signs.

Chicago...Kansas City...Nashville...Boise...Houston.

And now, Tumbleweed, Arizona.

"We kept on moving because after we'd be in a new city for a couple of months, I'd start to worry that Dominick might find us."

"How come?"

Elise rubbed her temple. "I don't know, exactly. We'd be walking down the street and I'd think I saw someone following us. Or the phone would ring, and when I'd pick it up, no one would be there."

Kelsey shivered. "So then we'd have to move."

Elise pressed her cheek against the top of Kelsey's head. "I know it's been tough on you, honey. Probably Dominick hadn't even found us at all. But I just couldn't take the chance."

It wasn't only Dominick Elise was worried about. The Boston district attorney's office had no doubt been furious to discover their star witness had flown the coop. They would have immediately broadcast word to law enforcement agencies all over the country, warning them to be on the lookout for Kelsey.

If an alert cop should happen to discover Elise's and Kelsey's true identities, the D.A.'s office would drag Kelsey back to Boston and force her to testify.

Except that Victor Dominick would never let her live that long.

Elise thought of Cole Hardesty, and that thoughtful, intelligent gleam in his eye. She'd seen instantly that here was a man who did his duty, and did it well. That was why she would have to avoid him completely from now on.

In spite of those shivery stirrings of attraction that seemed to nudge her toward him whenever they came face-to-face.

Especially because of those stirrings.

"Mom, are we gonna have to move away from Tumbleweed, too?" Kelsey was trying to sound casual, but Elise detected the anxiety in her voice.

She smoothed back Kelsey's bangs. "Do you like it here?"

Kelsey nodded enthusiastically. "I like my teacher, and I like my friends, and I like our house, and now I have Chester to go visit!"

Elise smiled. "Well, I like it here, too."

"Then we can stay?"

The hope in her daughter's eyes struck Elise like a rebuke. She would give *anything* not to have to uproot Kelsey again.

Her smile disintegrated. "I just don't know, Peach. I *hope* we can stay here for good, but..."

Her voice trailed off as she pictured Cole Hardesty's probing blue eyes, the skeptical slant of his dark brows, the determined set of his square jaw.

For some reason, she and Kelsey seemed to have aroused his interest. An interest that might eventually prove fatal.

"It just depends," Elise hedged, wishing she could promise Kelsey there would be no more spur-of-the-moment moves, that at last they'd found a permanent place to call home. "We'll just have to take it a day at a time, and hope for the best."

Kelsey straightened her spine. "Don't worry, Mom." She curled her lip scornfully. "That creepy old Dominick isn't going to find us." She wriggled off Elise's lap. "And you know what I'm gonna do if I ever see him? I'm gonna call the sheriff, that's what."

The prospect of Victor Dominick ever coming near her darling daughter made Elise shudder. "Just remember what we talked about, okay?" She wagged a scolding finger in front of Kelsey's button nose. "When someone comes to the door, *you* stay out of sight, young lady."

"Okay, Mom. I promise." She made a crisscrossing motion over her chest. "Cross my heart and hope to die."

Maybe it was just the ominous, unintentional irony of Kelsey's vow. But after her daughter went back to watching the nature program, Elise's thoughts drifted to the well-used road atlas tucked away on a shelf in her bedroom closet.

For the first time in months, she was haunted by the uneasy suspicion that it might be time to start putting some of those highway miles between the Grant family and Tumbleweed, Arizona.

Elise hated the thought of moving on. She'd come to appreciate and enjoy Tumbleweed's small-town environment, its desert scenery, warm climate and friendly people.

The only thing about it that bothered her, in fact, was its handsome, observant, all-too-competent sheriff.

Chapter 3

Cole felt warm, panting breath on the back of his neck. Followed by a cold, damp nose and wet, slurping tongue.

"Aaughh!" He squirmed to escape out of range, nearly veering the car off the road in the process. "Quit slobbering all over me, will you?" He wiped the slime off his neck in disgust. "I told you to stay down. Down!"

The puppy ignored him. Cole regretted the cruiser wasn't equipped with one of those steel mesh screens between front and back seats. Considering how rarely the Creosote County Sheriff's Department had cause to transport dangerous criminals, Cole had figured it wasn't worth the expense to install protective dividers in the department vehicles.

But that was before he'd known he was going to be playing chauffeur to a drooling, disobedient, extremely demonstrative basset hound.

Long, drooping ears tickled the skin just above the collar of Cole's uniform. He gritted his teeth and made another useless attempt to swat the dog away. This whole crazy escapade was probably going to be a waste of time, anyhow.

Cole told himself he was just trying to be nice to a little girl. But he'd never been much good at self-deception. Truth was, the dog was also a convenient excuse to see Elise Grant again.

Cole couldn't quite put his finger on what it was about her that intrigued him so. She was a knockout, for sure, but he'd met plenty of attractive women before. Must be some truth to that old saying about men in uniform, because a lot of those women had sure made it plain they wouldn't object to a little off-duty fraternizing.

Elise Grant, apparently, was immune to his uniform.

Was that it? Did she simply represent a challenge to the old male ego? Maybe Cole was only attracted to her because she seemed indifferent to him.

No, not indifferent. He made her nervous for some mysterious reason.

And Cole *hated* mysteries.

He hadn't been able to get Elise Grant off his mind since meeting her three days ago. That in itself was a mystery. For four years, Cole hadn't felt the slightest desire to pursue a woman. He hadn't felt much desire, period.

Not since Laura died.

This unexpected rekindling of sexual awareness had caught him off guard and made him edgy. It had him tossing and turning between the sheets at night.

Cole didn't much like *that,* either.

He'd done a little detective work during the last day or two. Besides tracking down the dog, that is.

"Cut that out, you mangy mutt!" he yelled as the dog started snuffling at his neck again. Cole tried to elbow him back, but the puppy ducked aside and began happily lapping at Cole's ear, his tail whisking to and fro against the back seat.

Cole resigned himself to enduring the exuberant display of affection, and tried to concentrate on what he'd learned recently about Elise Grant and her daughter.

At Tumbleweed Elementary School, he'd found out Elise had registered Kelsey in the third grade there last September. Some problem about previous school records, though. They'd gotten lost in the move, and Elise had promised to obtain replacement copies as soon as possible.

According to the school secretary, she hadn't gotten around to it yet.

No husband or father in the picture, either, it seemed. The secretary had the impression the Grants had moved to Tumbleweed from Minneapolis, and also recalled that Elise currently worked as a waitress at the Sagebrush Café downtown. Cole normally frequented a rival establishment for his meals and coffee breaks, which explained why he'd never run into Elise before her minor accident the other day.

The cause of that particular accident now started whimpering in Cole's ear.

"Hold on, we're almost there," Cole muttered. The dog lost his balance and skidded sideways on the back seat as Cole turned into Elise's driveway.

Maybe he should have checked to make sure Elise was even home, or whether she worked Saturday mornings. But Cole would have bet a week's pay that she scheduled her work shifts to coincide with Kelsey's schooltime.

Sure enough, there they both were, working in the yard. The sun simmered overhead in a brilliant lapis lazuli sky, baking the spring moisture out of the desert soil. Elise was on her hands and knees pulling weeds when Cole drove up. Though she subdued it quickly, there was no mistaking the dismay that flickered across her face when she saw him, like the shadow of a hawk's wing.

Kelsey was crouched down across the yard. She straightened up at the sight of Cole's car, clutching a fistful of wildflowers. Like her mother, she was clad in shorts and T-shirt.

Cole climbed out of the car. "Morning!"

"Hi, Sheriff!" Kelsey waved at him as if trying to flag down a taxi. She started across the yard.

Elise rose from the ground as gracefully as a ballerina. A ponytailed ballerina wearing gardening gloves and a smudge of dirt on her cheek. She smiled politely at Cole, but there was no welcome in her eyes.

Cole opened the back door of the cruiser, and the cooped-up canine barreled out of the car in a flurry of tail-wagging and lolling tongue. Immediately he put his nose to the ground and began to sniff in excited circles, his long ears dragging in the dirt.

Kelsey squealed. "It's the puppy!" Her bouquet of wild-flowers went flying back over her shoulder in a rainbow of confetti as she raced across the yard, weaving like a professional football player as she ran through the obstacle course of rocks and cacti.

Elise smiled again, and this time there was some warmth behind it. "Don't tell me you've brought the suspect out here for us to identify."

Cole chuckled. "One of Mrs. Applegate's neighbors called to complain about a stray dog digging in her garden. I take it this is the culprit who caused the accident?"

"Kelsey saw him better than I did. You'll have to ask her about that." Elise brushed sweat-dampened bangs out of her eyes with the back of her wrist. "Once she comes down from cloud nine, that is." Her eyes sparkled with doting affection as Kelsey hurled herself to her knees and flung her arms around the basset hound's neck.

Cole would have paid a pretty penny to have Elise gaze that fondly at him just once.

"Oh, puppy!" Kelsey crooned. "You're all right! I was so scared we hit you with our car...."

The dog gave her face a bath with his tongue. His tail was whipping back and forth so fast it was nothing but a brown-and-white blur.

Elise threw up her gloved hands in mock despair. "I've tried to get her to like animals, but..."

Cole kicked at a piece of gravel. "Well, now that you mention it, I did have an ulterior motive for coming out here."

Instantly, all the good humor evaporated from her face. "Ulterior motive?" The cords in her neck convulsed as she swallowed.

Cole sure wished he understood what she was so jumpy about.

"I know how Kelsey likes animals," he said. "Turns out this dog's probably been abandoned by his owner." Kelsey was stroking the dog's back and cooing sweet nothings in his oversize ear.

Cole lowered his voice, not wanting to get Kelsey's hopes up. "I thought maybe you two would like to keep him," he said to Elise.

Kelsey's audio antenna tuned in instantly. "Keep him?" she cried, looking up with an astonished expression of such joy and such pleading that something flipped over inside Cole's chest.

"Oh, Mom, can we? Can we keep him, please?"

"Peach, we've been over this about pets before...."

"But Mom, he *likes* me! Oh, please, please, please!" Kelsey clasped her hands together, kneeling on the gravel like a damsel in distress beseeching the villain for mercy.

Cole decided that if Elise could resist such a heartbreaking plea, she was made of a lot tougher stuff than he was. He felt guilty for putting her on the spot like this.

Elise opted for a delaying tactic. "You say his owner abandoned him?" she asked Cole, her forehead pleating with concern.

"Looks that way. Probably someone just passing through town, decided they didn't want the dog anymore, so they let him out of the car and drove off."

"How *mean!*" Kelsey exclaimed indignantly. "You poor boy. Well, maybe *they* didn't want you, but *I* do." She pressed her cheek against the dog's sagging jowls, holding his head in a neck lock.

"Seeing how he's just a puppy, it could be he was the last one of a litter," Cole said. "Owners couldn't find a home for him, so they just dumped him."

Elise shook her head. "It's hard to believe people could be so cruel."

Cole figured she must have led a pretty sheltered existence if she didn't realize that people were capable of far greater cruelty than abandoning a puppy.

She worried her lower lip in a way he found mesmerizing. "How do you know the owners left him behind on purpose?" she asked. "Maybe they made a stop here while traveling through, and the dog simply wandered off and got lost."

"Hmm? Oh." Cole tore his gaze from the enticing curve of her mouth. "In that case, they would have filed a police report when they couldn't find him, or put an ad in the newspaper or *something.*"

"I take it they didn't?" Now Elise was nibbling a finger-nail and studying Kelsey and the dog with a growing sense of resignation on her face.

"Nope. I checked around. Called all the neighboring towns. No report of a missing dog."

"I see."

"Oh, Mom, I *promise* I'll take care of him! I'll feed him and brush him and take him for walks and let him sleep in my bed at night." Kelsey was clinging to the dog so tightly, it looked like it might take major surgery to separate them.

"He'll sleep on the *floor* at the foot of your bed, young lady."

Kelsey's eyebrows jerked upward like a marionette's. "Does that mean I can *keep* him?" she squeaked.

Elise's eyes glazed with confusion, as if it had just dawned on her that she'd already agreed to keep the puppy. "I suppose," she said with a sigh of surrender familiar to parents the world over.

"Yippee!" Kelsey jumped up and down. The dog started barking.

Elise shucked off her gardening gloves. "Come over here, you." She crouched down on her heels and clapped her hands to get the dog's attention. Delighted to make yet another new friend, the basset hound trotted over, ears and tongue flopping like wet laundry in the breeze.

Elise scratched under his chin, patted his haunches. "Are you a good fella, huh?" The puppy launched himself at her face, panting and slurping with joy. "Oops!"

Knocked off balance, she started to topple backward. With lightning-quick reflexes, Cole caught her beneath her pinwheeling arms. He held on tight to keep her from sprawling on the ground, then hoisted her to her feet.

Somehow, they wound up face-to-face, with Elise clutching his shoulders for support. Cole kept his hands spanning her rib cage, telling himself it was because she still seemed dizzy and a bit off balance.

Under the soft covering of her T-shirt, her body was slender, her bones small and delicate. He could feel her pulse beating beneath his fingertips, and detected a faint acceleration as he continued to hold her.

This close up, she smelled like soap and cinnamon, a homey fragrance that evoked all kinds of pleasant memories. He could see tiny gold flecks scattered through her green eyes like shards of sunlight glinting on the sea. Undercurrents of shock and bewilderment swirled through those emerald depths as she stared back at Cole, breathing rapidly through her mouth.

All at once he was keenly aware of her breasts rising and falling, of her hands still gripping his shoulders, of the warm, pliant length of her body positioned so close to his.

Her parted lips were within kissing distance.

A shaft of heat speared through his loins. His sudden, sharp desire must have been reflected on Cole's face, because all at once Elise lifted her hands and used them to extricate herself from their near embrace.

"Um, thank you." She pushed back a few pale tendrils of hair that had escaped from her ponytail. Her cheeks blazed a fiery pink that had nothing to do with sunburn. "For catching me, I mean." She stooped to retrieve her gloves, avoiding Cole's eyes.

He'd meant to say "No problem," then realized he'd said "My pleasure," instead.

Elise yanked her spine straight. She tugged down the hem of her T-shirt, which only served to outline her breasts more distinctly.

Another stab of desire shot through Cole. Good God, what was happening to him? He felt like he was reverting back to a hormone-charged teenager.

Fortunately, Kelsey wasn't paying the least bit of attention to either one of them. "Sit," she commanded, pushing down on the aft end of the dog. "*Sit*, puppy."

The basset hound rolled over on his back and kicked his stubby legs in the air.

Kelsey pressed a fingertip to her chin. "Hmm." She tried a new tack. "Roll over," she said.

"What are you going to call him?" Cole asked Kelsey, watching Elise from the corner of his eye. All evidence indicated that she'd been as discombobulated to wind up in his arms as Cole had been to find her there.

He wondered if she'd felt the same startling thrust of desire he had.

Kelsey propped her chin on her fist. Her face scrunched up in concentration, like tightening drawstrings on a purse. "I know!" The drawstrings disappeared. "I'm gonna call him...Bob!"

Elise's hand crept to her mouth to conceal a smile. Cole himself was having some trouble keeping a straight face. "Bob, huh?" His mouth twitched. To hide it, he ducked his head to scratch behind the dog's ears—all the slobbering unpleasantness in the car forgiven. "Well, I think Bob's a fine name."

"Mom, when are we gonna get our car back, so we can drive into town and buy him some food? And some dog dishes and a collar. And we need to get one of those tags with our address and phone number on it, in case Bob gets lost."

Good heavens, Elise thought. *What have I gotten myself into here?* Kelsey hadn't even mentioned things like shots and vet bills. The repair work on the car had already made a hefty dent in the shrinking supply of cash Elise had hastily cleared out of her savings account just before they'd fled

Boston. What temporary insanity had made her think they could afford to keep a dog?

Still, the look on Kelsey's face as she cuddled the puppy was worth any price. For two years, Elise had felt guilty about denying Kelsey's repeated requests for a pet. But how could they possibly keep an animal when they were constantly on the move?

Maybe the fact that they'd actually stayed put in Tumbleweed for six whole months had given Elise a false sense of permanence and stability. Maybe she shouldn't have agreed to let Kelsey keep the puppy, knowing there was a definite chance they would have to leave him behind someday.

But she ached so *desperately* for Kelsey to have a typical childhood like other kids... at least as close a facsimile as Elise could manage under the decidedly *un*typical circumstances.

That was why she'd said yes to Bob.

She could only pray it hadn't been a mistake.

Now, Elise faced yet another quandary. What to do about Cole Hardesty.

After he'd been nice enough to give Kelsey the dog, how could Elise refuse to offer him at least a glass of lemonade? Her lack of hospitality was undoubtedly starting to seem conspicuous. The last thing she wanted was to seem out of the ordinary in any manner.

And in Tumbleweed, Arizona, ordinary people at least offered visitors something to drink.

Elise remembered the way the sheriff's arms had felt around her, how his broad, strong shoulders had felt beneath her hands. Something had happened between them during those few chaotic moments, something powerful and... nearly irresistible.

For a second, an intense, wistful yearning inside Elise had blotted out all memory of threatening pursuers. For the space of a heartbeat, she'd trembled on the verge of surrendering to those treacherous desires that urged her to move even closer into Cole's arms.

But protecting Kelsey, her child, was too deeply ingrained an instinct to be conquered by mere physical attraction.

Elise *was* attracted to Cole, she had to admit. Which was why she was so reluctant to invite him to hang around for one second longer than necessary.

Still, she forced the words out of her throat. "I've got lemonade in the fridge, Sheriff, if you'd like some."

He narrowed his eyes against the sun, studying Elise in that careful way of his that always made her fidget.

Before he could reply, Kelsey glanced up and said, "Mom, what about lunch?" She rubbed her stomach. "I'm *hungry.*"

Elise managed not to groan out loud. Now she was trapped into inviting him to stay for an entire *meal!* "We're just having tuna fish sandwiches, Sheriff, but you're welcome to join us," she said dutifully, injecting as much sincerity into her voice as she could. Which wasn't much.

Somehow, she sensed that he perceived her predicament and was actually enjoying it a little. "Thanks," he replied with a glimmer of amusement in his eyes. "Tuna fish is my favorite."

"Come on, Bob." Kelsey skipped into the house, the bounding basset hound nipping at her heels.

The sheriff retrieved his portable radio from the cruiser and hooked it onto his belt. "By the way, call me Cole," he told Elise as she led the way up the front steps.

"Oh. Er, all right." She paused for a second inside the front door to give their eyes a chance to adjust after the dazzling bright sunshine outside. "And, um, please call me Elise."

"All right. Elise."

The way he said her name made her shiver. She felt as if they'd just taken a significant step—a step in a dangerous direction.

"Make yourself at home," she said automatically. The *last* thing she wanted was for him to feel at home here. "I'll go fix those sandwiches."

Cole watched the subtle sway of her hips as she headed for the kitchen. Okay, he practically *leered* at her. What the hell had come over him, anyway? Cole wondered. One accidental taste of what it felt like to have her in his arms, and his dormant desires had sprung to life again. They made him itchy and restless and eager to have his hands all over her luscious body.

He hadn't felt this way in a very long time. And he wasn't sure he *liked* feeling this way.

Geez, she had fantastic legs! he thought. Slim and shapely, tapering from the hem of her shorts down to her sneakers. He could just imagine running his hand along the sleek curve of her calf....

Knock it off, Hardesty, he warned himself. *You'd be no good for her, even if she'd have you. Which I doubt.*

He heard noises coming from the kitchen—cupboards banging, dishes and utensils rattling, the murmur of Elise's and Kelsey's voices. Occasionally, the dog's toenails went *click-click-click* against the linoleum.

Homey sounds. Family sounds. And, as usual, Cole was on the outside looking in. He'd almost forgotten what it was like to have someone to come home to, to share meals and conversation with.

He steeled himself against the memories. Those days were gone. For good.

He meandered through the Grants' living room, absorbing the details of their everyday lives. Well, snooping, actually. Something about the place struck him as a little off kilter, though he couldn't quite put his finger on exactly what.

He catalogued the room as if it were a crime scene. Rattan couch and chair covered in nubby fabric, with peaches-and-cream-colored cushions. Woven rug on the hardwood floor, along with a few flourishing plants in terra-cotta pots. Kelsey's homework spread across the coffee table. TV, but no stereo or VCR. Arched doorways leading into the entryway and dining room.

A light, airy room that managed to feel cozy at the same time. But something was missing....

"Lunchtime!" Kelsey called from the dining room doorway.

Cole followed her out to the kitchen, where plates and glasses had been set out on a butcher-block table in the breakfast nook. With windows on all three sides to admit the morning sunlight, this would be a pleasant place to linger, Cole thought, to lazily enjoy a second cup of coffee and read the paper.

Just like he and Laura used to do on the rare mornings when neither of them had to work.

Cole slammed that memory back into its mental file cabinet and locked the drawer. Laura was gone. And so was any chance that he might ever find that kind of peaceful, simple happiness again.

"Want some lemonade, Sheriff?" As he seated himself in one of the Windsor chairs, Kelsey positioned a pitcher over his glass.

"Mmm, you bet." He held the glass steady while Kelsey very carefully filled it, her tongue poked out in concentration.

Elise removed his plate, then set it back in front of him with a sandwich on it. "Nothing fancy, I'm afraid." She darted him a quick look of apology before turning back to the counter.

"I'll bet it's even tastier than the sandwiches down at the Sagebrush Café," he told her. His mouth was already starting to water at the smell of pickle and onion.

Elise nearly dropped the bowl of fruit she was carrying. "What—? How did you—?" She set the bowl in the center of the table and skimmed her palms nervously along her thighs.

"That's where my mom works," Kelsey said through a bite of sandwich.

"I think the sheriff knows that already," Elise said. She could have balanced a book on her head with the stiff, straight-backed way she sat down. "Although *how* he knows that, I can't imagine." She bit into her sandwich as if she'd prefer to bite someone's head off.

Rats! Caught red-handed. Cole shifted uncomfortably in his chair and rasped a hand over his jaw. "I hope you don't think I was checking up on you or anything."

Elise finished chewing. "I suppose you're going to tell me you were just conducting... what is it they say on television? Ah! Routine inquiries."

Her tone was mild enough, probably for Kelsey's sake rather than his. But Cole could see a tiny vein throbbing at her temple, and her fingers were leaving dents in the hearty whole-wheat bread of her sandwich.

He'd had no business checking up on her behind her back. And now he had no choice but to plead guilty and throw himself on the mercy of the court.

"I'm sorry," he said, swallowing a bite of tuna fish. "I was just...curious, that's all." His glass left a damp ring on the table when he picked it up. "You see, I know most people around here, and I just wondered why I'd never bumped into you before. That's all." He sought refuge in his lemonade.

"And has your curiosity been satisfied?" Elise's eyebrows disappeared beneath her bangs.

Cole had the odd feeling that something important hinged on his answer. "Yes," he said.

No, he thought.

He'd just realized what had struck him as not quite right about the Grants' living room.

"Kelsey Grant, did I just see you feed a piece of your sandwich to Bob?"

The basset hound licked his chops and propped his head on Kelsey's knee, nose quivering expectantly.

Kelsey was the one with her tail between her legs. "But Mom, he's *hungry!* What am I *s'posed* to feed him?"

"After lunch I'll walk next door and borrow some proper dog food from the Morrisons. The car should be ready Monday, so we can go buy puppy chow after I pick you up at school." Elise snapped her fingers. "Bob, get down! Peach, we don't want him to learn the habit of begging for food at the table."

Kelsey reluctantly nudged Bob's paws from her lap. "Oh, okay." Her face brightened. "How 'bout if I feed him an apple?"

"Kelsey..." Her mother pursed her lips and donned a stern expression.

Just then, a burst of static erupted from Cole's portable radio. He unhooked it from his belt, acknowledged the dispatcher, then listened. "Got it. I'm on my way."

He shoved back his chair. "Sorry to eat and run, but duty calls." He grabbed the second half of his sandwich. "Mind if I take this with me?"

"No, of course not."

Judging by the relieved expression on Elise's face, Cole figured she wouldn't have minded if he took the kitchen sink with him, just so long as he left.

Kelsey's eyes were huge with excitement. "What did all those funny numbers mean, Sheriff?"

"It's the code for—well, never mind. Probably just means I've gotta go settle an argument, that's all."

"Wow!" Kelsey tagged after him to the front door, with Elise trailing some distance behind. "Can I have a ride in your sheriff's car someday?"

Cole heard a strangled sound from Elise. "Sure, kiddo." He winked at Kelsey. "You take good care of Bob now, okay?"

"Oh, I will. Don't worry." She dropped to her knees and hugged her arms around the puppy's neck to keep him from following Cole outside.

Cole raised his sandwich in a farewell salute to Elise. "Thanks again for lunch."

"You're welcome."

Cole noticed she didn't say he was welcome to come again, though.

Not that it mattered. He'd be back even *without* an invitation. Not that he had any legitimate professional reason for dropping by.

Call it a personal fact-finding mission.

Because what Cole had realized during lunch was that the Grants' living room—their entire house, for all he knew—didn't contain one single photograph.

No antique wedding photos of stiff-necked ancestors, no snapshots of family get-togethers, not even baby pictures of Kelsey.

Nothing to give any clue about what their lives had been like before they showed up here in Tumbleweed six months ago.

And in a house where there was such an obviously strong bond of family devotion, Cole found that mighty peculiar.

Definitely worth investigating.

Chapter 4

"Let me guess. The dog was curled up in bed with her the next morning, anyway."

"Nope." Elise's eyes sparkled like the shiny countertop she was wiping down during a welcome lull in Monday afternoon's pie-and-coffee rush. "When I went in to wake Kelsey, she and the dog were curled up together on the *floor,* thank you very much."

Roz's lavishly mascaraed eyes flew wide open. "The *floor?*"

"Snuggled up cute as can be. Kelsey had dragged the blanket off the bed to cover them, and the dog had his head plopped down on one of my new sofa pillows."

Roz erupted with a husky bark of laughter, sounding like a chain-smoking seal. "Get *outta* here." She gave her co-worker a playful shove on the shoulder. "That is just *too* hysterical for words. Did you get a picture?"

"Fresh out of film, I'm afraid."

"Kids." Roz swung an ample hip onto one of the counter stools and shook her upswept hennaed curls. "I raised four of 'em myself, and every time I figured nothing they could do would surprise me anymore, sure enough, one of 'em would come up with something new."

"Yes, well, I told Kelsey she was welcome to sleep on the floor if she wanted to, but I was *not* changing my rule about no dogs on the bed." Elise grabbed the coffeepot from its burner and came out from behind the counter to refill the cups of the café's only two customers. "Maybe I can get a load of dishes washed before the next wave of business hits," she said to Roz, who was still perched against one of the red vinyl stools.

Roz rolled her eyes toward the ceiling. "As if we didn't have enough work to do, waiting tables." She drummed her long, scarlet-lacquered nails on the counter. "Hey, Tiny!" she hollered. "When you gonna break down and buy a dishwasher?" She winked at Elise.

A gruff bass voice rumbled out of the kitchen. "Soon as I finish making the payments on my new yacht."

"Haven't you got that thing paid off yet?" Roz nudged Elise in the ribs as she called back, "Do you have any idea how many perfectly good manicures I've ruined? Not to mention what that awful dishwater does to my skin."

"Well, now, that's what these nice rubber gloves are for, sugarplum." Pots and pans struck up a cymbal symphony on the other side of the open ledge dividing kitchen from dining area. "'Sides, if you two gals would stop gabbing so much and didn't waste so much time harassing your poor employer, maybe you'd bring in some more business so I could *afford* to buy that dishwasher you're so all-fired anxious to get."

"My, oh my." Roz arched her carefully plucked eyebrows at Elise, and made an exaggerated display of being impressed. She flicked a vertical mark on an imaginary tally sheet hanging in midair. "Score one for the big guy, huh?"

Elise grinned as she hoisted the heavy plastic pan full of used dishes. That was one of the aspects she enjoyed most about her job—the friendly ribbing that seemed as much a part of the café's homey atmosphere as the smell of freshly brewed coffee and the ever-present sizzle rising off Tiny's grill in the kitchen.

The pay wasn't much, and Elise's feet inevitably ached by the end of her shift. But the good-natured teasing among her co-workers disguised a genuine sense of affection and camaraderie, and made Elise feel like she truly belonged.

Like she was part of the family. The only family she had these days, besides Kelsey.

Oh, and now Bob, of course.

"Put that dishpan down," Roz commanded with a flap of her hand. "It's my turn to wash."

"I don't mind doing them." Elise paused with her fanny backed up to the swinging door that opened into the kitchen. "Besides, I owe you for giving me a ride to work while my car's in the shop."

"Pooh, that's nothing." She shooed away Elise's gratitude. "You can return the favor sometime. That old rattle-trap of mine is due for a major breakdown any day now."

"The least I can do is—"

"Put those dishes back down, or I'll secretly fill all the sugar dispensers with salt and tell Tiny *you* did it."

Elise laughed. "All right, you win." She lugged the dishpan back behind the counter.

The bell over the door jingled as someone entered the café. Roz craned her neck to see who, then immediately twirled around, blocking Elise's view as she smoothed her blouse and patted her hair. "Well, hel-lo," she purred in a voice as smooth as fine whiskey. "To what do we owe *this* honor, stranger?"

"Hello, Roz." Only two quiet, slightly self-conscious words, but they were enough to unsettle Elise like an aftershock of a major earthquake.

The dishpan crashed onto its shelf with a clatter of glass and metal that *sounded* like an earthquake.

Roz hunched her shoulders up to her dangling gold earrings, then wheeled around to see what had happened.

The kitchen door swung open as Tiny poked his gleaming bald head out. "What's all the racket?" he boomed. "You gals aren't playin' Frisbee with my good china, are you? Why, look what the cat drug in! Howdy, Sheriff!"

Tiny lumbered out of the kitchen, all three hundred pounds of him. "Elise, honey, you watch yourself. Don't get cut on any of those broken dishes."

"I—it doesn't look like anything broke, after all." She completed her hasty inspection and glanced up, cheeks burning. She probably looked as red as the ketchup bottles spaced out along the counter.

She forced herself to meet Cole's eyes. "Hello."

"Afternoon." He nodded formally in her direction, having already removed his hat.

Roz perked up her ears like a cat who's just heard a mouse rustling behind the baseboards.

Tiny folded his arms over the white chef's apron that strained futilely to cover his massive chest. The arms themselves were as thick around as barrel cacti. "What happened, Sheriff? They kick you outta the Miner's Diner for using the wrong fork or somethin'?"

"Why, Tiny, I've been hearing you claim for years that you've got the best food in town." Cole dropped his hat onto the seat of an empty booth near the front window, then dropped himself beside it. "Thought it was about time I gave you a chance to prove it, that's all."

Roz whipped out a menu like a magician's bouquet. "We got some nice fresh peach pie today, just baked this morning. Elise'll be happy to warm some up for you, maybe put a scoop of vanilla ice cream on top of it."

Elise jerked her head up. Roz winked at her. "I'd get it for you myself, Sheriff, but I got a date with a big load of dishes."

Cole's gaze shifted to Elise, then back to Roz again. "That pie sounds real good, but I'll just have coffee, thanks."

"You're in luck! Elise just put on a new pot." She plucked the menu from Cole's hands. "That fresh coffee done yet, Elise?" She purposefully bumped Elise with her hip as she rounded the counter to retrieve the dishpan.

"What do you think you're doing?" Elise muttered from the side of her mouth.

Roz's eyebrows arched like a pair of croquet wickets. "Just doing the dishes, that's all." She lowered her decibel level by about ninety percent. "I saw that look the two of you gave each other. Not to mention the fact that your face is as red as a maraschino cherry." As she hoisted the dishpan, she kicked Elise's ankle and whispered, "Go for it, girl."

"It's not what you—I mean, I barely know the—*ohh!*" Elise blew a flustered stream of air through her bangs.

Roz gave her a knowing smile. "You think it's pure coincidence that a few days after meeting you, the sheriff sashays in here for the very first time in *ages?*"

"Sh!"

Roz lowered her voice, but her sly smile only increased in wattage. "Honey, I've worked here for the last eleven years.

You can bet your last nickel it isn't *me* the sheriff came hoping to see."

Reluctantly, Elise had to admit that Roz had a point. But that only made her feel even *more* uncomfortable, if that were possible.

"Come on, Tiny. You wash and I'll dry." Roz herded the boss back into the kitchen, prodding him with the dishpan.

"Nice try, sugarplum, but I'm right in the middle of fixin' up a batch of my special six-alarm chili."

"Well, then, you sure don't have time to stand out here yakking with the customers, do you?" Just before she backed through the kitchen door, Roz called out cheerfully, "What's the matter, Elise? You sprout roots or something? Get the poor sheriff his coffee. The man's parched with thirst—I can see it from here." She batted her lashes in Cole's direction. "Toodle-oo, Sheriff." Her words drifted out through the swinging door as she disappeared.

Elise turned and fiddled with the coffeepot, gaining a little extra time to collect herself before she had to face Cole. Er, the sheriff.

When she felt like her bright smile was securely pinned to her lips, she came around the counter and flipped over one of the clean coffee mugs already set out on the table in front of him.

"Cream or sugar?" Gee, what a brilliant conversationalist she was! At least she managed to keep her hand steady, so she didn't spill hot coffee all over his lap while pouring.

"Just black, thanks." He raised the mug and carefully blew steam off the top before sipping. "Mmm. Pretty tasty."

A genuine smile replaced her phony one. "I guess if you decide you don't want to be sheriff anymore, you could apply for a job as a diplomat."

"No, really." His leather belt creaked when he shifted his weight, as if he were discomfited by the fact she'd read him so easily. He took another sip and cocked his head to one side. "Well, it's nice and hot, anyway."

"Not as good as what they serve at the Miner's Diner, I guess."

He poked his cheek with his tongue, as if probing for another diplomatic answer. "This place has... other attractions."

Elise felt a flush spread across her skin like wildfire. By now she was used to customers flirting with her. She'd become quite expert, in fact, at dodging the occasional impertinent grope, which was one of the unfortunate drawbacks of being a waitress.

Coming from Cole, however, even that mildly suggestive comment left her tongue-tied. All of her snappy retorts went flying straight out of her head, as if she'd never had a man make a pass at her before.

Right away, Cole regretted his impulsive remark. What the devil had come over him, anyway? He hadn't meant to sound like he was coming on to her, but judging by the way Elise was blushing, that's exactly how she'd interpreted it.

Cole didn't want her to get the wrong idea. But then, he wasn't exactly sure himself what the *right* idea would be.

"Homemade peach pie, for example," he said quickly. "That's one of the attractions here. Or Tiny's six-alarm chili."

"I'll go see if he's got some ready yet, shall I?" Elise backed away from the booth, obviously relieved for an excuse to put some distance between them.

"No! Uh, I mean, I can't stay long. Just till I finish my coffee."

He noticed Elise didn't offer him a refill.

He noticed some other things about her, too, as he watched her over the rim of his mug while she bustled around the café, pretending to ignore him. Like the way her jade green blouse matched the color of her eyes. And the way her trim curves filled out the dark slacks she was wearing. And the way her mouth pursed so adorably when she was concentrating, like now.

He watched her adding up a bill in her head, tiny pleats gathered at the junction of her eyebrows, and wondered what it would be like to kiss that adorably pursed mouth.

With a grimace, Cole drained the slightly bitter contents of his coffee mug, and reached for his hat. He was just going to have to keep on wondering about that kiss, because it was never going to happen. His interest in Elise Grant was purely professional, and it wouldn't be right to take advantage of what might be a mutual physical attraction, just to make his job easier.

He strolled to the cash register and pulled out his wallet. Elise made a valiant effort to meet his eyes, but her gaze wandered off somewhere just over his left shoulder. "On the house," she said, waving his money away as if trying to shoo off a fly.

"'Preciate it, but I prefer to pay my own way." Cole set a five-dollar bill firmly on the counter next to the register. He knew most Tumbleweed cops got free coffee from the local eating establishments. No crime in that. He'd done it himself while on the force in Los Angeles.

But since accepting this job as sheriff, Cole had held himself up to a much more rigid code of behavior. Maybe it was part of his atonement for Laura's death. Maybe it was a way of distancing himself from his former existence. Or maybe it was just a way of rejecting the sloppier standards of the big city, where self-preservation so often won out over self-respect.

Elise counted out the change into his hand, careful not to touch him while she did so.

"How's Bob?" Cole asked.

"Bob?" Confusion reigned on her pretty face.

"The dog. Unless Kelsey's christened him something else already."

She thumped the heel of her hand lightly against the side of her head. "Oh, *Bob!*" Her smile warmed Cole even more than the coffee had, though he knew it wasn't specifically aimed at him. "Bob's fine. There was a small, unpleasant incident involving a pair of bedroom slippers, but we've smoothed that over and put it behind us."

"Glad to hear it." And glad that she seemed genuinely fond of the pup. Cole's conscience had been troubling him a bit, about the way he'd sort of manipulated her into taking him.

Now that they'd actually stumbled into a friendly conversation, Cole wished he could linger awhile longer, basking in the sunny rays of her smile. He assured himself that his reluctance to leave was only because he hated to waste this opportunity to steer the conversation around to the subject of her past.

Still, both of them had better things to do than stand here lollygagging around the cash register. Cole lifted his hat. "Well, guess I'd better be—"

"Not leavin' already, are you, Sheriff?" Roz poked her head out of the kitchen, across the ledge where the waitresses picked up the plates Tiny filled with food. In two seconds flat she was barging through the door, rubbing her hands with some kind of lotion. "Why, we haven't even had a chance to catch up yet! Sit down! Elise, get the man some more coffee, will you?"

Cole held up his hands. "Thanks, but I've gotta be on my way." From the corner of his eye, he detected unmistakable relief in Elise's expression.

Roz circled her lips into a pout. "Well, promise you won't be such a stranger from now on."

Cole crossed his heart and held up three fingers in the air. "Scout's honor."

Her pout dissolved as a gleam lit up her eyes. "Say, I've got an idea!" She snapped her fingers. "Elise, why don't we ask the sheriff here if he can drop you off at the repair shop to pick up your car? That way you won't have to wait till the end of our shift for me to drive you."

Elise was shaking her head before Roz even finished. "That's really not necessary. It's only another fifteen minutes till we're both off work, anyway."

"Exactly. So I can cover for you, easy. This way you can make it to school right at three, so Kelsey won't have to wait around for you."

"Really, there's no need—"

"I'd be happy to give you a lift," Cole said.

Elise was fighting a losing battle, and she knew it. She most definitely did *not* want to spend any time alone with Cole, even for the short ride to the repair shop. There was something a little too intimate about riding around in a man's car with him.

Especially a man she already found too attractive for her own good.

But to protest any further would sound funny. And the last thing Elise wanted was to draw any more attention to herself.

"All right. Thank you," she said, forcing herself to meet his eyes. They gazed back at her levelly, glowing an unblinking blue. Like warning lights on a runway.

"I need to get my purse out of the back," she said. "I'll only be a minute."

"No rush," Cole told her. With that unruffled, impassive demeanor of his, it was impossible to tell whether he was impatient, eager or indifferent about giving her a ride.

Roz, naturally, had a strong opinion of her own. The door into the kitchen didn't even have a chance to swing shut before Roz was plowing through it, hot on Elise's heels.

"Ooh, I am so jealous! That man's sweet on you, Elise. I can tell."

Elise strode into Tiny's office through a cloud scented with tomato and cayenne pepper. She grabbed her purse and spun around to confront her friend. "What do you think you're *doing?*" she demanded through clenched teeth.

"Doing?" Roz blinked. With her long, dark lashes, her eyes looked like two spiders clapping hands.

"Don't play Miss Innocent with me! You could hardly have been more obvious about it. Heaven only knows what the sheriff thinks about the way you were practically shoving me at him."

"Oh, pooh." Roz fanned the heavy, chili-fragrant air with her hand. "I'll tell you what he thinks." She propped her hands on her waist and angled forward. "The man's tickled pink, that's what!"

Elise struggled to keep a lid on her temper, reminding herself that Roz thought she was helping out. "I barely know the man. I think you're reading way too much into this."

"*Re-e-eally?*" Roz's face blazed with triumph, like a prosecutor who's just trapped a defendant in a lie on the witness stand. "Well, answer me this, then. The sheriff claimed he came in here today to try out the food, didn't he?"

"So what?" Elise was starting to fidget. She stared longingly at the office window, which could easily provide an escape route into the back alley.

"Well? Did you see him eat anything?" Roz flung out her arms. "Did you see the man take even one...single...bite?"

Elise picked at a loose thread on her blouse. "Uh ..."

Roz leaned back against Tiny's desk and extended one arm to inspect her manicure. "You don't have to thank me," she said graciously. "Just ask me to be maid of honor at the wedding."

"There isn't going to *be* any wed—"

"Just remember," Roz interrupted, hustling Elise out of the office and past the stove where Tiny was sampling a spoonful of chili with a blissful expression on his moon-shaped face. "One, I refuse to wear anything with puffy sleeves and a bow on the back. And two—"

She pushed Elise into the front part of the café and called through the swinging door in a loud stage whisper, "I look terrible in pink!"

Driving through downtown Tumbleweed was like entering a time warp and stepping out a hundred years ago. With its brick-and-adobe false-fronted buildings, its narrow sidewalks overhung by wooden balconies, First Street looked much as it must have during Tumbleweed's heyday. Back then, hordes of boisterous miners had crowded the shops and saloons and bawdy houses, and the thriving copper and silver mines nearby had poured a steady cascade of wealth through the town.

The copper and silver were all gone now, along with the bawdy houses, most of the saloons and three-fourths of the population. From its peak of fifteen thousand in 1895, the size of the town had dwindled, eventually stabilizing at its current four thousand residents.

Right now, Sheriff Cole Hardesty was interested in one particular resident.

"Which garage did you take your car to?" he asked Elise. She sat next to him in the passenger seat with her spine ruler-straight, elbows drawn in to her sides, hands firmly clasped over the purse in her lap, as if worried something in the sheriff's cruiser might go off if she touched it accidentally. She gave the rifle in its rack an especially wide berth.

"Art's Auto Repair," she replied. Those were the first three words she'd spoken since she got into the car.

Cole made a right turn onto Arroyo Avenue. "Art's a good mechanic," he said. He reached over and turned down the volume on the police radio, which erupted frequently with bursts of garbled chatter interspersed with static. "Honest, too." He thought of Elise, struggling to raise her daughter on a waitress's salary. "Hope the repair bill didn't set you back too much."

Judging by the unhappy crimp of her mouth when she gnawed her lip, it had. "No," she said.

Cole felt bad for bringing the subject up. He cast about for a less worrisome topic of conversation, and came up with the one thing he knew they both had in common.

"Quite a change, isn't it, moving to a small town like this from the big city?"

From the way she whipped her head around to stare at him, it was as if Cole had asked if she'd like to pull over for a quick tumble in the back seat.

"Big city?" she echoed warily.

Cole threw her a sideways glance. "Last time I looked, Minneapolis was a big city, right?"

"And just how exactly do you know I'm from Minneapolis?" Her voice was as taut as her posture.

"Same way I found out where you worked," Cole replied. "I asked around."

Elise's knuckles turned white, as if she were attempting to throttle her purse into submission. "I thought I made it clear that I don't appreciate you prying into my personal life."

Cole turned the radio down even further. This conversation was getting more interesting by the minute. "In my job, curiosity sort of comes with the territory," he said mildly. "Guess I don't blame you for being put out, but I certainly meant no harm by it."

"No. No, I'm sure you didn't." She turned her head to gaze at the passing scenery, though Cole was willing to bet she wouldn't have noticed if a flying saucer set down right in the middle of the parking lot in front of the Shop-Rite Supermarket.

"I visited Minneapolis myself, once," he said, undeterred by the silence that lay between them heavy as desert heat on an August afternoon. "Went there for a law-enforcement seminar on the latest developments in forensic techniques."

"Really?" That one word was laden with caution, as if she expected him to launch into a detailed recitation of all the dull, dry, scientific procedures for evidence collection.

"Minneapolis is a beautiful city," he continued.

"Mmm."

"All those lakes, lots of trees . . ."

"Uh-huh."

Cole braked gently as they approached a stoplight. "One night a couple of buddies and I took in a play at that famous theater—what's the name of it?" He made a rolling motion with his hand and glanced at Elise for help.

"Um . . ." She wore the slightly panicky expression of a student called on in class who hadn't done her homework the night before.

"You know the one I mean," he said. "Near downtown? The one where the audience sits in a big curve around the stage?"

"Yes, uh—"

"It's right on the tip of my tongue. The Gifford? The Garrett?"

"Er..."

"The Guthrie, that's it!" Cole snapped his fingers. "The Guthrie Theater. Boy, was that place impressive."

When the light changed, he turned his attention back to the road. But not before he noticed the relief that swept across Elise's face like shifting sands in a windstorm.

Up ahead, he spotted the sign for Art's Auto Repair. "I take it you're from the big city yourself," Elise said, surprising Cole with the sudden friendly warmth in her voice.

"Los Angeles," he replied.

"That *is* a big city." Her pretty green eyes widened momentarily. "How'd you wind up here?"

Cole massaged the nape of his neck. Funny how the tables had turned. Now *he* was the one who wasn't all that anxious to supply information about his past. "Guess I wanted a change," he said carefully. "I got tired of all the indifference, the callousness, the me-first attitude of the big city."

He must have revealed more than he'd intended, because a faint note of compassion, or perhaps sympathy, crept into Elise's voice. "Not everyone in the big city is callous or indifferent."

"No." He swung the cruiser into Art's. "But too many of them are." He shifted the transmission to park just as another burst of chatter erupted from the radio. This time the call was for him.

He switched on the mike and spoke to the dispatcher, aware that Elise was watching him from the corner of her eye. He seemed to have sparked *her* curiosity now, just the way she'd sparked his.

"I'm on my way," he said. He switched off the mike.

"Thanks for the ride." Elise opened the door, then paused, as if she didn't want to appear too eager to get out. Just like that awkward, end-of-the-date moment.

"No trouble." Cole felt an unexpected impulse to ask her out.

He squelched it. He had no business getting involved with a woman, letting her believe there might be a chance for a relationship between them.

Cole was incapable of forming any lasting attachments. His heart simply wasn't in it anymore. Not since Laura.

"Well...see you." Elise got out and shut the door, bending down to give Cole a little wave through the window before she walked off.

He watched the way her hips swayed with unintentional seductiveness, the way a faint breeze lifted her blond hair from her shoulders. He shoved the transmission into drive.

"You'll be seeing me, all right," he said under his breath as he headed out to respond to the radio call.

Because, even though Cole had no intention of following up on his *personal* attraction to Elise, his *professional* interest in her had just clicked up a couple of notches.

Take that Minneapolis business, for example.

Cole hadn't purposely tried to trip her up, but she'd given herself away when he'd drawn a blank on the name of the Guthrie Theater. He knew, even from his brief visit, that the Guthrie was a local landmark, centerpiece of the local cultural scene. *Anyone* who'd ever lived within a hundred-mile radius of Minneapolis should have instantly been able to produce its name.

But Elise hadn't.

Then there was the way she'd turned the tables and started asking Cole about himself. Maybe she was truly interested in hearing his autobiography, but Cole doubted it. His instincts told him that her questions were merely an effort to divert attention from herself and her own increasingly mysterious past.

Elise Grant was hiding something, all right.

And Cole intended to find out what it was.

Chapter 5

Thursday after school, Elise and Kelsey sat at the kitchen table, planning. "And I want a chocolate cake with chocolate frosting, and chocolate ice cream to go with it!"

Elise made a face. "Sounds a little too chocolaty to me."

"Mom! You said I got to decide what we're having!"

"But what if one of your guests doesn't *like* chocolate?"

Kelsey rolled her eyes as if her mother were hopelessly ignorant. "*Everyone* likes chocolate."

Well, probably everyone in the third grade did, Elise conceded. But she made a mental note to buy some vanilla ice cream just in case.

"Okay, okay." She held up her hands in surrender. "Chocolate it is, then."

Beaming with triumph, Kelsey grabbed her pencil and carefully added this latest detail to their party-planning list. Waiting for her to laboriously spell out the word *chocolate* three times gave Elise another opportunity to second-guess herself about the whole birthday party business.

During the years they'd been on the run, Elise had regretfully discouraged Kelsey from inviting friends home from school. She hated to come off like the Wicked Witch of the West, but allowing children into their home inevitably meant allowing their parents in, too.

Elise hadn't dared risk the chance that one of them might accidentally spot something that revealed a clue about her and Kelsey's past. Even the most casual comment a visitor might later make about Elise could have dire consequences, if spoken to the wrong person.

But Elise was also worried about the eventual psychological damage she might create if she continued to deprive Kelsey of the normal joys and tribulations of childhood friendships.

Besides, the parents would only be coming here to drop off their kids, not snoop through Elise's dresser drawers and root through the closets.

So this time she'd told her flabbergasted daughter *yes* when Kelsey had made her annual plea for a party.

"Okay, now for the games." Kelsey sucked on the pencil's eraser, hastily yanking it from her mouth when she intercepted her mother's disapproving frown. "Mom, I was thinking." She twirled one of her ponytails around her finger. "Can we have a clown that does magic tricks, like a girl at school did when we lived in Houston?"

Elise pictured their dwindling savings, stashed away in a shoe box on the floor of her closet. "I was thinking more in terms of Pin the Tail on the Donkey."

Kelsey groaned. "Mom, that's for *babies*."

"Peach, we just can't afford a clown. Why don't you think of another game you'd like to play, and we'll—"

Just then, a series of muffled bangs erupted from somewhere close by.

Bob, snoozing under the kitchen table, twitched one ear, yawned, then went back to sleep.

"What on earth—? Kelsey, you stay there." Elise speared a warning finger at her daughter as she peeked cautiously through the breakfast nook window. Maybe she was just edgier than usual at the prospect of a bunch of strangers descending on her home. But that familiar panicky feeling of danger was threatening to make a comeback.

She didn't want to alarm Kelsey, though.

"You sit here and think up some games for your party, and I'll go see what's making that racket." The banging started up again as Elise hurried through the dining room, every nerve in her body on red alert.

The noise seemed to be coming from the far side of the house, near the carport. Elise sidled next to the living room window and drew back the curtain a fraction of an inch.

When she spotted the sheriff's cruiser parked in the driveway, she sagged against the wall with relief. Not a response Cole Hardesty had ever stirred in her before.

She was so glad he wasn't Victor Dominick, though, she could have flung her arms around his neck and kissed him.

She unlocked the door and ventured outside. "Cole? Is that you? What are you—?"

Elise braked to a halt while her brain tried to assimilate the surprising scene in front of her.

Cole was kneeling on the ground, hammer in hand, a cluster of nails clamped between his lips. Next to him sat a stack of lumber. A brand-new plank bridged a gap in the fence that Elise had temporarily blocked with cardboard.

Cole shoved himself to his feet and plucked the nails from his mouth. "Afternoon," he said. "I noticed last time I was by that your fence needed some fixing. Thought I'd take care of it for you."

Once Elise's astonishment ebbed, embarrassment surged in to take its place. Was her precarious financial state so obvious that Cole felt sorry for her?

"You don't need to do this," she said, cheeks flaming. "I'm going to pay someone to repair it as soon as I have the...chance."

Cole wiped a film of sweat from his brow with the back of his wrist. He scrutinized her so thoroughly, Elise was gripped by the unpleasant certainty that he could read all her secrets in her eyes.

"This isn't charity, you know," he said, zeroing in on the source of her discomfort. "I feel obligated to you for taking that dog off my hands." He gestured at the dilapidated fence. "This is just my way of repaying a debt, that's all." His back was to the sun, so she knew the twinkle in his eye wasn't merely a reflection. "Can't have old Bob making a break for it, can we?"

Once again, Elise was startled by the abrupt jolt of a connection between them. As if on some primitive level, they already shared the kind of soul-deep intimacy that couldn't be explained by such a brief acquaintance.

Something moved inside her, like a fragile seedling stretching toward the sun. And Elise realized that, despite her best efforts to the contrary, she was starting to *like* Cole Hardesty.

She stepped over to the pile of lumber and picked up another board. "Well, you should have at least told me you were here. And now that I know, the least you can do is let me *help* you," she said.

A grin broke across his handsome face, shifting the rugged planes and angles into an even more attractive array. And at that moment, Elise knew she was in trouble. *Big* trouble.

"Deal," he said, extending his hand.

She shifted the board to her left arm. When their hands joined, lo and behold, it was just like in some romantic fairy tale. An electric current *did* seem to flow between them, setting up a magnetic field that made it difficult for Elise to let go. Or to breathe.

"How about if you hold this board in position while I nail it?" Cole suggested.

Working side by side gave Elise a chance to absorb lots of little details about him. She'd never seen him out of uniform before, but today he was wearing jeans and a short-sleeved cotton shirt casually unbuttoned at the collar. A fine sprinkling of dark hair rippled along the muscles of his forearms as he wielded the hammer and nails.

She watched a tiny drop of sweat creep down from his hairline, across his temple, along the solid shelf of his jaw. Tiny strands of coal black hair were plastered to his forehead. Elise inhaled deeply, trying to be subtle about it, filling her lungs with the mingled scents of fresh-cut pine and Cole's uniquely masculine fragrance.

It was warm out in the sun, but she suddenly experienced a rush of heat that had nothing to do with the weather.

A half hour later, Cole gave the nail a final tap and stood up to inspect their work. "There, that oughtta do it. Unless Bob decides to tunnel his way out, I'd say he'll be safe and sound in the backyard from now on."

Elise gathered up the remaining scattered nails and dumped them back into their brown paper sack. "I can't tell you how much I appreciate this."

"Like I said, it's the least I could do." Cole gripped her elbow as she rose to her feet. Elise didn't actually require any assistance standing up. She could tell by the way his hand lingered on her arm that Cole knew it, too.

Move away, Elise, she commanded herself.

"Let me carry those," Cole said as she bent over to pick up the leftover boards. "They're heavy."

"Piece of cake, compared to juggling half a dozen plates full of food all at once," Elise replied. But she left half the load for him to carry.

The trunk of the cruiser gapped open a few inches. Elise nudged it wider and slid the lumber in. "Ouch!" She examined her palm.

"Sliver?" Cole quickly deposited his armload of wood. "Here, let me see."

"It's nothing, really. I—"

But he was too quick for her. He lowered his head close to hers while he studied her imprisoned hand like a palm reader. Hopefully, the lines there didn't reveal too much.

Elise found herself observing the texture of his skin...the concerned furrows crinkling his forehead...the faint, emerging shadow of his beard. He kept holding her hand while he dipped into his jeans pocket and produced a red Swiss Army knife.

"You're not planning to operate, are you?" Elise asked warily.

He flashed that subdued yet devastating grin at her. "Only with these, I promise." He freed her hand and extracted a tiny pair of tweezers.

"You certainly come prepared, don't you," she murmured, trying to ignore the little frisson of pleasure she felt when he grasped her hand again.

"Me and the Boy Scouts," he replied. He hovered over her hand, brow creased in concentration. "This is going to hurt you worse than it hurts me," he warned.

"Your bedside manner leaves a little something to be desired." Elise winced as he produced a little tug with the tweezers.

"Must be why I never made it into med school." He slid his tongue over his lips. "Aha!"

"Ow!"

Cole held up the tweezers and squinted at the splinter. "Boy, that was a nasty one." He flicked it away and tucked the tweezers back into place. "Let's see your hand."

"It's fine. Hardly—"

He gently but firmly pried open her fingers. "Mmm. Got any antiseptic in your medicine cabinet?"

"I think so. Yes. I had to use some on Kelsey's skinned knee a few weeks ago."

"Let's go, then." He ushered Elise toward the house, his hand resting solicitously on the small of her back as if she'd just fallen off the roof, rather than jabbed herself with a teeny fragment of wood.

She didn't bother protesting. After all Cole had done for her, she would have had to invite him inside for a cool drink, anyway.

As they entered the house, a chair scraped against the kitchen floor. Kelsey came barreling through the dining room, the puppy snuffling along in her wake. "Mom, where'd you go? Oh, hi, Sheriff!" As soon as she noticed Cole, she gave him a sunny smile he found completely irresistible.

"Hi, yourself, kiddo." He grinned back.

"Mom, what was all that noise?"

Elise sort of drifted away from Cole, as if she were uncomfortable standing so close to him in front of her daughter.

"The sheriff was nice enough to come by and fix the fence for us," she said, sending him a look that managed to be both grateful and guarded at the same time. "That was hammering we heard."

"Oh." Kelsey stooped down to tickle the dog's chin, popped up like a jack-in-the-box, then dropped herself into a chair and began to swing her legs back and forth. She seemed to have a surplus of energy that kept her constantly in motion. "Mom, can we have a piñata at my birthday party? Filled with candy and stuff? You could tie a blindfold around our eyes and we could use my baseball bat to swing at it."

Elise tilted her head to one side, a pensive gesture that made her look a lot like her daughter. "I don't see why not."

"Yay!" Kelsey catapulted to her feet.

"When's your birthday?" Cole asked.

"In eight more days," Kelsey replied promptly. She sounded like she could probably tell him exactly how many hours and minutes, too, if he were interested. "But we're having my party a week from Saturday, 'cause that makes it easier for people to come."

Then her eyes widened into silver dollars. Cole could practically see a light bulb pop on over her head. "Hey, would *you* like to come to my party, Sheriff?"

"Peach, the sheriff's pretty busy," Elise said quickly. "Besides, I don't know how much fun he'd have, being the only adult at the party."

"But *you'd* be there, Mom," Kelsey pointed out innocently.

Elise awkwardly cleared her throat.

"I'd love to come," Cole said, eliciting a sharp glance from Elise. "A week from Saturday, is it? I'll mark it on my calendar right away."

"Goody!" Kelsey's twin ponytails danced as she hopped up and down. "And don't forget, I'm going to be nine years old."

Cole was absurdly touched by her invitation, even though Elise obviously didn't share her daughter's enthusiasm. Her lips were sewn into a tight seam, as if to prevent any objections from spilling out.

She would have been even more unenthusiastic if she'd known what Cole had discovered about her recently. Repairing her fence wasn't the only project involving Elise that he'd tackled this week.

"Now, about that antiseptic..." he said.

"Hmm? Oh, yes." She glanced down at her hand as if she'd completely forgotten about the splinter. "Kelsey, why don't you take Bob outside to play, and I'll bring out some lemonade in a few minutes."

"'Kay." Kelsey spun around like a top. "Come on, Bob." The dog trotted happily after her, his new metal name tag jingling against his collar.

Elise turned to Cole. "Why don't you join them? It's fairly pleasant sitting in the shade."

"Your hand..."

She made a scoffing sound. "I'm perfectly capable of dabbing on a little antiseptic. Heaven knows, I've had enough practice with Kelsey's bumps and scrapes."

Cole could hardly insist on accompanying her, not unless he wanted to insult her by implying she was some helpless female incapable of taking care of herself.

It occurred to him Elise might be afraid of what a glance at her medicine cabinet might reveal. An old prescription label, perhaps, containing the name of some doctor in another city?

Or had she been as careful to obliterate any trace of her past from the bathroom as she'd been in the rest of the house?

As he stepped into the backyard, Cole knew one thing for certain. Whatever city Elise and her daughter had lived in before moving to Tumbleweed, it wasn't the one she claimed it was.

Cole had done a little investigating since the last time he'd seen her. And discovered that no one named Elise Grant had owned property, paid for utilities, registered a car or possessed a driver's license anywhere in the vicinity of Minneapolis, Minnesota. At least not during the last ten years, which was as far back as he'd checked.

Furthermore, no child named Kelsey Grant had ever been enrolled in the city's public schools.

Now, Cole could come up with logical explanations for some of that. Maybe Kelsey had gone to a private school, whose records he hadn't had access to. Maybe Elise had had a husband who'd kept everything in *his* name.

Still, it seemed awfully unlikely that she hadn't left even the slightest trace of herself in the public records.

So Cole was proceeding on the assumption that Elise had either lied about her name, or lied about living in Minneapolis, or both. Which raised the intriguing question of what *else* she might have lied about.

Maybe she still *had* a husband. Maybe he was some brutal, abusive monster, and Elise had been forced to change her identity to escape from him.

Or maybe Kelsey's father was a perfectly decent guy, and Elise had stolen their child from him after a bitter custody battle.

God, he sure hoped not.

"Hey, Sheriff! Wanna pitch to me?" Kelsey lobbed a softball up and down in one hand. A baseball bat dangled from the other.

"Sure!"

She tossed him the ball, then positioned herself near the fence, scuffing her toe in the dirt with the serious concentration of the leadoff batter in the opening game of the World Series.

Cole wound up and let the first underhand pitch fly. Kelsey watched it with disdain as it sailed past her and clunked into the fence. "Ball one," she called.

"Sorry." Cole had pitched occasionally for the sheriff's department softball team, but an eight-going-on-nine-year-old's strike zone was pretty small.

He tried again. This time, Kelsey connected with a solid *thunk!* that sent a speeding grounder just out of Cole's reach. Bob began to bark furiously and chased after the ball.

Kelsey jumped up and down, shrieking with laughter. "Look at him go!"

Cole scratched his head. "Maybe we can teach Bob to play outfield."

Elise stuck her head out the back door. "Kelsey Grant, what did I tell you about playing baseball in the backyard?"

"Oops!" Kelsey covered her mouth with her hand and looked as sheepish as Cole felt.

"Uh, sorry about that," he told Elise. "I didn't realize..."

She waved aside his apology. "I wouldn't worry, except Kelsey's gotten to be such a good hitter, I'm afraid one of these days she's going to smack a home run right through the kitchen window."

"She's got a pretty impressive swing, all right."

Elise flashed Cole a smile brimming with maternal pride. "I'll be right back with the lemonade." She disappeared into the house.

Kelsey was struggling to wrestle the ball from the dog's jaws. Loose folds of skin jiggled like jelly as he shook his head back and forth, growling good-naturedly.

Something swept over Cole as he watched them, a wave of feeling so intense it took him a minute to identify it as longing. What would his life be like today if he and Laura had had a child? He could have had a terrific kid like Kelsey himself... if only things had turned out differently.

"I bet if you let go of the ball and pretend you're not interested, he'll drop it," Cole suggested.

Kelsey followed his advice, making a big show of turning her back on the basset hound and folding her arms across her chest. Sure enough, within seconds Bob dropped the ball and began sniffing around Kelsey's sneakers.

"Hey, you were right!" She snatched up the ball and held it high in the air, like a fielder who'd just made a spectacular catch to save the game.

"Maybe you and I could go to the park sometime and, uh, work on my pitching a little." Even as he spoke, Cole couldn't believe those words were coming out of his mouth. He didn't know the first thing about kids, and the last thing he wanted was to get attached to a sweet little girl whom he might have to turn over to her real father someday.

"Neat-o! Can we take Bob?"

"Why... sure." Like it or not, Cole appeared to be committed.

"I wanna learn how to play just like Ted Williams when I grow up." Kelsey scrunched up her freckled nose. "You know who Ted Williams is?"

Cole pantomimed swinging a bat. "Only one of the greatest hitters of all time."

"That's right! And he played for the Boston Red Sox, who are my very favorite team."

Cole went still for a second. "The Red Sox, huh?"

"Yup." She bobbed her head emphatically, then dropped to her knees to give the squirming dog a hug. "'Course, I wanna be a veterinarian when I grow up, too." She shrugged. "Guess I'll have to decide which one I really, *really* want to be."

"Maybe you could be a vet during the off-season," Cole suggested. But his mind wasn't entirely on Kelsey's career dilemma at the moment.

The back door opened. "Lemonade!" Elise called.

Kelsey and Bob raced over to the shady area beneath the white canvas awning that extended from the back of the house. Cole followed at a more restrained pace. He felt like a heel, accepting Elise's hospitality under false pretenses.

If she'd known how he was snooping into her background, she would be tossing him out on his ear rather than graciously offering him one of the lawn chairs arranged in the shade.

"I didn't even ask if you'd rather have something else to drink," she said, setting the tray of glasses onto a small table. A curtain of blond hair slipped forward to screen the side of her face. She reached up to tuck it back behind her ear. "I have iced tea, or soda..." Her lips puckered in apology. "Nothing stronger, I'm afraid."

"Lemonade sounds delicious." When she handed him a glass, Cole noticed the small bandage on her palm. It had tiny cartoon characters frolicking all over it.

Whatever else she might be, Cole had certainly seen plenty of evidence that Elise was a thoughtful, devoted mother.

Who are you, Elise Grant? he wondered. *And what kind of trouble are you in?*

It might not be too long before he found out. Because, although it had never been Cole's intention to pump an eight-year-old child for information, Kelsey had inadvertently supplied him with a couple of new clues.

He just wished he didn't have to use Elise's own daughter to solve the mystery of her past.

Ice cubes tinkled pleasantly as Cole sipped his cold lemonade. But all he could taste was the bitter flavor of guilt.

Chapter 6

"**Y**ou sly fox!" Roz wagged a lollipop red fingernail and leered at Elise.

"I don't know what you're talking about, but boy, am I glad to see you." Elise grabbed the plastic shopping bag dangling from Roz's wrist and towed her friend into the house. "I can't believe I forgot to buy birthday candles, of all things! Kelsey would never forgive me. The guests will be here any minute, and if you hadn't bailed me out, I don't know what I would have done!"

"Good heavens, take a deep breath! You'd think you were hosting a state dinner for the king of Timbuktu, instead of a kids' birthday party." Roz swung the shopping bag tantalizingly out of reach. "Uh-uh-uh! Before I hand over the candles, you have to tell me *everything*."

Elise absentmindedly plowed her fingers through her hair. "I still don't know what you're talking about," she said, trying to remember where she'd put the red bandanna she planned to use as a blindfold while the kids were trying to whack the piñata.

Roz's face was the picture of utter exasperation. "I'm talking about one specific entry on your guest list? A particular partygoer who's *not* in Kelsey's class? A certain someone who's got the hots for you?"

"Oh," Elise said. "You mean Cole." Butterflies stirred in her stomach. "Don't be silly. He doesn't have the hots for me."

"No?" Roz twirled the shopping bag and wiggled her hips like a burlesque performer vamping with her feather boa. "Then why is he coming to Kelsey's party? Not to play Pin the Tail on the Donkey and eat birthday cake, I'd imagine."

Elise made a lunge for the bag and managed to nab it. "How do you know he's coming to the party, anyway?"

"Puh-*leeze.*" Roz rolled her eyes. "Haven't you lived here long enough to realize the amazing efficiency of the local grapevine?" She cupped her hand to the side of her mouth and whispered loudly, "He was seen in Beekman's Toy Store, shopping for a present for a nine-year-old."

"Really?" Elise snatched the box of candles from the bag and headed for the kitchen. "That was nice of him. Wonder what he got her."

"Nothing." Roz tagged close behind. "At least, he walked out of Beekman's empty-handed." She made a swatting motion as if trying to drive away a cloud of gnats. "Never mind that. I want to hear all about the stroke of genius that inspired you to invite our sexy sheriff to Kelsey's party."

Elise counted out nine candles and began to poke them into the cake. "I didn't invite him. Kelsey did."

"Ooh, aren't you the clever one? Getting your kid to do it for you. I must say, I'm impressed." She speared out a finger to snitch a dab of chocolate frosting. "Never knew you were such a master of manipulation, Elise."

Elise slapped her hand away. "I didn't manipulate anybody. It was all Kelsey's idea, and Cole was polite enough to accept her invitation."

"Polite, my grandma's nightie! That man is interested in you, Elise. The whole town knows it."

"That's ridiculous." Still, she couldn't help feeling a bit flattered.

Roz ticked off points of evidence on her fingers. "He drops by the café just to see you, he comes over here on his day off to fix your fence, and if that's not enough, *now* he's showing up for your kid's birthday party!" She shook her head. "Boy, if that's not proof the man's crazy about you, I don't know what is."

"He's just being nice, that's all." But a delicious, warm glow made Elise feel sort of giddy inside. She hadn't forgotten the danger Cole could pose to her and Kelsey. But she was too honest to deny her own attraction to him, or to pretend she didn't enjoy the boost it gave her feminine ego to know the attraction was mutual.

Roz swiped another bit of frosting. "If he was just being nice," she said, her voice muffled by the finger in her mouth, "why would he be going all over town asking questions about you?"

Elise's hand jerked, so that she dropped one of the candles onto the gooey chocolate frosting. Her warm glow evaporated instantly. "What do you mean, asking questions about me?"

"Oh, you know." Roz shrugged. "Where you're from, if you're divorced or widowed...just the sorts of things a man would ask if he was scoping out the territory before making his move."

Elise forced herself to fish the candle out of the frosting, pluck another one from the box and proceed as if cake decorating was her biggest concern in the world right now.

Maybe Roz was right. Maybe all the snooping Cole was doing was pure curiosity, prompted by a romantic interest in her.

Or maybe he suspected something.

Fear began to simmer in her stomach.

The loud rapping of the front door knocker sounded like a round of artillery fire. Elise jumped, nearly dropping another candle.

Roz made a beeline for the front window, then snapped her fingers in disappointment. "Darn, it's not him." She stuck her head back into the kitchen. "Looks like the first wave of little darlings has arrived."

Elise opened the back door. "Kelsey! Your guests are here."

Kelsey came racing across the backyard. "Can I let 'em in?"

"Unless Roz has already beaten you to it. No, Bob, you have to stay outside during the party. Remember those cookies you stole off the counter last week?"

"Roz is here?" Kelsey cried. "Roz, are you gonna stay for my party?"

"'Fraid not, sugar pie." She rustled Kelsey's hair. "I've gotta get back so I can baby-sit a couple of my grandkids this afternoon."

Kelsey scrunched up her face in puzzlement. "But you're not *old* enough to be a grandma."

Roz grinned broadly. "Sweetie, you just made my day." She pinched Kelsey's cheeks. "Go on, let your guests in. Elise, what an absolutely *perfect* child you've raised!"

"I know. But I try not to say it within her hearing too often." Elise nervously licked a smear of chocolate off her thumb. Until a few minutes ago, entertaining a rambunctious group of third-grade girls for two hours had loomed as the major worry in her life. But Roz's offhand remarks had jolted matters back into perspective.

All that truly counted in the grand scheme of things was keeping Kelsey safe. And the man who could very well pose a threat to her safety was about to arrive on their doorstep any minute.

"Here he comes!" Roz announced, peering out the window. She stretched her mouth into a grimace of mock horror at the lively mob of little girls now swarming through the living room. "All I can say, Elise, is that you're a braver woman than I am." She wiggled her fingers in farewell. "Good luck!"

She sidled out the front door, primping her hair as she waltzed down the steps. "Why, hello, Sheriff!" Elise heard her sing out.

An ominous crash made Elise spin around. One of Kelsey's classmates had knocked over a terra-cotta planter, strewing a mixture of pottery shards, soil and philodendron leaves across the floor. The culprit stood frozen with guilt, her eyes enormous, her lower lip quivering as if she were about to burst into tears.

Elise swallowed a sigh as a comforting smile sprang to her lips. "Don't worry, Amanda. It was just an accident." She gave the little girl a reassuring hug as she knelt to gather up the sharp pieces. "It was just a silly old plant, anyway."

Amanda blinked back tears. "I didn't mean to—"

"Of course you didn't, sweetheart."

"Mrs. Grant?" Another girl whose name escaped Elise at the moment stepped forward. "My mother says to tell you I'm not allowed to eat sweets. Do you have any yogurt or fruit instead? Only not strawberries. I'm allergic to strawberries, and I don't like apples or bananas, either."

Just then, Bob galloped into the living room, eliciting a chorus of squeals as he attempted to make each girl's acquaintance by leaping up to leave an imprint of his dirty paws on the front of her party clothes.

"Drat! I must not have shut the back door tight." Elise was still hunkered down on the floor, her hands full of broken pottery. "Kelsey, grab him, quick!"

From the corner of her eye, she glimpsed a pair of well-worn cowboy boots. Her gaze traveled upward along hard, muscled legs clad in black denim...over a teal blue shirt buttoned across a broad chest...to a handsome, square-jawed face that managed to look both somber and amused at the same time.

He wore a tan sport coat and a bolo tie, and cradled an elaborately wrapped gift in his left arm. To her dismay, Elise felt her pulse pick up its pace, and knew that worry wasn't the sole source of her reaction.

Cole's dark brows quirked upward. "Can I help?" he asked.

Kelsey held court in the backyard, surrounded by a sea of discarded wrapping paper and ribbon. A bright yellow bow was stuck to the cone-shaped party hat on top of her head.

Her eyes widened in delight when she ripped open the gift in her lap. "Wow, the newest Rainbow Street Detectives book!" She opened it and greedily scanned the inside jacket cover. "In this one, Peter and Jessica try to find out who kidnapped the class guinea pig over Christmas vacation." She beamed at the friend who'd given it to her. "Thanks, Sara!"

In one corner of the yard, near the battered remnants of the unfortunate piñata, Bob's leash anchored the prostrate basset hound to a fence post. Every once in a while, he perked up his drooping ears, blew a wet, mournful sigh through his jowls and plopped his head back down on his oversize paws. Obviously, he was feeling a mite left out.

Cole knew just how he felt.

As he surveyed the cluster of giggling, whispering, chocolate-smeared little girls sprawled in a semicircle around the picnic blanket, Cole felt like an alien intruder from another planet.

As out-of-place and conspicuous as King Kong at a square dance.

Elise wasn't helping matters any. Ever since Cole's arrival, she'd treated him like a gate-crasher she was too polite to throw out. A week or so ago, she'd acted as if she were finally warming up to him. Though he was definitely rusty when it came to the cautious signals men and women exchange during the initial steps of the mating dance, Cole could have sworn that the undercurrent of physical attraction had flowed both ways.

Not that he had any intention of following up on that attraction, to see where it might lead.

He'd been busy, though, following up on some other leads. Kelsey's declaration that the Boston Red Sox was her favorite baseball team had given Cole a place to start. How would a kid in Arizona develop such loyalty to a team that played two thousand miles away, unless she'd once lived there?

Weak, maybe, but it was all Cole had to go on. Along with Kelsey's birth date, which she'd also conveniently provided him. He was counting on the chance that whatever other facts Elise might have altered about their past, her daughter's birthday wasn't one of them.

Armed with those two questionable clues, Cole had contacted the proper bureaucrats in Boston and asked them to compile a list from computerized records of all children born in the Boston area on that date, with the first name Kelsey on their birth certificates.

Cole was making another assumption here—that Kelsey was, in fact, the child's real first name. But it seemed to him much easier for an adult to adopt a false name than to teach a child to respond to a brand-new one. Hopefully, Elise hadn't gone to the trouble of changing her daughter's *first* name, at least.

A list of seven children had arrived from Boston three days ago.

Cole intended to follow up on all of them, if necessary, but one pair of names had leaped out at him. Father— Thomas Christopher Jordan. Mother—Elizabeth Marie Jordan, née Winfield.

Elizabeth Jordan ... Elise Grant? Elizabeth ... Elise?

Coincidence, maybe. But Cole would find out soon enough. A copy of Elizabeth Jordan's Massachusetts driver's license, along with those of the other six mothers, would be faxed to the Creosote County Sheriff's Department as soon as the authorities in Boston got around to processing his request.

The pictures on the licenses would reveal to Cole which one of the women—if any—was now going by the name Elise Grant.

While the crowd of exuberant little girls oohed and aahed over Kelsey's latest gift, Cole slanted a speculative glance across the yard. Elise was leaning against the back-door frame, hands pancaked behind her back, watching the festive proceedings with an absent smile on her face.

Absent, yet vaguely anxious, too.

He noticed that her eyes never once flickered in his direction. She'd been giving him a wide berth all afternoon.

Almost as if she knew what Cole had been up to all week.

Kelsey stuffed a birthday card back into its envelope and looked around. "Any more presents?" she asked hopefully.

Elise shielded her eyes and shook her head with embarrassment.

Dumb, but suddenly Cole felt nervous. "One more," he called to Kelsey, producing the gaily wrapped package from where he'd half hidden it behind his lawn chair.

What if she didn't like it? He'd spent days traipsing through stores all over town in search of the right gift, but at the moment he couldn't imagine what had possessed him to buy this particular one. What the heck did he know about nine-year-old girls, anyway? He should have gotten her a doll, probably, or a video game or a stuffed animal.

Kelsey tore off the paper eagerly. She got the box turned right side up, and studied it silently for a moment.

Cole sucked in his breath. *You idiot,* he thought. *Of all the stupid presents to give to a little girl . . .*

All at once, Kelsey's face lit up like a cake full of birthday candles. "It's a hummingbird feeder," she exclaimed, bouncing with excitement. "Look, Mom! I can hang it outside my window, and hummingbirds will come and *eat* there!"

Relief spread through Cole like a soothing balm. Elise finally looked over at him. Only for a split second, but long enough to convey the approval and appreciation in her eyes.

"What do you say to the sheriff, Peach?"

Kelsey aimed a thousand-watt smile at him. "Thanks, Sheriff!"

"You're welcome," Cole replied, absurdly pleased that his present had been such a hit. "It comes with a book so you can identify the different hummingbirds." The pleasure flowing through him must have loosened his tongue.

"My wife had one she used to hang outside our dining room window."

Elise flung an abrupt, startled glance in his direction.

"Your wife?" Kelsey cocked her head at a quizzical angle. "I didn't know you were married."

Cole could have bitten his tongue off. He adjusted the sleeves of his sport coat, fiddled with the ends of his tie. "My wife died," he said, clearing his throat.

Elise's hand crept up to cover her heart.

Kelsey's mouth curved down at the edges. "That's too bad," she said, studying him with an innocent curiosity that made Cole want to squirm. "What happened to her?"

Elise clapped her hands. "Okay, girls, your parents will be here soon to pick you up. Let's see how fast we can gather up all this wrapping paper. Everyone make sure you have your share of loot from the piñata!"

Though her voice was cheerful, her face had gone pale. When she stared briefly at Cole over the heads of a dozen scrambling third-graders, he saw the troubled storm sweeping through her eyes like a cloudburst over the desert mountains.

"You didn't have to do this, you know. Stick around and help me clean up."

"I know. I believe you've already mentioned that once or twice."

One last streamer of crepe paper dangled limply from the light fixture over the kitchen table. Elise plucked it out of the air and stuffed it into the black plastic trash bag. "Well, anyway, I certainly appreciate all your help."

Cole's eyes twinkled as he handed her a yellow twist tie to close the top of the bag. "I believe you've already mentioned *that* once or twice, too."

"Have I?" Elise plopped the bag down by the back door. "Guess I must be repeating myself in my old age."

The two of them smiled cautiously at each other.

The last paper plate had been tossed away, the last blob of ice cream wiped off the wall, the last pile of cake crumbs swept off the kitchen floor.

Cole leaned back against the counter and crossed one boot over the other. "Nice party," he said.

Elise rolled her eyes. "Especially if your idea of a good time is complete and utter chaos." She blew a gust of air through her bangs. "I had no idea a group of perfectly sweet little girls could act as rowdy as a bunch of drunken Mardi Gras revelers."

Cole chuckled. "I've busted up bar fights that weren't as lively as this."

"Bet you didn't know what you were getting into when you accepted Kelsey's invitation."

"I wouldn't have missed it for the world."

Something in his tone told Elise he really meant it. There was certainly a lot more to Cole Hardesty than met the eye, she thought. On the surface, he seemed so competent, so sure of himself, so self-contained. He was the stereotype of every terse, rugged, fast-drawing lawman who'd ever sauntered across a western movie screen to rid the town of bad guys.

But beneath that cool, chiseled exterior that so rarely gave anything away, Elise sensed that Cole might not be as invulnerable as he seemed. Every once in a while, she caught a sad gleam in his eyes or a wistful note in his voice that made him seem kind of...oh, lonely or something.

Maybe she was just being fanciful. But the more Elise thought about it, the more Cole appeared to her like a man haunted by a powerful yearning for the one thing on earth he could never have. There was an air of resigned acceptance about him, but conflict, too, as if he couldn't quite force himself to surrender that last thread of hope.

Oh, for heaven's sake, she thought, dusting her hands together in disgust. *Quit trying to psychoanalyze him. And quit being so melodramatic, while you're at it.*

She was just feeling an artificial closeness to Cole, that was all. Because of the astonishing bombshell he'd quietly dropped during the party, about having a wife who'd died.

Just because they had similar tragedies in common didn't give Elise a road map to the darkest recesses of his soul.

Still, discovering this unexpected bond between them made Cole seem less of a threat, somehow.

"I—I was sorry to learn about your wife," she said.

Cole shifted his feet and immediately looked uncomfortable. "Oh. Uh, thanks."

Elise didn't realize how far she'd let her guard down until she heard herself blurting out, "My husband died, too."

Cole's head shot up. "He did?"

Elise wedged her thumbnail between her bottom front teeth. Well, now that she'd revealed *that* much, might as well go all the way. She was probably just being paranoid, anyway, fretting so much about letting the least little information about her past slip out.

She drifted over to the table, where Cole had draped his sport coat over a chair before pitching in with the cleanup.

"We'd only been married three years," she said carefully, still not reckless enough to mention Tom's name. "He was a...workaholic," she continued, managing to tell the truth without revealing that the work in question had been as a stockbroker. "He came down with what turned out to be pneumonia, but kept right on driving himself... wouldn't even slow down long enough to go to the doctor to find out why he kept coughing all the time."

Cole listened silently, though his eyes conveyed his sympathy more plainly than words.

Elise dropped her hands to the back of the chair. "Finally, he collapsed at the office one day and had to be taken to the hospital by ambulance." Her fingers clutched the shoulders of Cole's jacket. "I barely had time to get there before he was gone."

She blinked, not with tears, but in a sort of daze. "His death sent me straight into shock, of course, but one thing I remember clearly is how *surprised* I was to learn what killed him. I mean, people aren't supposed to die of pneumonia these days. Not young, otherwise healthy people."

"Elise..."

"I just kept asking the doctor over and over, how could he die of *pneumonia?*"

"Elise." Cole gently placed his hands over hers. Elise realized she'd been grinding her fingers into his jacket, kneading the cloth as if she were massaging Cole's shoulders instead of the chair back.

His hands were warm and reassuring. Or else hers were cold and trembling—it was hard to tell which. He drew another chair from beneath the table. "Why don't we sit down?"

"It's...been a long time since I thought about his death," Elise said, pressing shaking fingertips over her eyelids. *Over two years of being on the run, when I had to shove those memories deep down inside so I could focus on protecting Kelsey...*

Cole squeezed her other hand. "It must have been a nightmare, trying to cope with such a terrible loss, *and* continue to care for your child at the same time."

Elise realized if she were smart, she would move her hand away from his. She didn't. "Kelsey was born four months after my husband died,'' she said softly. ''She never knew her father.''

Cole's grip tightened. Normally, his face was like the shutter of a camera, allowing only the briefest flashes of illumination to expose his emotions. But now that shutter snapped all the way open, showing Elise a picture of raw anguish that obviously had a more deeply buried source than the sad story she'd just told him.

''How did your wife die?'' she asked softly.

For a minute, while she watched Cole struggle to close that shutter again, she thought he wasn't going to answer.

''She was killed during a mugging,'' he said finally. The words sounded as if he had to physically pry each one out of his throat.

Elise's breath hitched in her chest. ''Oh, Cole.'' She clasped both her hands around his.

Although he was gazing straight into her eyes, Elise knew he was seeing something very far away. A scene he must have played over and over in his head, until countless repetitions had etched every terrible detail into his visual memory like acid.

''Laura was a social worker,'' he said slowly. ''I was an L.A. police detective. We'd been married almost two years.''

His own voice sounded distant to Cole's ears. Detached. The way it did while he dictated reports into a recorder for his secretary to type up later.

''One night, I was invited to a bachelor party for one of the guys on the squad. Laura tried to be a good sport about it, but I could tell she was a little annoyed.''

He took a deep, steadying breath. ''God knows, with the crazy hours I worked, it was pretty rare for the two of us to get to spend an evening at home together, and here I was, going off to 'guzzle beer all night, leer at some bimbo jumping out of a cake and in general behave like an overgrown adolescent whooping it up while Mom and Dad are out of town.' ''

Surprisingly, Cole felt the taut line of his mouth jerk into a crooked smile. ''That was a direct quote from Laura, by the way.''

Elise returned a tentative flicker of a smile. ''Obviously a very perceptive woman.''

''And not one to sit around drumming her fingernails and stewing over a done deal. She was a real go-getter when it came to her work, and after I left that evening, she decided to pay a home visit to one of the troubled kids she'd been counseling.''

A light film of sweat made Cole's forehead feel clammy. This was where it started to get bad.

''The kid lived in a rough neighborhood, one I never would have let Laura go into alone at night if I'd known about it. But the parents had been uncooperative, not showing up for appointments during office hours, dodging her phone calls and so on, so Laura figured she'd catch them at home in the evening and *make* them sit down and discuss their child's problems with her.''

Cole felt that old familiar sick feeling slide into the pit of his stomach. Elise's eyes were huge as she listened to him— vast, twin seas shimmering in the fading rays of daylight that filtered into the kitchen.

''It happened while she was walking back to her car, after trying to talk to the parents.'' A heavy weight settled on Cole's chest, making it hard to breathe. ''Someone jumped her...grabbed her purse...maybe she resisted, I don't know. It would have been just like her.''

He swallowed the taste of bile. ''For whatever twisted reason, the guy stabbed her. Over and over.''

Horror splashed across Elise's face, like a rush of spilled blood across the pavement. Her nails dug convulsively into Cole's hands, but he barely noticed.

"She lay there, in the gutter, her cries growing weaker and weaker. Witnesses later admitted hearing her. But it was nearly twenty minutes before anyone bothered to call for help."

Elise's face crumpled. She covered her mouth with her hand. "Dear God," she said in a broken voice.

"By the time the paramedics got there, she'd already bled to death."

Tears brimmed in Elise's eyes. One of them trickled down her cheek. "I'm so sorry," she whispered.

"Laura..." Saying the next part was like forcing splinters out of his throat. "She was three months pregnant with our first child."

Chapter 7

Shadows draped the kitchen in darkness. Through the west-facing windows, the nearest mountain ridge was visible only as a collection of hulking black shapes against the orchid-hued remnants of sunset.

Elise could barely make out the rugged, haunted contours of Cole's face. She suspected she wasn't the only one grateful for the concealing veil of gloom.

Still, they couldn't sit here in silence forever, while the lingering echoes of tragedy and grief swirled and settled around them, like desert sand over bare, bleached bones.

Elise reached for a switch behind her. Light exploded into the room, making them both blink. A chair scraped, a throat cleared, and both of them discovered a sudden fascination for the wood grain in the kitchen table.

They were both, it seemed, suddenly embarrassed by the painful disclosures, the secret sorrows that had somehow been easier to share in the descending darkness. They had stumbled into a deep, unexpected chasm of intimacy by accident, by daring to expose aspects of themselves they normally kept hidden from the world.

Now they found themselves bound together by a powerful emotional connection that, under the revealing flood of light, seemed awkward... and perhaps something to be regretted.

It was the way Elise imagined she might feel waking up in the harsh glare of dawn, after having spent the night with a stranger.

She pushed herself to her feet. "I didn't realize how late it was getting," she said, summoning a strained smile. In the now-opaque reflection of the dark window glass, she saw that her smile looked as stiff as it felt. "Time to start cooking supper already."

Cole rubbed his eyes with the heels of his hands, as if they felt gritty. He shoved his chair back. "Guess I should be going."

Elise opened the refrigerator and stared into it as if trying to decide what to fix. But she was really just buying time while she wrestled with a different decision.

"Would you like to stay for supper with Kelsey and me?" she asked finally, letting the door swing shut as she turned around.

Maybe the startling bond of closeness they'd just shared had given Elise a false sense of security. But all those reasons why she'd worried so much about having the sheriff hanging around her house had flown straight out of her head.

Now it was Cole who seemed uncomfortable with the idea. His mouth yanked into a tight curve that was more grimace than smile. "Thanks, but I should be on my way." He shrugged on his sport coat. "How 'bout a rain check?"

Elise couldn't tell if he was sincere, or just trying to be polite. Amazing how just a short while ago, she'd thought she had him all figured out. Now she couldn't even tell if he was trying to give her the brush-off or not.

"Sure." She combed her fingers through her hair and surreptitiously pinched her cheeks to bring some color back into them. She could just imagine what a mess she must look, her eyes all red and puffy with the residue of tears. "Well . . . thanks again for the thoughtful gift you gave Kelsey. I know she'll love watching the hummingbirds."

Just like your wife did, she thought, and saw the same idea ricochet beneath the surface of Cole's controlled features.

Now that she'd had a glimpse of the buried grief and rage that were as much a part of Cole as his dedication to his work, Elise understood what a struggle it was to mask his feelings behind his impassive, granitelike facade.

Surprisingly, she found she was genuinely disappointed he wouldn't be staying for supper.

"Thank *you* for the party," Cole said. "And for . . . well . . ." He made a rolling, at-a-loss-for-words motion with his hand, as if to encompass all that had passed between them. "For listening," he finished.

His shirt collar had gotten a little bunched up when he'd put on his coat. Elise had to squelch an inappropriate, wifely urge to straighten it for him.

"Anytime," she said. Though she figured it would be a snowy day in summer before Cole Hardesty made the deliberate choice to unburden himself to her again.

There was enough illumination spilling out of the kitchen to walk him to the front door without switching on any more lights. Just as well. Elise felt as if her emotional circuits were already overloaded from seeing too much. She suspected Cole felt the same way.

But she flipped on the porch lamp so he could make his way to his car. He paused in the doorway. Beneath the muted golden glow, shadows pooled in his eyes and in the carved hollows beneath his cheekbones.

"I . . . never told anyone else all that stuff about Laura's death before." His gruff voice was edged with a hint of amazement.

Elise felt strangely touched. "Don't worry. I don't intend to go blabbing the story all over town."

Cole chuckled quietly. "That's the last thing I'd worry about, believe me." He brought his hand to the side of her face.

Elise caught her breath. His skin was so warm, his touch so unexpected.

"I have a feeling that one thing you're very good at," he said, bringing his face close to hers so she could see blue flames in his eyes, "is keeping secrets."

Now, what on earth is that supposed to mean? The question skittered across her mind and evaporated almost instantly. Because all at once, Elise realized that Cole was about to kiss her.

She could have backed away, mumbling something incoherent and retreating behind the safety of that sturdy front door.

Instead, she tilted her head up to meet him.

There was a deliberate, focused quality to his kiss, as if it were his first one and he was worried about doing it right.

He needn't have worried.

His lips were warm and firm as they moved over Elise's. She was shocked by the powerful spasm of desire that shot through her the moment their mouths joined. Dear God, but it had been a long time since a man had kissed her like this! Since a man had kissed her, period.

That must explain the sudden rush of heat and dizziness, as if Cole's touch had ignited an instant fever. Elise felt her heart flutter wildly against her ribs as her insides turned to liquid.

As if the air itself had turned to liquid, too, her hand moved in slow motion as she glided it beneath his jacket...slipped it partway around his waist...brought it to rest just above the level of his belt. His hammering pulse reverberated throughout his lean, hard frame, transmitting his heartbeat to Elise's fingertips.

He tasted, naturally, of chocolate. A flavor Elise had never been especially partial to, but which right now she couldn't seem to get enough of.

A brief rumble rose from Cole's throat as he wove his fingers through Elise's hair and readjusted the angle of his head to slant his mouth more snugly over hers.

A sharp stab of hunger lanced through her, and she parted her lips instinctively. She splayed her fingers across his rib cage, tracing the strong web of muscles beneath his shirt.

He touched the tip of his tongue to hers, once, and a slight shudder rocked his body. Almost immediately, Elise felt him start to withdraw. Beneath her fingers, his muscles went rigid, as if he were struggling to rein himself in.

She forced herself not to cling to him, to fight off the disappointment that lashed through her.

Though she knew perfectly well this kiss could never lead anywhere, it was astonishing how reluctant she was to have it end.

Cole broke the contact between their lips, then brushed his mouth lightly over hers, once...twice...three times. Elise's scalp tingled as he sifted his fingers through her hair.

When he finally drew back, she breathed deeply, intending to infuse her racing blood with some sanity-restoring oxygen. Instead, she filled her lungs with the provocative male scent of him. It reminded her of the pleasant, pungent fragrance of sagebrush leaves when you crushed them between your fingers.

It made her mouth water.

Cole, too, was breathing hard. The silver tips of his bolo tie glinted against his shirt as his chest rose and fell. Now his eyes were back in the shadows, so that Elise felt as if she were gazing into the bottomless depths of two mysterious, impenetrable caverns.

He dropped his hand from her face, letting the strands of her hair fall away like folds of precious silk. "Tell Kelsey goodbye for me." Elise heard a hint of unsteadiness in his voice, as if he'd been as strongly affected, as caught off guard by their kiss, as she'd been.

"I'll tell her." Her words emerged as thin wisps of sound. She had to devote all her internal resources just to remain motionless, to keep from swaying toward him.

Cole caught her hand and brought it to his lips in a curiously gallant gesture. Elise's eyelids fluttered shut for a moment as that same seductive heat radiated all the way to her fingertips.

"Good night," he said. He squeezed her hand in farewell. Then she was listening to his boots scrunch down the gravel driveway.

Not until Elise heard the sound of his cruiser fade away in the distance did she whisper, "Good night."

The first star of the evening—or maybe it was a planet—hovered over the horizon. Even this far into spring, the desert air still cooled down rapidly once the sun had set. Elise shivered.

All at once, the sky seemed incredibly dark and vast and full of the unknown. A faint rustling noise stirred across the yard. A car started up, somewhere off in the distance.

Then something swooped suddenly out of the darkness, arcing across Elise's field of vision with a speed that made her gasp.

A bat, probably. But it made her all too aware of how unprotected she truly was against the dangers of the night.

She stepped hastily back inside and shut the door with more force than necessary. With lightning-quick fingers she snapped the dead-bolt locks into place.

The image of Victor Dominick swooped through Elise's memory, just like the bat. As malevolent and threatening as Count Dracula himself.

She'd only seen the man in person once, on her way to a meeting with the detective in charge of the murder case. Dominick had been coming out of Boston police head-quarters with his lawyer. Elise had recognized his sinister, bearded face from newspaper accounts of his arrest.

Their glances had intersected for only a fraction of a second, and Elise had hurried up the steps past him as fast as she could. But the stone-cold ruthlessness she'd glimpsed in his eyes, as cruel and unrelenting as the distilled essence of evil, had seared an indelible imprint into her memory.

Time and again during the next two years, while rounding a busy sidewalk corner or glancing in her rearview mirror at the driver stopped behind her at a red light, Elise had had to stifle a scream when she thought she spotted those same evil eyes pinning her in their sights.

Even though she knew intellectually she was just imagining all these close calls with Dominick, they jolted Elise so badly that it was never long before she and Kelsey were on the run again.

She hadn't had one of those frightening, all-too-vivid hallucinations since moving to Tumbleweed, Arizona. Which was another reason she was keeping her mental fingers crossed that she and Kelsey would be able to settle down for good this time.

Funny. For weeks, she'd been so jumpy about the way Cole seemed to be nudging his way into their lives. Now, after he'd driven off into the night and left her and Kelsey alone, Elise realized the only time she actually felt *safe* from Victor Dominick was when Cole was around.

She knew she still had to be careful around Cole, not to let anything slip that might lead to his discovering the truth. After all, he had taken an oath as sheriff to uphold the law, and the law wanted Kelsey back in Boston to testify.

Back in Boston, where Dominick could make another attempt on Kelsey's life. And Elise doubted he would fail the next time.

She shuddered. She skimmed her fingertips over her lips, where she could still feel the delicious, dizzying impact of Cole's kiss.

She couldn't allow a repeat of that kiss. She couldn't let Cole get any closer. She wasn't sure where he hoped the winding road of their relationship might lead, but it was time for Elise to post a Dead-End sign.

She had to, for Kelsey's sake. Even though Elise knew that Cole would never deliberately let anything bad happen to either one of them. Even though she believed with all her heart that he would risk his life to protect them.

Cole was a man of courage and honor. He was a man who stirred feelings inside Elise that had lain dormant for a long, long time.

But he was also a man devoted to his job and to his duty.

And that was where the danger lay.

Cole pushed open the glass door of the one-story, beige stucco building that housed the Creosote County Sheriff's Department. The heels of his boots echoed loudly on the marble floor as he strode down the hallway toward his office.

Pam Taylor, the weekend dispatcher, looked up from her computer terminal when Cole stuck his head into the room. Her eyes widened in admiration while she gave him a thorough, head-to-toe once-over. She was grinning when she pulled off her headphones.

"Anything I should know about?" Cole asked.

"Pretty quiet for a Saturday night, Sheriff." Her eyes twinkled. "Dressed up awful fancy, aren't you?"

Cole drew a blank. He glanced down at his clothes, vaguely surprised to find he wasn't wearing the uniform that was practically like a second skin to him.

Pam winked. "Hot date tonight, huh?"

"Just came from one," Cole replied easily, trying to push back the sharp, arousing memory of Elise's lips on his. "With a nine-year-old girl and a bunch of her friends."

"Ooo, sounds kinky." She reached for the can of diet cola near her elbow. "Well, whenever you decide you want to play with someone your own age, you just let me know." She hoisted her eyebrows along with the soft-drink can and took a sip.

When Cole had first taken this job as sheriff, his businesslike—some might call it aloof—behavior toward his colleagues had eventually conveyed the message that there was a certain line not to be crossed.

It hadn't taken long for any female in the department who had designs on him to realize that Cole was not in the market for even the most casual hanky-panky.

Once they got used to thinking of him strictly as a fair, honest, hardworking boss, Cole had lowered his reserve a little. Not enough to let anything like true friendship develop, but enough so that he'd come to enjoy the camaraderie and conversational banter that now substituted for any meaningful relationships in his life.

Normally, Pam's good-natured, brazen flirting didn't bother Cole. Both of them knew nothing would come of it.

Tonight, however, he himself had crossed a line. One he'd had no right to cross. And Pam's suggestive comments were conjuring up images that made Cole feel uncomfortable. Guilty, actually.

He tipped her a farewell salute with two fingers. "I'll be in my office, if a crime wave happens to develop."

She waved at him before she put on her headphones and swiveled back to the computer. "You'll be the first to know," she promised.

There he'd been, spilling his guts to Elise at her kitchen table—kissing her on her front doorstep, for God's sake! While behind her back, he was busy conducting an investigation that might very well turn Elise and her daughter's lives upside down.

It was despicable behavior on Cole's part. Unforgivable. Chalk up another mark on the guilty side of his slate.

"Evenin', Sheriff!" Zack Brewster, one of Cole's deputies, passed him in the hall. His voice was muffled by the sloppy, overstuffed sandwich he was shoveling down. A strand of lettuce dribbled down the front of his shirt.

"Hey, Zack." Cole's stomach grumbled. Too bad he'd had to decline Elise's invitation to supper. But how could he share a cozy meal with them, asking Elise to please pass the salt, complimenting her cooking, while secretly repaying her hospitality with treachery?

Besides, how could he look her in the eye in that cheerful, bright kitchen after burdening her with the tragic story of Laura's death?

He thought about all he *hadn't* told Elise.

How Laura's killer had turned out to be a two-bit thug whom the robbery detail Cole was assigned to had been trying to catch for weeks.

How if Cole had put in just a few more hours, followed up on a couple of more leads, they might have nailed the bastard before Laura became his first murder victim.

How if Cole had stayed home that night the way Laura had wanted him to, she wouldn't have been walking down that dark, dangerous street where some vicious piece of filth was waiting to butcher her.

Cole's job was to protect people. But he hadn't even been able to protect his own wife and unborn child.

All of a sudden, he didn't feel hungry anymore.

"By the way, Sheriff..."

He wheeled around when Zack hailed him again. The deputy wolfed down a huge bite before gesturing in the direction of Cole's office with the remainder of his sandwich. "A fax came in for you a while ago. From back East somewhere. Boston, maybe?" He shrugged. "Anyway, I put it on your desk."

"Thanks, Zack." Normally, Cole would have been impatient to check out any new puzzle piece that might or might not be part of a case he was working on. But he found his feet dragging as he walked the rest of the way to his office.

All he could think about was the way Elise had felt in his arms. How her mouth had responded so warmly to his. How she'd pressed the soft, innocently seductive curves of her body against him and sent powerful desire coursing through his bloodstream for the first time in years.

She was kind. Generous. Compassionate. For the span of that sweet yet utterly sensual kiss, she'd made Cole feel like a whole man again.

And now he might have to betray her.

He entered his office, closed the door and rasped his palms over his cheeks before approaching the desk.

The fax was right on top, just where Zack had left it. Cole absently flicked away a shred of lettuce curled over one corner.

He pushed his chair aside and remained standing while he scanned each page, carefully averting his eyes from each photograph until he found the copy of the driver's license issued to Elizabeth Jordan.

Her eye color was listed as green. The height, age and weight seemed about right.

Cole took a deep breath and looked at her picture.

The hair was shorter, clipped into a carefree wedge. Her face appeared a bit fuller. And the self-conscious, driver's license smile definitely didn't do her justice.

Cole's heart plummeted like a runaway elevator.

Bingo.

Chapter 8

"Bye, Mom!" Kelsey waved enthusiastically from Mrs. Applegate's doorstep.

Elise rolled down the car window and stuck her head out. "I'll be back to pick you up at five."

"Are you sure you won't stay and have a snack with us?" Mrs. Applegate asked for the third or fourth time since Elise had brought Kelsey by. "I baked some delicious peanut-butter cookies earlier."

"Thank you. They sound yummy, but I have some errands I need to run." Elise let the car inch backward. "Thanks again for inviting Kelsey over to play with Chester."

"Why, she's welcome to come any time." Mrs. Applegate waved a corner of her apron in farewell.

"Have fun," Elise called to Kelsey. "Give my regards to Chester."

"'Kay." Kelsey disappeared with Mrs. Applegate before

Elise even finished backing out the driveway. Hot on the trail of the elusive cat, no doubt.

She turned the car toward home, untroubled by the slightest twinge of guilt about the little fib she'd told Doris Applegate. It wasn't errands that awaited her this afternoon. It was a long, hot bubble bath, complete with a glass of wine and a thick, juicy paperback novel she'd borrowed from Roz just for the occasion.

Elise sighed at the prospect of such glorious self-indulgence. Though Kelsey meant everything in the world to her, she couldn't help looking forward to having a couple of hours to herself. She couldn't even remember the last time she wasn't either surrounded by people at work, or at home with her daughter.

The bottle of wine and the scented bath crystals she'd splurged on were stashed in a sack in the back seat. Maybe she could even dig up some candles...? Of course! Kelsey's leftover birthday candles would help provide the proper decadent mood!

Elise smiled. Not exactly "Lifestyles of the Rich and Famous," but for her the next two hours loomed ahead like an orgy of blissful luxury.

She eased her foot off the accelerator and checked her rearview mirror as she approached the turn for Saguaro Road.

Immediately, her heart catapulted into her throat.

Some type of law-enforcement vehicle was flashing its red lights directly behind her. Adrenaline exploded into her bloodstream with a sickening rush. She felt as vulnerable, as defenseless as a guppy pursued by a shark.

For two years, Elise had never once crept over the speed limit or failed to come to a complete halt at a stop sign—never so much as jaywalked across the street. Because she was terrified that the most innocent brush with the law could somehow tip off the Boston authorities about where to find Kelsey and her.

Her instinctive reaction to those red lights flashing behind her now was pure, gut-wrenching fear.

No other cars in the vicinity. She was the one he was pulling over, all right.

Easy, she commanded herself. *You're not Ma Barker. You haven't got a chance of outrunning him, even if you were stupid enough to try it.*

She coasted to a stop on the gravel shoulder of the road. The flashing red lights pulled up right behind her. Elise gripped the steering wheel with both hands to keep them from shaking. But there was no way she could control the flip-flops in her stomach.

In her side mirror she watched, paralyzed with dread, as the door opened. When she recognized the emblem of the sheriff's department, hope made a frantic leap inside her. Maybe she could talk her way out of this by claiming friendship with Cole.

Except maybe this guy hadn't pulled her over for a traffic violation. Maybe the cops in Boston had finally tracked her down and sent this local emissary of the law after her, in which case even the most blatant name-dropping wasn't going to do her a bit of good.

Oh, God, maybe he'd seen her drop Kelsey off at Mrs. Applegate's ... maybe at this very moment Kelsey was sitting in the back of another cruiser, being whisked straight back to Boston and the man who intended to kill her....

Then Elise recognized the figure approaching her. A flood of relief washed away her fear, leaving her light-headed in its wake. Cole!

Her heart was still pounding like a jackhammer. As she climbed out of her car to meet him, her legs nearly gave way.

"Gosh, I thought I was in for a ticket!" she exclaimed, breathless relief making her babble. "I saw your lights, but I didn't recognize you, and I couldn't figure out what I could have done to get pulled over...." Her voice trailed off. She couldn't see his eyes behind his sunglasses, but the rest of his expression certainly seemed grim.

"You're going to have to write me a ticket, anyway, aren't you?" she asked. She should have known Cole would never dole out special favors. Well, that was all right. It was one of the things she admired about him, in fact.

"Elise, we have to talk," he said.

A little voice inside her head whispered that something was wrong. But if she could just keep things light, make a joke out of it...

"Boy, if *those* aren't the most ominous words in the English language," she said, rolling her eyes.

But there was something genuinely ominous in the rigid set of his jaw, in his tense, feet-apart stance, in the way he maintained this formal distance between them.

Elise clutched the edge of her car door. "It's not...Kelsey, is it?" Her voice quavered. "I just dropped her off at Doris Applegate's a few minutes ago. Surely there's nothing wr—"

"I know." Cole held up his hands as if to ward off her fears. "Kelsey's fine."

"Oh." Elise sagged against the car. Her relief glands were sure getting a workout today. Cole's words sank in. "But then . . ." She studied him warily. "What do you mean, you know?"

The planes of his face shifted just a little. "I set it up."

"Set *what* up?" None of this was making sense.

"The invitation to Mrs. Applegate's."

"You—"

"I arranged it."

"What do you mean, you arranged it?"

He poked his cheek with his tongue before replying. "I needed to talk to you. Alone. So I dropped a suggestion or two to Mrs. Applegate."

Elise's face grew warm with indignation.

"It's not like some big conspiracy," Cole said quickly. "Mrs. Applegate is fond of Kelsey. She was delighted to invite her over for the afternoon to play with her cat."

"Wait a minute." Elise felt her temper inch upward. "Are you saying you deliberately manipulated us like chess piec—"

Cole cut her short with his next words. "Does the name Elizabeth Jordan mean anything to you?"

Shock zapped down Elise's spine like a lightning bolt. Her mouth went dry. "Should it?" she heard herself ask. Her ears were ringing, and her voice sounded very far away.

"It ought to." Cole plucked a folded piece of paper from the breast pocket of his uniform. He extended it between two fingers. "Your long-lost twin, maybe?"

Shock had left Elise numb, but she could feel panic starting to creep around the edges. Like a robot, she lifted her hand and accepted the paper.

It took forever to unfold. She felt Cole's gaze on her the whole time, those unflinching blue eyes drilling into her from behind his dark glasses.

Then she was looking at a photo of herself. Or rather, a photo of the person she used to be. Elizabeth Jordan, mild-mannered housewife. Single mother, suburbanite, member of the upper middle class.

It was like staring at a picture of someone who was dead.

She refolded the paper carefully, as if it were a delicate work of origami. All the while her mind was racing, half of it screaming at her to run, to lie, to brazen her way through this, while the other half warned her to stay calm.

She handed the paper back to Cole. "What now?" she asked dully.

"For starters, how about an explanation?" He tucked the paper back into his pocket without removing his gaze from her.

"You seem to be pretty good at figuring things out," Elise replied, stalling for time until she could figure out how much he already knew. "I doubt anything I say would enlighten you very much."

"Enlighten me." He folded his arms across his chest.

What if he *didn't* know the reason she and Kelsey were living under false identities? If she thought fast, maybe she could concoct a story that would satisfy him and put an end to his infernal snooping.

Unfortunately, Elise's face must have telegraphed her mental fancy footwork. Cole's mouth tightened impatiently. He grasped her wrist. "Come on. Let's go for a ride."

Instinctively, she wrenched away. "What are you going to do, drive me to some secluded spot and pistol-whip me into confessing?" she demanded, desperation making her reckless.

A muscle twitched irritably along his jaw. "You know better than that."

"Where are we going, then?" If she could just make an excuse to get away from him for a little while, she could grab Kelsey, stuff a few possessions into their suitcases and be on the road in less than half an hour.

Bob. What was she going to do about the poor dog?

"The way I see it, a nice, peaceful drive might be just what you need right now." Cole stepped around her, retrieved her purse from the front seat and shut the car door. "Give you a chance to think things through. Sort out your options. Maybe give your common sense time to reassert itself before you decide what you're going to tell me.''

He was walking back to his cruiser with her purse. Elise had little choice but to follow. ''What if I decide not to tell you anything?'' she asked, experimenting with the bravado approach.

He pinched his lips together as if disappointed with her. ''Guess I'll just have to keep on investigating.'' He held open the passenger door for her. ''Till I track down the whole truth for myself.''

The stern set of his features left no doubt that that was *exactly* what he would do. Elise felt like the jaws of a trap were closing around her as she slid into the cruiser.

Cole drove them away from town, turning off the main highway, then onto an even narrower road that snaked up slopes studded with spiny ocotillo plants and jumping cholla cacti. Pretty soon, there wasn't another house, vehicle or human being in sight.

Elise's thoughts were spinning so rapidly, it was amazing they weren't audible. But the only sound in the cruiser was the crackle of the police radio, until Cole reached over and switched it off.

And that one gesture told Elise how dead serious he was about prying the truth out of her. She knew it went completely against Cole's nature to make himself unavailable to the dispatcher, in case duty should call.

The road they were on eventually turned to gravel as it climbed into the mountains, past sentries of tall saguaro cactus. Off in the distance, Elise occasionally spotted the remains of some old mine building or prospector's shack built back around the turn of the century. Their gray, dilapidated walls, scoured by sand and weather, canted crazily to the side, as if they were on the verge of giving up the exhausting struggle against gravity.

Right now, Elise felt as beaten by fate, as dragged down by exhaustion, as those old wooden ruins looked.

She was so tired of running, of hiding, of lying. But how could she risk putting Kelsey in danger by telling Cole the truth?

If he didn't know it already, that is.

The road grew narrower, bumpier, its traces more overgrown with scrubby desert plant life. Finally, it petered out altogether.

Cole switched off the ignition. An oppressive silence filled the car, disturbed only by the tick of cooling metal.

"Let's walk a little." Cole broke the silence finally and unfastened his seat belt. He sailed his hat into the back seat and climbed out of the car without waiting for Elise's response.

When she stepped from the car, a dry desert wind lifted her hair from her shoulders. She drew in a bracing lungful of air, inhaling the spicy scent of creosote bush.

Cole strolled on ahead, stopping when he reached the edge of a steep drop-off framed by limestone boulders on each side. Swallowing a lump of trepidation, Elise reluctantly walked after him.

But not without one final wistful glance at the car. Maybe Cole had left the keys in the ignition. Maybe she could . . .

No. Forget it.

Elise's heartbeat picked up its tempo as she approached Cole. She still didn't have a clue what she was going to tell him.

He waited with his foot propped on a rock, his forearm braced crossways over his knee. "Not exactly Lovers' Lane," he said, sweeping his hand to indicate the view. "But I've always liked it up here."

Elise ignored the panoramic desert vista, the town of Tumbleweed spread out below, the ranks of buff-colored mountains marching off into the distance. "Do you always bring your suspects up here to interrogate them?" she asked sourly.

Brilliant idea, Elise. Why don't you try to antagonize him and see how far that gets you?

To her surprise, she recognized hurt among the jumbled chorus of emotions clamoring for her attention. She'd convinced herself Cole was attracted to her. Now it turned out his interest had been only a diversion, a way to distract her while he was secretly digging into her background.

Amazing what a good actor he was. She could have sworn the kiss the other night was for real.

"You're not a suspect, Elise," he said quietly, scanning the horizon. "I'm not even sure what I'm supposed to suspect you of yet."

"I haven't done anything wrong!" The words burst out of her unexpectedly. For heaven's sake, she was the *victim* here, not some sort of criminal! For the umpteenth time in the last two years, she cursed the unfair twist of fate that had led Kelsey into the woods that day to cross paths with Victor Dominick.

Cole drew off his sunglasses and dropped them into his shirt pocket. When he altered position to lock his gaze directly onto hers, Elise found his eyes no more readable than they'd been a minute ago.

"I could have kept on investigating," he said with a matter-of-fact shrug. "Sooner or later, I could have tracked down the answers I was looking for. But I wanted to be honest with you."

"Honest?" she scoffed in as disdainful a voice as she could summon. "You call it honest, snooping around behind my back? Pretending to be interested in me? Pumping my nine-year-old daughter for information?"

For some reason, that last dart apparently struck a bull's-eye. *Something* pricked a sensitive nerve, at any rate.

His coal black brows dove together in anger. "I never deliberately used Kelsey. She's a great kid, and the last thing I'd want to do is take advantage of her."

Elise shoved wind-swirled hair out of her face so she could look Cole squarely in the eye. "That's the *least* of what you could do to her if you don't just forget about whatever it is you've learned."

Cole abandoned his stance and grasped Elise's shoulders. "What are you talking about?"

Her eyes flickered back and forth over his in a desperate plea. "I'm asking you to walk away from this. To pretend that we never met—that Kelsey and I don't even exist."

He shook his head. "You know I can't do that."

"Kelsey's *life* is at stake!" Elise's cry whipped away on the wind.

Cole dented her flesh with his fingers. "Talk to me, Elise."

"I can't!"

He licked his lips. "Look, I didn't have to give you this chance to tell me your side of the story. I could have kept digging until I discovered whatever it is you're trying so hard to hide." His fingers eased their pressure, although he didn't let go of her.

"But I already felt guilty about sneaking around behind your back," he went on. "And after the other night, I felt like I owed it to you to be honest about what I'd found out."

Elise tried very hard to control the trembling in her voice. "What's the other night got to do with anything?"

He shifted his gaze past her shoulder, obviously becoming uncomfortable. "All that stuff I told you about Laura . . . it meant a lot to me that you listened."

Despite the terrible decision that still confronted her, Elise's eyes flared with surprise. "I didn't do anything special, Cole. I—I was flattered that you felt you could share it with me."

He slid his hands slowly up and down her arms. "And then I kissed you."

"Yes." Even now, when Cole posed such an immediate threat to her, a faint ribbon of desire uncurled inside Elise in response to that memory. The delicious feel of his mouth, the masculine smell of his skin, the intoxicating warmth of his breath mingling with hers . . .

"I had no right to kiss you," he said, shattering Elise's foolish little fantasy into a million pieces. "Because nothing can ever come of it." His hands burned trails of heat through her sleeves. "Because I have nothing to offer a woman—any woman. And you deserve better than that."

A shadow of regret skimmed across his eyes like the dark outline of a hawk circling against the brilliant azure sky. "That's the reason I decided to come clean with you about my investigation. And the reason I owe you a chance to be honest with *me,* too."

You may be awfully smart, Cole Hardesty, Elise thought. *But you're dead wrong about one thing. You've got plenty to offer some lucky woman.*

Any woman but me.

Life on the run meant you traveled light, and that meant no room for heavy emotional involvements.

Even if Cole *didn't* force her and Kelsey to go back to Boston.

Cole wrapped his strong fingers around Elise's wrist. Like handcuffs. "Come on. Let's sit." He picked out one of the smoother boulders nearby and drew her down beside him.

Elise glanced behind them at the abrupt drop-off that created such a stunning view. Right now, she felt as if she were perched on the edge of a far more perilous cliff.

Tell Cole the truth.

Tell him nothing.

Tell him any story you can make up that will buy you enough time to grab Kelsey and run for it.

She teetered helplessly on the brink. Cole would eventually uncover the whole truth, anyway. Even if Elise and Kelsey had time to escape, Elise didn't exactly relish the prospect of adding stubborn, single-minded Cole Hardesty to their list of pursuers.

But what finally tipped her decision in the end was a fragile, completely unexpected seedling of trust that chose that moment to take root inside her.

Cole was a decent, honest, fair-minded man. She couldn't believe he would ever do anything to bring harm to Kelsey or her.

Maybe, just maybe, she could trust Cole to do the right thing.

So Elise took a deep breath, and told him about Victor Dominick.

Chapter 9

"Oh, for heaven's sake! How many times do I have to show you? You have to push the control key at the same time. Here." Cole's white-haired secretary leaned over his shoulder and jabbed two crooked fingers at the computer keyboard.

The departmental budget figures scrolled onto the screen.

"Uh, thanks, Mildred." Cole sheepishly hunched his shoulders. "Don't know why I can't seem to remember that."

Mildred Simmons had worked for a long line of Creosote County sheriffs. Her exact age had been mysteriously purged from department personnel files while they were being computerized a number of years back, but the general assumption was that she'd already been around for a while by the time Warren G. Harding was president.

No one who worked with her, however, would dare hint that Mildred consider hanging up her Dictaphone and start enjoying a well-deserved retirement.

She fixed Cole with a reproving frown. "All it takes is a little concentration," she said. "Use your noodle!" She poked the side of his skull, sounding like an exasperated schoolmarm. "What's got into you today, anyway? Every time I come in here, you're staring off into space, woolgathering."

Without giving him a chance to reply, she turned to march back to her desk. When she got to the doorway, she fired back one last piece of advice. "Best clear those cobwebs out of your brain before some criminal gets the drop on you."

Cole propped his chin in his hand and watched the door shut behind her with a curt click. Mildred was right. He was going to have to snap out of it, and soon.

With a muffled curse, he forced himself to focus on the screenful of budget figures. But over the steady hum of the computer, he kept hearing the tortured, halting cadence of Elise's words when she'd told him about Victor Dominick yesterday.

Cole was convinced she'd told him the truth. No one could have artificially injected the raw fear he'd heard in her voice while she described Kelsey's narrow escape from death.

No one could possibly have faked the revulsion that shuddered across her pale, pretty features whenever she mentioned Dominick's name.

Cole stared at the computer monitor, but all he could see was the silent, desperate pleading in Elise's eyes when she'd finished her story. Begging him not to betray her.

Damn it, what was he supposed to do? Pretend he wasn't sworn to uphold the law? He gave up on the computer, tipped back his chair and propped his feet on the desk while he wrestled with the fix he was in.

GOOD NEWS! You can get up to FIVE GIFTS – FREE!

If offer card is missing, write to:
The Reader Service, PO Box 236, Croydon, Surrey, CR9 3RU

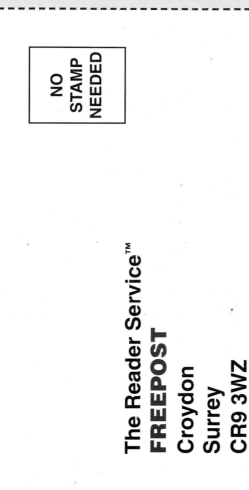

NO STAMP NEEDED

The Reader Service™
FREEPOST
Croydon
Surrey
CR9 3WZ

FIND OUT <u>INSTANTLY</u> HOW TO GET
UP TO 5 FREE GIFTS IN THE
LUCKY
CARNIVAL WHEEL

▼ SCRATCH-OFF GAME ▼

Scratch off ALL 3 silver areas

S7GIB

YES! I have scratched off the 3 Silver Areas above. Please send me all the gifts for which I qualify. I understand I am under no obligation to purchase any books, as explained on the opposite page. I am over 18 years of age.

Mr/Mrs/Ms/Miss _____

BLOCK CAPITALS PLEASE

Address _____

_____

_____ Postcode _____

Kayla Daniels

He was beginning to wish
around in Elise's past. Or *Eliz*
hell he was supposed to call her

A brusque rap on the door di
warning to remove his feet fro
stuck her head back into his off
ing look over the tops of her s
Grant out here to see you.''

Cole hastily lowered his feet
He busied himself with the she
posed to be comparing to the nu
Elise stepped hesitantly into his
pencil against his desk, forehea
to resemble deep concentration.

She cleared her throat. Cole
rose to his feet and indicated
''Please, sit down.''

''Thank you.'' She perched
seat as if preparing to take fligh

''Can I get you some coffee o

Her hands were clasped prim
her knees, her ankles welded to
her tailored slacks. Not for the
had very nice ankles.

She gave a nearly imperceptib
thank you. I—I can't stay long
from school at three.''

''Guess we should get down t
tled back in his swivel chair and
chin. ''I must say, I'm kind of s
''Oh?''

''Thought you might have ski
conversation yesterday.''

Her mouth worked for a minute as if she were tasting the flavor of various responses. "That was my plan," she finally admitted with a defiant toss of her head.

"I figured as much." Cole nodded. "So, why didn't you run?"

She gazed at him levelly. "I decided we wouldn't get very far before you caught up with us." She lifted one shoulder, let it fall. "For all I knew, ten seconds after you dropped me back at my car, you could have radioed in and had roadblocks set up, or our house staked out."

"Mmm." He crossed his arms. "That the only reason you didn't run?"

She hesitated, nibbling her lower lip in an unconsciously sensual manner that Cole found distinctly arousing. A distinctly inappropriate reaction on his part, considering the circumstances.

"No," Elise said finally. "The other reason I decided not to run was because . . . well . . . because this town feels like home to us now."

"Does it?" For some reason, that pleased him.

"Kelsey's settled in school, she's made lots of friends. . . ."

"What about you?" Cole asked. "Have *you* made lots of friends?"

"Me?" She brushed a lock of hair from her eyes, appearing flustered by his question. "I—no. Not really. I can't afford to get too friendly with people."

"Must be pretty lonely for you."

"Well, I enjoy the company of the people I work with. And Roz has been a good friend." She mumbled something Cole didn't catch.

"Pardon?" He leaned forward.

She fiddled with the clasp of her purse a few seconds before looking him straight in the eye. "I said," she repeated with a note of self-mockery in her voice, "then there was *you.*" She gave a short laugh tinged with bitterness. "Of course, that was before I found out the real reason why you were being so nice to us."

"Elise..."

She popped out of her chair like a jack-in-the-box. "Look, none of that matters anymore. The reason I came here is to find out what you intend to do about—about this situation."

When Cole rose to his feet, he towered over her. They were mere inches apart, but Elise held her ground. That was yet another quality he admired about her—the way she dug in her heels and refused to budge when she felt threatened.

"Truth is, I haven't quite figured out *what* I'm going to do," Cole admitted. He rubbed the nape of his neck. "I know what I'm *supposed* to do."

Her eyes glinted with emerald sparks. "Turn us in to the Boston police," she stated bluntly.

"This time they'll be sure to protect Kelsey," he assured her. Because that's what he was supposed to say.

"That's what they told me they'd do the last time!" Elise exclaimed. "And Dominick nearly got to her, anyway!"

"That won't happen again."

"How can you be so sure?" she demanded, her face pale and drawn with tension. "How can you even consider risking my daughter's life this way?"

The weight of duty compressed Cole's chest like steel bands. "It's my job," he said.

"It's your job to protect people, not to push little children into danger!"

The steel bands grew tighter. "Elise, there are rules. Rules set up to protect society from the likes of Victor Dominick. They're not always easy to live by sometimes, but—"

"I don't give a damn about protecting *society,*" she burst out angrily, slamming her purse onto his desk. "All I care about is protecting my *child!* Don't you understand?"

Instantly, Cole remembered his own unborn child, the child who'd never had a chance to live.

The child he hadn't been able to protect.

The pressure in his chest was so intense, he had to struggle to breathe. "Yes," he replied harshly. "I understand."

"You couldn't," she muttered through clenched teeth, "or all your precious rules wouldn't matter compared to Kelsey's life." She angled her chin up scornfully. "If you understood, then just this once, you'd forget about doing your damn job!"

Her anguish was hard to witness. Cole's chest felt like it was about to implode. "If I'd done my job properly before," he growled, forcing the words from his throat, "my wife and child would still be alive."

Elise stiffened, as if shocked by a high-voltage wire. Her eyes flared with surprise and confusion. "What—what are you talking about?" she asked, sounding as if the wind had been knocked out of her.

Immediately Cole regretted his words. "Never mind."

Elise's gaze darted back and forth across his face. "You think that your wife's death was somehow *your* fault?" she asked, half inquiring, half incredulous.

Obviously, she wasn't just going to let this go.

"The punk who attacked Laura was someone we'd been after for weeks." Thunder pounded in Cole's ears. "If I'd done my job properly, we'd have caught him before he killed her."

Elise's lips parted in astonishment. "You can't seriously blame yourself for that."

"Laura wanted me to stay home that night. If I hadn't gone to that bachelor party, she'd have been safe at home with me, instead of getting stabbed to death out in the streets.''

Cole felt powerless to stem the flow of words tumbling out of him. What irresistible quality did Elise have, anyway, that prompted him to spill his guts whenever he was around her?

She brought her hand to the side of his face. "Cole, that's just second-guessing, all of it." Her touch was gentle—cool and soothing in contrast to the boiling turmoil inside him. "It's unfair and completely unreasonable to blame yourself for not being able to see the future."

Cole scanned the depths of her eyes. Instead of the recriminations, the guilt, the shame he saw when he looked in the mirror, he found only a tender upwelling of compassion and sympathy.

"Look, I know all about guilt. When Tom died, I tortured myself for months with all those what-ifs and why-didn't-I's. Why didn't I nag him to stop working so hard? Why didn't I force him to go to the doctor when he got sick?"

Cole was struck by the irony of this situation. Elise had come here with her child's well-being foremost in her mind, to make a last-ditch plea for Cole to keep their secret. Yet somehow, she'd wound up trying to ease *his* troubles.

"There are all sorts of things I would do differently if I could go back," Elise said softly. "But I can't go back. None of us can. We just have to keep plowing ahead through life, making the best choices we can, accepting the fact that some of them may turn out to have terrible consequences we couldn't possibly have foreseen."

Something loosened inside Cole's chest. A heavy weight lightened just a little. Not that he was prepared to jettison the burden of guilt he'd been lugging around for so long. But for the first time, he sensed a dim flicker of hope that perhaps someday he might be able to set down some of that emotional baggage and move on with his life.

Gratitude warmed the icy, numbed reaches of his heart. Gratitude... and something more.

"I have to set you straight about something," he said hoarsely. He touched Elise's hair, letting it slide through his fingers while he marveled over its soft texture. "What you said a little while ago... about me being nice to you and Kelsey."

Elise's eyes shone round and luminous. "Yes?" Her hand still lingered on his face, her fingers gentle and ethereal as butterflies.

"It wasn't some kind of ruse," Cole said, letting his thumb caress the delicate slope of her jaw. "I didn't start coming around just so I could figure out what you were up to."

Doubt shimmered in her eyes like summer heat waves rising from noonday pavement.

"Kelsey's a great kid," he said. "And you're a beautiful woman, Elise." His fingertips picked up the rapid pulse beat in her throat. "Not just on the outside, but on the inside, where it counts."

A self-conscious smile quirked the corners of his mouth. "Guess that sounds kind of corny, but it's true."

He could tell by the subtle, shifting interplay of her features that she was struggling to believe him.

"This...chemistry between us. This crazy...connection I feel to you sometimes." Cole rummaged through his vocabulary for the right words, but somehow they were all inadequate to describe the attraction that had grown between them during the last few weeks.

"Whatever you want to call those feelings, they're real, Elise." He closed the narrow distance between them. "Just like this is."

Cole tipped back her head and kissed her. Even though he had plenty of reasons not to. Ethical reasons, not to mention personal and practical ones.

Right now he held Elise's future in the palm of his hand, and it was wrong to take advantage of her vulnerability.

He'd already let himself get too involved with her, and every time he kissed her made it that much more difficult to extricate himself from a relationship that could lead nowhere.

Besides, Mildred was liable to poke her head into his office any second and catch them both red-handed. Not to mention red-faced.

This is crazy, Cole warned himself. It was his last rational thought for a while.

Elise didn't return the kiss at first, apparently caught off guard by his rash, impulsive action. But gradually she began to respond, her lips growing warm and pliant under his. He could feel the tension melting from her limbs, allowing the sweet, soft curves of her body to nestle more snugly against him.

Cole's hunger for her expanded. He wrapped his arms around her, drawing her even closer. He dragged his mouth from hers and moved it over her eyelids, her temples, her hair. God, she was so lovely! Her skin was so velvety, so warm... and she smelled like a bouquet of the wildflowers that miraculously carpet the desert after a late-winter rain.

Cole's lips felt the vibrations as a faint moan of pleasure escaped Elise's throat. She circled her arms around him, sliding her hands up the slope of his back. Desire hurtled through him like a runaway mine train when he felt the lush swell of her breasts press into him.

He wanted her... God help him, but he wanted her! Not just because it had been so long since he'd made love with a woman, but because this particular woman was an oasis of

kindness and compassion and decency in a bleak world that
was too often devoid of such things.

Despite the ugly, bitter experiences that had hardened and
disillusioned him, Cole discovered that deep down inside, he
still wanted to believe that goodness existed.

Even in a world that could turn its back on Laura's dying
cries.

He framed Elise's face between his hands and captured
her mouth again with his. The heat in his loins spurred him
on recklessly. There were no rules, no such thing as duty, no
reason to hold back. There was only the two of them, clinging to each other in a whirling vortex of passion and need.

Cole deepened the kiss, exploring, plundering, worship-
ing her with his tongue. Elise responded in kind, parrying
him thrust for thrust, her fingertips kneading the taut muscles of his back.

Cole felt the tenuous threads of his self-control snap, one
by one. When he lowered his hand to her breast, Elise's eyes
flew wide open with shock. Shock, but also with the unmistakable flare of desire.

She broke the contact between their lips. "I—I should
go," she murmured breathlessly.

Cole's pulse thundered in his ears like a herd of gallop-
ing mustangs. He dropped his hand from her breast and
linked his arms loosely around her waist, reluctant to let go
of her quite yet. He tipped his forehead against hers, giving
them both a chance to collect themselves.

Elise averted her gaze. Her cheeks bloomed pink, as if
she'd only now noticed the hard proof of desire pressing in-
timately against her, just below the vicinity of Cole's belt
buckle. Without actually pushing him away, she managed
to maneuver out of his embrace.

The color of rose petals lingered on her cheeks. "It's
nearly three. I have to pick up Kelsey." She made a big pro-

duction of searching for her purse, giving herself a convenient excuse to avoid his eyes.

Cole took a deep breath. It had been inexcusable, letting his hormones get the best of him. He had nothing to offer Elise or any other woman, and he had no right to give her the wrong idea by acting like he was...courting her or something.

Courting? That was certainly a polite word for it. How about making a pass at her? Leading her on? Seducing her?

There was no doubt in Cole's mind that if they'd been somewhere slightly less public than a government office, he would have tried his damnedest to cajole Elise into bed.

The force of his desire for her had stunned him like a blow to the head. But he wouldn't do either of them any favors by denying it.

"Elise, I—I shouldn't have done that. I'm sorry."

She straightened her blouse, then combed back her hair with trembling fingers. Her face was still flushed, her eyes vaguely accusing.

Only Cole wasn't too sure, exactly, what she was accusing him of.

"Please think about what I said," she requested in a strained voice. "About protecting Kelsey."

"I can't make any promises."

Her chin came up a fraction of an inch. "Yes, I'm well aware of that."

Once again, Cole wasn't sure they were talking about the same thing.

"But you'll at least *consider* not turning us in?" The ill-concealed desperation in her eyes made him feel like even more of a heel.

"Don't worry," he said. Though he knew that's *all* she would do.

She took a deep breath. "Thank you."

The last thing you owe me is thanks, he thought.

Then she slipped out the door and was gone.

Cole settled back against the edge of his desk. Elise's visit had stirred up a whole bunch of feelings he would just as soon not have to deal with. All at once he felt restless, itchy, raring to hop in the cruiser and floor it up to a hundred miles an hour.

He also felt horny as hell.

Well, that was no one's fault but his own. He'd made a damn fool blunder by letting things spin so fast and so far out of control.

And he wasn't about to make yet another mistake by letting his heart—or any other part of his anatomy—overrule his brain when it came time to make tough decisions.

Cole was a by-the-book kind of guy. Deep down inside, he'd known all along what he had to do.

He dragged a hand over his face. Even behind closed eyelids, he could still see Elise's half accusing, half pleading expression.

With a muffled oath, he reached for the phone.

"Mom, how come you call me Peach?"

Elise had been trying in vain to concentrate on her daughter's steady stream of chatter ever since picking Kelsey up at school. But the disastrous dilemma currently facing them kept clamoring for her attention.

Along with the unsettling, still-vivid memory of that steamy embrace in Cole's office.

Even now, recalling what his mouth and hands had felt like made Elise's knees go weak. And remembering the passion of her own response made her cheeks flame.

She forced herself to focus on Kelsey. "I'm sorry, Peach. What did you just ask me?"

Kelsey rolled her eyes in exasperation. "I *said,* how come you always call me that?"

"Peach?"

"Uh-huh."

A sentimental smile danced across Elise's lips. "Because when you were a little baby, your cheeks were just as chubby and pink and fuzzy as peaches."

Kelsey screwed up her face. "Oh, *brother!*"

Elise laughed. "How about...because I think you're peachy keen?"

Kelsey tilted her head doubtfully. "What's that mean?"

"Peachy keen? It means terrific. Wonderful. The best."

"Hmm." Kelsey tugged on one of her braids, considering.

"Know what, Mom?"

"What?"

"I think *you're* peachy keen, too."

The road ahead of them blurred as Elise's eyes misted over. For a second or two, she couldn't speak past the lump in her throat.

A torrent of love swept through her, so sharp and fierce it was almost a physical ache.

Equally sharp and fierce was her determination to protect her darling little girl, no matter what the cost.

Right then and there, she vowed that at the first sign Cole had contacted the Boston cops, she was going to grab Kelsey and run.

Never mind that they would be fleeing from the first place in two years they could truly call home.

Never mind that it would mean starting all over again in a strange town, a strange school and a strange job.

Never mind the irony that they would be running from the very same man who had come to occupy such a special place in both their hearts.

Nothing was more important to Elise than Kelsey's safety. The instinct to protect her child was as deeply ingrained as her instinct to breathe.

She'd sensed from the beginning that Cole could be trouble. But along the way, the physical attraction she felt for him had become inextricably tangled with a complex jumble of emotions.

It was too soon to attach a label to those feelings. But Elise would be lying to herself if she pretended that leaving Cole behind wouldn't leave an aching void in her life.

She couldn't let that matter. She'd already made a long list of sacrifices to keep Kelsey out of danger, and had done so willingly. Becoming a fugitive had cost Elise her home, most of her savings and any contact with family and friends.

What did one more loss matter, compared to the all-important priority of keeping Kelsey safe?

As she drove down the highway that someday soon might lead them out of Tumbleweed forever, Elise tried her best to forget how wonderful Cole's arms had felt around her.

"The district attorney's office has been after this guy Dominick for years. You can imagine the uproar that ensued when their star witness and her mother pulled a disappearing act right underneath their noses."

Cole recalled the echo of terror in Elise's voice when she'd recounted for him how that car had nearly run down Kelsey, mere yards from the cop who was supposed to be protecting her.

He scowled into the phone. "You can hardly blame the mother for taking off after you guys screwed up."

"You mean the attempt on the kid's life? Not *my* screw-up, old buddy. But you can bet some heads rolled over in Homicide after *that* incident. The D.A. was furious."

"I'll bet." While placing his call to the Boston police earlier this afternoon, Cole had remembered Tony Clareview. Tony and he had gone through the L.A. Police Academy together and had kept in touch until Tony moved to Boston seven or eight years ago to take a job on the force there.

Somehow, the idea of casually scoping out the situation with an old friend had tasted a lot more palatable to Cole than cold-bloodedly turning Elise in to whomever happened to be handling the Dominick case these days.

After their initial conversation, Tony had called Cole back a little while ago to let him know what he'd found out.

"The D.A.'s on his way to some charity banquet or something. They're trying to track him down right now to see how he wants to handle this."

"You think he still wants the little girl to come back and testify?"

"Hell, yes!"

Cole uncrossed his fingers with a sigh. There was always the chance that in the last couple of years, the authorities might have found some other way to nail Dominick—one that didn't require Kelsey to take the witness stand.

Tony's unequivocal response dashed his hopes. "Listen, this Dominick's an incredibly slippery character. Criminal charges just slide right off him like mud off a greased pig. Plus, he's got more high-powered connections than the electric company."

"That so?" Cole's heart sank at the picture of one sweet, freckle-faced little girl going up against a clever, vicious, seemingly invincible thug like Dominick.

"He runs the gambling operations all over this part of the state. And hey, lots of people in positions of power like to gamble. Politicians, judges, heads of major corporations—even cops. So, let's say one of these upstanding citizens runs up a huge gambling debt. Dominick, out of the goodness of his slimeball heart, magnanimously agrees to write it off. Then, guess what?''

''He's got that powerful person sewn up in his pocket forever,'' Cole finished grimly.

''Bull's-eye.''

Cole didn't like the image *that* conjured up one bit.

''That's how come he was able to get free on bail, even on a murder rap,'' Tony continued. ''And that's why the D.A.'s office, now that they have a witness who can send him away for years, isn't about to let that witness slip through their fingers again.''

Elise, please try to understand. I did what I had to do, Cole thought unhappily.

''Look, I gotta go,'' Tony said. ''But keep me posted, all right?'' He whistled. ''Boy, I'd sure love to see that bastard Dominick locked up for good. We all would.''

''Keep me posted from your end, too, all right?'' Cole wasn't sure where all this was going to lead. But he had no intention of simply handing Elise and Kelsey over to the Boston authorities and then forgetting about them.

How could he forget about a wonderful kid who wanted to be both a baseball player and a veterinarian when she grew up?

How could he forget about a woman who crept into his dreams more and more frequently at night? Who'd shown him that kindness and compassion did still exist in the world...

Who'd begun to thaw the icy shell around his heart, and bring to life passionate yearnings Cole had thought were long dead and buried.

No. He wouldn't abandon them to face alone whatever fate awaited them back in Boston. He'd already crossed the line where that was possible.

Mere minutes after Cole had hung up the phone, it rang again, jarring him from his thoughts.

"Yes, Mildred?"

"The district attorney from Boston is on the line."

"Put him through, please."

Cole pinched the bridge of his nose. His skull throbbed with the ominous beginnings of a headache. Like distant drums growing closer.

"Sheriff Hardesty? Michael Dunnigan, Boston D.A."

"Yes, Mr. Dunnigan."

"Someone from my staff has filled me in on the situation down there. Am I to understand that Mrs. Jordan isn't aware you've contacted us?"

"That's correct." A barb of guilt pricked Cole's conscience. "However, she's aware that I know her real identity and has voluntarily explained to me the circumstances under which she and her daughter left Boston."

"Ah, yes. They were certainly...unfortunate." In the background, Cole could hear the low murmur of voices, punctuated by the clink of crystal and silverware. They must have tracked Dunnigan down at his charity banquet.

"Look, Sheriff, this is a rather, ah, tricky situation. In the past, Victor Dominick has proven to be a rather...ah, elusive quarry for our office."

"I sort of got that impression," Cole said diplomatically.

"Unfortunately, there have been some leaks. Within my office, the police department, God knows where else. The man has a network of high-level contacts you wouldn't believe. That's why I'm calling you from a pay phone. For all I know, he could have both my home and office phones tapped."

"Sounds like a real rattlesnake."

"He's dangerous, all right. And that's why I'm going to ask a favor of you."

"What favor is that?" Those ominous drums in Cole's head began to beat a little louder.

"You've already established a certain rapport with Mrs. Jordan, correct?"

"I guess you could call it that." He thought of the powerful sense of connection that drew them together at times, that made him want to tell Elise things he'd never shared with another human being.

Yeah. You could certainly call that rapport. *But there were other words you could call it, too.* Words Cole wasn't quite ready to voice yet, not even to himself.

"Although I hate to admit it," Dunnigan said, "the truth is that Mrs. Jordan and her daughter are probably safer staying put right where they are for the time being."

"You mean, you're not going to bring them back to Boston?"

"Not right away. Our case completely fell apart when we lost that little girl two years ago, and I need time to reorganize and rebuild it on a strong, solid foundation before I spring the murder charge on Dominick again."

"So you're going to allow the Gran—I mean, the Jordans to stay here for the time being?"

"Yes. But I can't afford the risk that they'll decide to disappear again."

"What do you want me to do, lock them up?" If that was the favor Dunnigan was asking, Cole was by God going to refuse.

"I'd rather not. The last thing I want to do is alienate Mrs. Jordan any further. Without her cooperation, the kid could decide to clam up, and there goes our case again."

"What's your plan, then?"

"That's where you come in."

"How's that?" Cole asked, dreading the answer.

"I need you to keep an eye on them for me. Sort of a protective surveillance, if you will."

Alarm raised the hackles at the nape of his neck. "You think there's a chance Dominick might discover their whereabouts and come after them?"

"Listen, where Dominick's concerned, the only thing I know for certain is not to underestimate him. That kid is the only person who can connect him to this murder, and he knows it. Believe me, he's not sentimental when it comes to children. If there's a leak, and he finds out where she is, he'll do everything in his considerable power to make sure she doesn't live to testify."

Determination sliced through Cole's voice like a steel blade. "I'll make sure no harm comes to either one of them."

"I checked up on your record before I called, Hardesty. You're good. Damn good. But in any contest with Dominick, you have to be damn lucky, as well."

"He won't get to them." He hadn't been able to protect Laura. But by God, he wasn't going to let any murdering thug hurt Elise and Kelsey!

"Oh, one more thing, Sheriff." The D.A. raised his voice to be heard over a swell of applause in the background. "I can't take the risk of letting our only eyewitness slip through our fingers again. So it's absolutely imperative that you don't let Mrs. Jordan or her daughter know that you've been in contact with me."

Cole frowned. "Don't you think that's unfair? After all, Mrs. Jordan has a right to know that Dominick may have been tipped off to their whereabouts."

"That's exactly what I *don't* want her to know," Dunnigan exclaimed. "I don't want her getting spooked and taking off again."

Cole remained silent, but evidently his disapproval carried through the phone lines all the way to Boston.

"Look, you claimed you could protect them," Dunnigan said. "So what's the problem? This way, you'll spare her unnecessary worry."

I'll be lying to her, he thought.

"You do your job, and let me do mine. When we're ready for the little girl's testimony, I'll let you know."

And then Elise will find out I've been spying on her.

"I'll touch base with you every few days or so." The D.A.'s voice grew stern. "Remember, Hardesty. Under *no* circumstances are you to let Mrs. Jordan know you've contacted me."

In the silence after he hung up the phone, Cole heard the echoes of what he'd told Elise earlier today in that very office. *There are rules. Rules set up to protect society from the likes of Victor Dominick. They're not always easy to live by sometimes....*

Cole's own words, it seemed, had come back to haunt him.

Chapter 10

"Strike two!"

At the plate, Cole slowly wheeled around and fixed Elise with a skeptical glare. "I believe that was high and outside."

"It was a strike!" Kelsey hollered from the pitcher's mound.

Elise thumped the softball into her mitt a couple of times. "Hey, I just call 'em like I see 'em," she retorted with a smirk. She threw the ball back to Kelsey.

It was Saturday afternoon in the park, where they were playing their own three-man version of softball. Well, *four*-man, if you counted Bob, who did a pretty fair job of chasing line drives, whenever they could get him to stay in the outfield.

Kelsey wound up for her next pitch, swinging her arm around like a propeller. This time, the ball got past Elise and hit the chain-link backstop with a metallic *clink!*

"Ball three," she called.

Cole tapped the end of his bat into the dirt. "That's more like it."

"Mo-om!" Kelsey complained.

"Peach, it wasn't even close."

"Oh, *okay.*"

Elise threw her the softball, then crouched down to await the next pitch. It was kind of difficult to keep her mind on the game, however, with Cole hunkered into his batter's stance right in front of her.

His biceps flexed as he took a couple of little practice swings. Elise had never seen him wearing shorts before today. She found herself fascinated by the dusting of dark hair revealed on his long, lean legs, and by the way his thigh and calf muscles rippled while he was chasing fly balls.

It was hot beneath the blazing April sun, and sweat dampened his T-shirt so that it clung to the solid contours of his chest and shoulders. Beneath his baseball cap, commas of dark hair were plastered to the nape of his neck.

Elise felt a bead of sweat trickle down between her breasts, and for a split second allowed herself to imagine what it would feel like if Cole...

Despite the heat, she shivered.

"Bob, no! Come back here!"

There was a slight delay of the game while Kelsey chased after the errant basset hound, who'd invited himself to someone else's picnic a short distance away.

Cole chuckled. "Guess he prefers food to playing center field."

"He prefers food to *everything.*" Elise lifted her bangs to let a little air move through them. "Except Kelsey, that is. He'd follow her to the ends of the earth, even if it meant leaving his supper dish behind."

"So I've noticed." Cole pitched an intimate smile at Elise.

He'd certainly had plenty of *opportunity* to notice. Over the last several weeks, it seemed to Elise that Cole had spent the vast majority of his off-duty hours hanging out at the Jordan house.

No, it was still the *Grant* house, she reminded herself. She wasn't about to drop the smoke screen of their false identities as long as Victor Dominick was out there somewhere.

Or until the long arm of the law reached out from Boston and dragged her and Kelsey back there kicking and screaming.

The first few days after she'd confessed the truth to Cole, Elise had jumped at the slightest sound, positive it was the Boston authorities banging on her front door. But as the weeks passed, she'd gradually started to relax again.

Or at least to return to the constant state of vigilance in which she'd lived for the last two years.

Since the day she'd gone to Cole's office, Elise hadn't asked him again whether or not he intended to turn them in. She'd pleaded her case once, and she wasn't about to keep begging. But as each day passed with no sign of the authorities, gratitude and relief eased in to replace her fear.

Her instincts, apparently, had been right all along. She could trust Cole.

"Okay, ready?" Kelsey returned to the pitcher's mound after restoring Bob to the outfield.

"Let's see, the count's three balls and one strike, right?" Cole called.

Kelsey stamped her foot. "*Two* strikes!" she yelled.

Cole tipped back the brim of his cap and scratched his head. "Are you sure?"

"Three balls and *two* strikes!" She made a V with her fingers and waved it in the air for emphasis.

"Well, okay," he said doubtfully. "If you say so."

"Nice try," Elise told him cheerfully as he resumed the batter's position. "Aren't you ashamed of yourself, trying to cheat a little girl?"

"Hey, all's fair in love and baseball," he mumbled out of the side of his mouth. "Haven't you ever heard that?"

Maybe she'd just been out in the hot sun too long, but hearing the word *love* come out of Cole's mouth made Elise feel slightly dizzy. Not that she was hoping he would someday say it to *her* or anything.

All signs seemed to indicate he was still in love with his late wife, anyway. How else to explain the fact that, ever since Elise had gone to his office to plead with him to keep her secret, Cole hadn't done so much as give her a peck on the cheek?

He kept finding excuses to drop by their house in the evenings, though—always making sure to arrive after they were finished eating until Elise finally started inviting him to supper. Nowadays, he was a regular fixture at the dinner table.

Weekends, he'd taken to proposing outings for the three of them. A nature hike to enjoy the brief burst of blooming wildflowers. A trip over to Tucson to visit the Arizona-Sonora Desert Museum. A picnic and softball game in the park.

Elise was touched by the way he always included Kelsey. Her infrequent, unsuccessful forays into the dating world after Tom died had taught her that most men weren't exactly wild about the idea of a child tagging along.

But Cole had never once suggested that Elise leave Kelsey with a baby-sitter. He'd never maneuvered to get Elise alone. Even after Kelsey had gone to bed, while he and Elise sat together on the couch and talked for a while before he left, Cole was always the perfect gentleman.

A little *too* perfect, in fact.

Though she hated to admit it, Elise missed the excitement and passion of his kisses. She missed the safe, solid, connected feeling of having his arms around her. And she missed the secret, forbidden thrill of wondering where their next embrace might lead.

Obviously, Cole didn't feel the same way.

Elise almost *wanted* to believe he was still in love with Laura.

Because otherwise, she might have to believe that Cole had just been faking his attraction to her. That it had only been a convenient means to learn more about her past once his initial suspicions had been aroused.

Maybe now that his curiosity about Elise had been satisfied, so had any desire he might have felt toward her.

But then . . . why was he still spending so much time with Kelsey and her?

Elise sighed. Maybe she *could* trust Cole. But she certainly couldn't understand him.

The crack of bat against softball knocked her from her baffled speculations.

Kelsey shrieked as the ground ball whipped past her. "Get it, Bob! Get the ball, quick!"

Elise jumped up and down. "Hurry, Kelsey!"

Cole was hustling up the first-base line. Running backward.

This was one of the rules they'd agreed on beforehand, to even up the odds a little. Another rule was that the batter was only required to run to first base and back. Returning safely to home plate meant scoring a run.

Bob was having trouble understanding the urgency of the situation. Kelsey raced past him to retrieve the ball. When she turned around and saw Cole running backward, arms pinwheeling in an exaggerated display of effort, she collapsed into giggles.

"Peach, throw me the ball!" Elise managed to holler through her own laughter. "Hurry up, or he's gonna score!"

Bob sniffed the ground at Kelsey's feet, then started barking. Cole reached first base, looped around it and began backpedaling for home, flailing his arms over his head and whooping loudly.

Kelsey was still doubled over in hysteria at his antics. Her feeble throw to home plate dribbled out halfway across the infield grass.

Bob chased after it, still barking, his tail whipping back and forth like an out-of-control metronome.

Elise was laughing so hard, she had tears in her eyes. "Come on, Bob," she gasped, beckoning frantically. "Bring the ball here. Good boy!"

From the corner of her blurry vision, she saw Cole looming ever closer as he continued his backward base-running. Kelsey recovered enough to screech, "He's coming! Hurry, Mom!"

Bob crouched on stubby bowed legs, ball clamped between his jaws, long ears sailing from side to side as he flicked his gaze uncertainly from one crazed human being to another.

Elise made frantic, coaxing kissing noises and clapped her hands. "Come here, Bob!"

Finally, the basset hound got the idea and trotted obediently forward. Weak with laughter, Elise huddled near home plate and struggled to draw air into her lungs. She heard Kelsey's excited squeals, the jingle of Bob's collar, the thud of Cole's feet....

"Cole! Look out for—"

Dog and humans collided at home plate. Elise heard an indignant yelp, a muffled *oomph!* and suddenly found herself entangled in a jumble of arms and legs and floppy ears.

By the time it was all straightened out, she was lying in the dirt, head cradled in Cole's lap, staring up at the bright turquoise sky.

Cole's worried face blocked her view of the heavens. "Elise, honey, are you all right?"

He called me honey, she thought happily. "I think so," she replied.

"Don't try to get up," he ordered, although abandoning her current position was the furthest thing from her mind. Cole's thigh provided a warm, hard pillow beneath her head. The side of her face rested against his flat stomach, and she could feel his chest heaving with exertion.

He smelled sweaty and masculine and wonderful.

"God, Elise, I'm so sorry! I couldn't see behind me, and then I tripped over Bob—"

"How is he?"

"Bob? He's fine." Cole smoothed her damp bangs off her forehead. "It's you I'm worried about."

"I don't think anything's broken."

"Broken?" Alarm sped across his handsome face. Immediately he ran his hands over her limbs. "Does this hurt? Can you wiggle your toes? Bend your elbow?"

"Nothing hurts," Elise murmured. Just the opposite, in fact.

"How many fingers am I holding up?"

"Mmm...three?" She made it sound as if she were hazarding a guess, though she could see perfectly well.

Cole spanned her rib cage with his broad hand. "Any pain when you breathe?"

Elise took a deep breath, releasing it in a drawn-out sigh. "No."

She would have been gloriously content to lie there with her head cradled in his lap, malingering while Cole tenderly fussed over her nonexistent injuries, except...

"Mom, are you okay?" Kelsey's wide-eyed, dirt-smudged face hovered next to Cole's. She had her baseball cap on backward and looked like she was trying hard not to be scared.

Elise struggled to sit up.

"Careful." Cole supported her back with one strong arm and eased her upright.

Elise blinked.

"Dizzy?" he asked, watching her closely.

She gave her head a sharp shake, more to clear it of silly, wistful fantasies than to sweep it of cobwebs. She smiled reassuringly at him. "I'm fine." She reached up and affectionately yanked one of Kelsey's pigtails. "At least I didn't let him score," she said with a wink.

Kelsey's face split into a relieved, conspiratorial grin. "Yeah! He was out by a mile!"

"What?" Cole yelped. He poked Kelsey in the ticklish spot beneath her ribs. "Hey, I was safe! The score is now five to four, ladies."

Kelsey clutched her side, giggling. "No, it's not."

"Is too!"

"Is not!"

"Too!"

"Not!"

Bob snuffled over and finally propelled Elise to her feet by nudging his cold, wet nose behind her knee.

"Easy." Cole maintained a secure grip on her elbow as she stood up.

For perhaps half a second, Elise considered swooning into his arms. But only for half a second.

"I'm fine," she repeated, dusting off her hands and the seat of her shorts. "Only my pride was bruised."

Cole released her—reluctantly, she thought. Or hoped.

"What d'you say we call the game a tie and go out for some ice cream?" he suggested.

"Bob, too?" Kelsey asked quickly.

Cole knuckled up the brim of his cap. "I think there might be some pesky health-department regulation about dogs in ice-cream parlors."

"But it's too hot to leave him in the car," Kelsey pointed out.

"You're absolutely right." Cole scooped up the mitt Elise had been wearing before it was dislodged in the collision. "So what we'll do is tie Bob outside someplace where there's shade, and bring him a bowl of water. Then we can watch him from where we're sitting inside."

"Eating our banana splits?" Kelsey asked hopefully.

"Eating our *one* scoop of ice cream," Elise corrected her, playfully swatting her daughter's backside.

"Only *one?* I can't decide on just *one* flavor, Mom."

Elise snatched off Kelsey's cap and jammed it onto her own head. "As if you ever order anything but chocolate!"

Kelsey jumped up, straining and stretching as if trying to grab the brass ring from the merry-go-round. "Gimme my Red Sox hat!"

"You've gotta catch me first!" With a ribbon of mischievous laughter trailing back over her shoulder, Elise took off across the park with Kelsey and Bob hot on her heels.

Cole watched her graceful, bounding flight with a complex brew of emotions simmering in his blood.

Relief, because she was obviously unhurt by his clumsiness.

Regret, because he had a feeling these lighthearted moments between mother and daughter had been all too rare these past couple of years, ever since the sinister shadow of Victor Dominick had fallen over their lives.

And of course, guilt, which had been his constant companion ever since he'd secretly promised Dunnigan to keep an eye on Elise and Kelsey.

Cole picked up the baseball bat and propped it over his shoulder as he started after them. He'd certainly kept his promise to Dunnigan. He was amazed Elise and Kelsey weren't sick of him, the way he'd been horning in on practically every moment of their free time lately.

But the cost to his conscience and his self-control had been enormous. It went against every honest fiber in Cole's body to worm his way into their lives under false pretenses. He certainly didn't have to pretend that he enjoyed their company, but the secret he was hiding still rankled.

And it was pure torture to spend so much time close to Elise without being able to touch her.

But Cole would never be able to face himself in the mirror if he pursued a more intimate relationship with Elise at the same time he was deceiving her. How could he kiss her, caress her, maybe even take her to bed, knowing that she would shove him angrily away if she knew what he'd done?

So, ever since he'd contacted Boston, Cole had stuck to a "hands off" policy where Elise was concerned. Until today, when he'd barreled into her at home plate, knocked her to the ground and realized that the awful throbbing in his chest was fear.

He'd felt so helpless, holding her against him, not knowing how seriously she was hurt. The relief he'd felt when she opened those beautiful green eyes and smiled up at him had been indescribable.

And it had forced Cole to face a fact he hadn't wanted to admit before.

He was starting to care for Elise. A lot.

Which, ironically, made it even more imperative that he resist these fevered dreams and urgent desires that kept him thrashing beneath the sheets at night.

Because, in the end, making love with Elise would only mean hurting her more.

Up ahead, she and Kelsey and the dog were playing an impromptu game of tag on the way back to the car. Something about the happy chime of Elise's laughter and the way her ponytail danced across her shoulders while she romped with the others, struck Cole as sweetly innocent. Completely trusting.

And all too vulnerable.

Anyone watching Cole approach them across the grass would have assumed they were a family. They wouldn't realize that Cole was the outsider. That he would forever remain the outsider because of the course he'd chosen to follow. Because of the decision he'd made to deceive them.

Even though it was for their own good.

Hunched down in the dry creek gully, Victor Dominick adjusted his binoculars. Then he slapped the back of his neck and cursed. Damned bugs!

Sweat trickled into his eyes, making them sting. *Geez, it was hot out here in this miserable, godforsaken desert!*

Eyes burning, he aimed the binoculars across the no-man's-land of cactus and brush that separated him from the one-story stucco house a couple of hundred yards away. A tall wood fence blocked his view of the backyard, but from his vantage point he could see most of the front of the house, as well as anyone coming or going.

Two hours he'd been stuck out here, roasting like a pig on a spit, target for snakes and scorpions. And he still hadn't seen any sign of the little brat or her mother.

Now his binoculars picked up a car turning onto the gravel road leading to the house. There was already a car parked under the carport, but instinct told him the house was empty. Maybe, he considered, she'd hitched up with some guy during the last couple of years, and they'd all gone somewhere in a second vehicle.

If so, tough luck for the poor slob. He'd have to be disposed of, too.

All at once, Dominick nearly dropped his binoculars. Holy hell! It was a cop car pulling into the driveway!

He crouched even lower, so only the binoculars and the top of his head rose above the edge of the gully. This was *just* what he needed. Some cop coming to haul the kid back to Boston. Damn it, why couldn't the D.A.'s office have waited just another day or two?

Dominick realized that this was going to make his job difficult. Difficult maybe, but not impossible.

He made out the word *Sheriff* on the side of the cruiser as it coasted to a stop in front of the house. To Dominick's surprise, three of the doors opened.

What the—? Either cops out here in the sticks wore awfully casual uniforms, or this one was off duty.

Dominick smiled as the other two figures emerged from the car. *Gotcha!* He pumped his fist. There they were—the kid and her mother. Trailed by some kind of weird-looking mutt.

His triumphant smile wilted as he watched the group proceed into the house. The cop had seemed pretty chummy with the girl and her mother. Even with the dog. It was almost like he was . . . part of the family.

Dominick consoled himself with the knowledge that at least the cop wasn't there to escort them back to Boston. Which meant there was still time to finish the job he'd come to do.

He would just have to come up with a new plan, of course. One that factored in the cop. But now that Dominick had finally laid eyes on the quarry he'd been hunting for two years, he was confident of success.

He jammed the binoculars into the case around his neck and crept down the gully a prudent distance before striking out across the bleak terrain toward the place where he'd left his van.

Chapter 11

"Dinner was delicious, Elise." Cole spiked her coffee with a splash of the coffee-flavored liqueur he'd picked up on a weekend trip to Nogales, Mexico, a couple of years back. It had collected dust in his kitchen cupboard until he'd brought it over to share with Elise last week. Now it had become part of what was practically an evening ritual after Kelsey was tucked into bed.

"Thanks, but macaroni and cheese is hardly what you'd call haute cuisine." Elise waited until he'd poured liqueur into his own coffee before taking a sip of hers. "It is, however, one of Kelsey's favorite foods."

They settled back against the sofa cushions, both still dressed in shorts from the afternoon softball game.

Cole adjusted his leg ever so slightly, so that his knee touched Elise's. "How about letting me take you out to dinner tomorrow night, to repay you for all the free meals I've been getting lately?"

Elise stroked her thumb along the curved handle of her coffee mug. ''I—don't want to leave Kelsey with a baby-sitter.''

''No need to.'' Cole swallowed some coffee. ''Kelsey's included in the invitation, of course. That goes without saying.''

Elise nibbled her lip. Her brows feathered together as if she were troubled. Cole waited.

Finally, she shifted her gaze to meet his and said, ''What's all this about, Cole?''

''All what?'' he asked cautiously.

She made an expansive sweep with her hand. ''All the outings you've organized. The picnics in the park. The dinners together every night.''

He set his mug on the coffee table. ''Elise, if I've been making a pest of myself—''

''It isn't that.'' Her mug clinked against his when she set it down. ''Kelsey and I have both enjoyed your company. And you're welcome to stay for dinner anytime. But I'd just like to understand what—what the reason is for all this...togetherness.''

Cole wrinkled his forehead. ''Are you asking me what my intentions are?''

''Well...yes.'' When Elise noted the twinkle in his eye, she broke into a sheepish grin. ''I guess that sounds a little old-fashioned, huh?''

''I like old-fashioned.''

''It's just that I don't want Kelsey to grow too dependent on you.''

''Kelsey, huh?''

''She's had to grow up without having a man around the house, and I know she absolutely adores all the attention you've been giving her. I'm just afraid that if—things change, and suddenly you're not around anymore, Kelsey might get hurt."

Cole laid his hand on her arm. "I would never do anything to hurt Kelsey. Or you, either."

Elise stared down at his hand. "I'm sure you wouldn't, intentionally. But if I could just explain the situation to Kelsey, maybe she wouldn't . . . count on you so much."

"Elise." Cole nudged up her chin with his knuckle. "Is this about Kelsey? Or about you? About us?"

She drew in a deep, tremulous breath. In the muted lighting, her eyes glowed a luminescent green. "I guess it's really about us," she admitted.

Cole took her hand in his. What could he tell her? That the reason he'd been spending so much time with her and Kelsey was because he was under strict but secret orders from the Boston D.A. to protect them? That somewhere along the way, his continuing involvement in their lives had become not just a duty, but something he looked forward to?

No. He couldn't tell Elise any of that. Because then he would have to tell her he'd been lying to her.

So he decided to *show* her how he felt, instead.

When their lips met, the joining seemed so inevitable, so right, that Cole nearly forgot he'd promised himself not to do this. Elise's mouth was warm and welcoming, her hair silky soft as it slipped through Cole's fingers. He cradled the back of her head in his hand, and adjusted their positions to deepen the kiss.

At first he was content just to savor the taste of her, to explore her subtle reactions when he touched her tongue with the tip of his, or moved his hand just so. He was in no rush. Like a traveler entering an exotic, enchanted land, he wanted to take his time, to let his heightened senses absorb all the strange, wonderful magic of his surroundings.

He was aware of everything simultaneously, from the gentle friction of the sofa pillows against his bare arm, through the faint, lemony fragrance of dish soap rising from Elise's hands, to the lush, velvety mingling of her tongue with his.

He felt her pulse throbbing delicately yet rapidly in her neck, like the wings of a butterfly. When his hand touched her breast, Cole heard the catch of her breath, and sensed the desire uncurling inside her.

Like a match to dry timber, her response seemed to ignite flames of urgent need inside him, so that all at once he had to force himself to hold back. God, how he wanted her! She was kind and sweet and loving, and she'd made him feel whole again. For the first time in years, Cole dared to hope that the rest of his life might contain some joy, might serve some purpose besides atoning for his past failures.

But this wasn't only about *his* desires, *his* needs.

Reluctantly, he parted his mouth from hers. "Elise, maybe I should go. Maybe this isn't such a—"

"Don't go," she whispered between his lips. Her eyes were huge, gleaming like candles, sure and unwavering.

"No," Cole said gladly. "I want to stay."

Then he was plunging into her warmth, her sweetness, again, melding his mouth to hers, sliding his hand beneath her shirt to stroke the soft, bare expanse of her skin. She arched against him, pressing the tantalizing curves of her body into him, so that they fit together like two pieces of a puzzle.

When she wound her arms around his neck, Cole felt like he'd come home.

Desire spilled through him like molten impatience. He slid his hand up her spine and located the clasp of her bra. His clumsy fingers seemed to take forever at their task. Then, at

the long-awaited moment of triumph, Elise broke their kiss
and pushed against his chest.

Raw, aching disappointment lashed through him. So she
couldn't bring herself to go through with this, after all. Cole
swallowed. Well, no doubt it was for the best—

"Kelsey," she whispered.

For a second or two, his overloaded nervous system was
incapable of transmitting the meaning of the message to his
brain. But as soon as it registered in his thick skull, Cole
yanked back his hands and whipped his head around guiltily, dragging himself back into a more or less upright position.

Elise made a tiny sound behind her fingers. Not until he
noticed the crinkles smiling from the corners of her eyes did
he realize the sound had been one of merriment.

"Kelsey's not here," she assured him in a gentle voice.
"But in case she gets up for a glass of water or something,
I'd just as soon she didn't find her mother making out on
the couch."

"Good grief, no." Cole's shoulders slumped with relief,
even while he shuddered at the picture Elise had brought to
mind. "So, er, what do we...I mean, I wouldn't want
to—"

Elise scooped her hair back from her face and rose to her
feet, smiling. "Want to come look at my etchings?" She
held out her hand.

Cole took it. "Surely you don't expect me to fall for *that*
old trick," he scoffed. He *was* falling for Elise, though.
Hard.

She led him down the hall. At the far end, a door stood
ajar. Rhythmic, wet snores drifted from the darkened room.
Cole scratched his head. There couldn't possibly be a man
sleeping in there, but it seemed equally unlikely that a cute
little nine-year-old girl could produce such a racket.

Elise caught the look on his face. "That's Bob," she murmured with amusement.

Of course—the dog! Cole chuckled quietly. "I'm amazed Kelsey gets any sleep," he whispered.

"Fortunately, Kelsey could sleep through a chain saw convention." Elise's heart was hammering wildly when she drew Cole into her bedroom. She was stumbling into unfamiliar territory now, bringing a man into her bed while Kelsey slept peacefully beneath the same roof.

When she closed the door and locked it behind her, the faint metallic click was like a signal marking the start of a new stage in her life. Never before had she put a locked door between her and her child.

Because up till now, she'd never met a man who was worth it.

She'd boldly led Cole into her bedroom, but now her courage was faltering. How did one go about this, exactly? Should she turn on the light or leave them standing in the dark? Was she supposed to wait for Cole to make the next move, or was it her turn?

It had been at least twelve years since she'd faced this type of awkward dilemma. And nine years since she'd shared her bed with a man. She was definitely out of practice.

She sensed a sudden hesitancy in Cole, too, and wondered if he was thinking about the wife he'd lost.

With a pang of sympathy and understanding, Elise lifted her hand to the side of his face. Cole turned his head and pressed his lips into her palm. Blinded by darkness, she used her fingertips to trace the solid, square wedge of his jaw, the pleasant, bristly rasp of his emerging whiskers.

"Elise, there's something I need to tell you...." His words were muffled by her palm until he moved his mouth away and wrapped his hand around hers. "There's something you should know about, before we—"

"Sh . . ." She crossed his lips with her finger. "I know all I need to know about you."

"But—"

"Whatever it is, it doesn't matter." She knew Cole was still in love with the memory of his wife. Maybe he always would be. But Elise wasn't asking for forever. That was a word that could have no place in her vocabulary until the day she was certain Kelsey was safe once and for all.

She hadn't planned on meeting someone like Cole. She hadn't intended to let a man into her life as long as Kelsey was in danger. But, however, it *had* happened. Whether she'd planned it or not, Elise had come to care for Cole. More than she ought to.

Even though their relationship could lead nowhere, even though they were both trapped by the consequences of tragic events in their pasts, why shouldn't they turn to each other for whatever brief moments of happiness they could capture?

This might be the last chance she would ever have to find passion with a man who knew all her secrets. A man she could trust.

Maybe he could never love her. But Elise had learned not to look too far ahead. To live each day as it came, because you never knew when your happiness might come to an end.

She linked her wrists behind Cole's neck, drawing his head down to hers. "Kiss me," she whispered into his mouth. "Make love to me, Cole."

She felt the tendons straining in his body, as if he were fighting against himself.

Laura would want you to rebuild your life, to find happiness again, Elise thought.

But she didn't have a chance to say it, because with a muffled groan that sounded half desire, half despair, Cole crushed his mouth against hers.

Elise leaned into him as his arms came around her waist. Excitement swept through her like wildfire. His mouth was hungry, hard, greedy. His heart thundered in his chest, sending reverberations through her own body. His hands were in constant motion, stroking her back, exploring the curve of her waist, cupping her hips to draw her more snugly against him.

She let her head tip back as desire flowed through her. Cole branded the sensitive flesh of her throat with burning kisses.

He slipped his hand beneath her shirt, kneading a trail of delicious circles that climbed her rib cage until his fingers pushed aside her loosened bra. When he caressed her bare nipple with his thumb, pleasure sped through Elise with an intensity that took her breath away.

Somehow, they moved toward the bed in a clumsy tango. Cole reached down, fumbling for a moment with the lamp on the nightstand.

"There," he said with a grunt of satisfaction when amber light spilled across the room. "I want to be able to see you while we make love." In the shadows cast by the dim light, Elise saw doubt slide over his rugged features. "You don't mind, do you? Because I can turn it back off if—"

She silenced him the most effective way she knew how.

Cole lowered her onto the bed without breaking their kiss. Elise heard twin thumps as his sneakers hit the floor. She was barely aware of kicking off her own shoes, so caught up was she in the whirlwind of sensation and anticipation that created a loud rushing in her ears and sent blood pounding through her veins.

Her emotions shifted as quickly as desert sands in a dust storm. One moment, she was apprehensive. The next, impatient. Now, hesitant. Then, bold. Above all, she burned with the need for Cole's touch. With a powerful craving to fulfill the promise of that emotional link she'd felt toward him from the first, to make it a physical link as well.

She helped him tug her shirt over her head, shedding the rest of her clothes in short order. Amazingly, she didn't feel the least bit shy in front of him. This was Cole, after all. The man she'd already entrusted with her most important secret.

His eyes gleamed with lustful admiration as he gazed down at her. ''Elise, you're so beautiful....''

She hadn't felt sexy for a long time. Her primary focus for the past nine years had been on her role as a mother. But this...chemistry that she and Cole shared had reminded Elise that she was still a vibrant, adult woman with needs of her own.

Cole made her feel desirable again. And in the process, reawakened passions she'd almost forgotten could exist.

With a seductive, feminine smile, she reached for the snap of his shorts.

Hastily, he peeled off his shirt, never taking his eyes from her. The faint rasp of his zipper was about the sexiest sound Elise had ever heard. He stepped out of his shorts and underwear and skimmed off his socks.

Elise unabashedly drank in the sight of him. Bathed in gold light, he stood as unselfconsciously, as unaware of his magnificence, as the statue of a Greek god. His broad chest was shaded with a scattering of dark curls that tapered to a V over his belly, pointing like an arrow toward the proud evidence of his desire.

His legs were long and straight, sheathed in muscle. Chasing criminals must be good exercise, Elise decided. She swallowed when her mouth actually began to water. God, but he was gorgeous!

Excitement laced with anxiety erupted inside her when he lay beside her on the bed. What if this wasn't like riding a bicycle? What if she couldn't remember what to do, or proved inadequate in some way?

Then, Cole brushed away her fears with the sweep of his hand down the length of her body. "So soft, so smooth," he murmured.

Her skin tingled wherever he touched her, which covered a lot of territory. Elise responded in kind, acquainting herself with the exciting, unfamiliar terrain of his nude body. The wiry hair along his legs crinkled deliciously under her palm.

At the top of his thigh, she traced a two-inch pucker of skin with her fingertips. A scar left by some bad guy's bullet? She shuddered to think of the dangers Cole had faced as a big-city cop. It was comforting to know he was a small-town sheriff now, and unlikely to encounter the brand of ruthless, violent criminals that prowled the urban streets.

He misinterpreted her shudder. "Cold?" he asked in concern.

Cold? She was on fire. "How are you planning to warm me up?" she asked innocently.

Cole chuckled, even as desire sprang into his eyes. "Here, let me show you."

He kissed her mouth, her eyelids, her temples, caressing her with his hands and his lips. Elise's temperature was definitely going up, all right. She was positively melting in his embrace.

When he lowered his head and took her nipple in his mouth, she gasped, clawing at his back. Dear heaven, she'd never felt anything so wonderful before! Circles of pure pleasure spread out from her breast like ripples in a pond.

She reached for him, wrapping her fingers around his hardness, provoking a groan deep in his throat.

After a minute or two, he lifted his head. His eyes were wild, his mouth glistening. "Elise...honey..." He paused for a ragged breath while his eyes closed briefly. Opening them, he said, "Sweetheart, I—I'm not going to last much longer if you keep that up."

"Want me to stop?" she teased softly.

"No—yes...I mean, no!" He skimmed his hand down below her belly, using his fingers to open her gently, like the petals of a flower.

Elise sucked in her breath. "Cole..."

"There," he said through his teeth. "Now we're even."

Every time she thought he couldn't possibly increase the intensity of her pleasure, Cole surprised her. She arched blindly against his hand, practically delirious with the incredible sensations he was arousing inside her. She felt herself rising, soaring, straining toward the sky....

When she managed to choke out his name, it sounded like a plea.

Swiftly, Cole raised himself above her. Their eyes met, linking them with that same powerful connection that had pulled them toward each other from the beginning.

I love you, Cole.

Whether or not he received her mentally telegraphed message, Elise didn't know, nor have time to discover. Because Cole eased himself inside her, filling her with an ecstasy that promptly blotted all thought from her mind.

"Ah...Elise." The cords in his neck stood out as he moved back and forth inside her. "You feel so good."

"Yes," she whispered. "Oh, yes..."

She matched her rhythm to his, while every stroke lifted her to a new level of pleasure and passion. She relished the weight of his body on top of hers, the delightful friction of skin against skin as he thrust into her, deeper, faster....

She writhed against him while an almost unbearable pressure mounted inside her. She thought Cole called her name, but she couldn't be sure, because of the rushing sound that filled her ears, as if she truly *were* rocketing toward the stars, up and up and—

"Cole!" she cried out.

"Yes!" he hissed fiercely.

As fireworks exploded inside her, Elise glimpsed the expression on his face and knew that he, too, was sailing through the heavens with her.

Afterward, it felt as if she were slowly awakening from a dream, as if the details of their surroundings were sifting back into place bit by bit. Gradually, the spasms in Elise's body stilled, the tingling of her skin faded, the scattered shards of her consciousness pieced themselves back together.

Cole stirred on top of her. Elise lazily stroked his back. She couldn't recall ever experiencing another moment of such utter bliss and contentment. She would gladly have lain there forever with Cole sprawled on top of her—

Except for that pesky oxygen problem. Reluctantly, she prodded his shoulder. "Darling," she whispered. "I'm... having a little trouble... breathing."

Instantly, Cole rolled off her, his eyes wide with remorse. "Elise, honey, I'm sorry, I didn't realize—"

"It's okay," she assured him with a smile and a touch of her finger to the tip of his nose. "I was kind of oblivious to everything myself for a while."

Relief blunted the sharp angles of his face. He gathered her into his arms. "Does that mean it was—did I—I mean, did you, uh..." He blew a disgusted stream of air through his lips. "Boy, I don't exactly sound like Mr. Cool, do I?"

"Nope." Elise snuggled happily into his embrace. "But the answers to all your other questions are yes, yes and yes."

"Yes?"

"*Oooh*, yes."

"Mmm." He hugged her tighter. "Well, I give it an emphatic yes vote, too."

"It's unanimous then." Elise twined a curl of his chest hair around her finger and sighed. She waited for the cold touch of regret to chill her, now that the heat of passion had subsided to a warm glow.

There was none. No regrets, no second thoughts, no wishing she could go back and do everything all over.

Well, actually, *some* parts of this evening she wouldn't mind doing all over. And over, and over, and—

"What are you smiling at?" Cole asked, grazing his knuckle across her cheek.

"Need you ask?" Playfully, Elise nipped his finger with her teeth. She felt about twenty years old again. Life seemed full of magic, full of possibilities, full of hope.

You still have no future with this man, Elise warned herself. *Making love with Cole doesn't change anything.*

Still, despite her insistent denial, it felt like it had changed *everything*.

With a growl of satisfaction, Cole nuzzled her neck. Elise giggled. When her roaming fingers encountered the ridge of scar tissue on his thigh, she asked, "What's this from? A bullet?"

Cole flicked his tongue across her earlobe. "Nothing nearly so glamorous, I'm afraid."

Elise shivered at his warm breath in her ear. "What, then? A knife or something?"

He propped his head on one hand and gazed down at her. "Truth is, a sharp branch skewered me when I fell out of a tree as a kid."

Elise winced. "Ouch."

"You can say that again. And I *did,* too. Quite a few times that day." He grinned. "Usually I tell people I was wounded in the line of duty."

Elise made a twisting motion over her sealed lips, then mimed throwing away a key. "Your secret's safe with me. After all, turnabout is fair play."

Cole's grin sagged at the edges.

"I mean," she said quickly, "that now I know all your secrets. Just like you know all mine." She nestled her head into the crook of his shoulder, sorry that the subject of her complicated past had intruded into this special time together.

Cole lay motionless for a minute, then began to stroke her hair. "Elise..."

She could feel the tension tightening his muscles. "Mmm..." She yawned sleepily, determined to distract him from further discussion of the subject she herself had been careless enough to bring up.

Cole cleared his throat. Darn it, he wasn't going to drop it! Hardly a surprise, considering how stubbornly persistent he could be when he latched onto something. But the last thing Elise wanted to talk about right now was her past. Or Cole's past. Or their nonexistent future together.

So, she thought of a more effective way to distract him.

And did.

Under cover of darkness, Victor Dominick watched the sheriff slip out of the Jordan woman's house. He'd been parked across the street for nearly five hours, slumped down behind the steering wheel of the passenger van he'd rented under a phony name in Tucson.

Finally, his patience paid off. He'd been starting to think the two lovebirds had settled in for the night. But he hadn't been willing to end his surveillance until all the lights went off.

Now he'd uncovered the useful nugget of information that, cozy as things might be between the kid's mother and her cop friend, the sheriff didn't make it his habit to spend the night.

Dominick wasn't quite ready to make his move yet. He still had a few details to work out, but his plan was definitely coming together.

Especially now that he knew he didn't have to worry about finding the sheriff sound asleep in Elizabeth Jordan's bed.

Chapter 12

"What's bowl—bool—boil..."

"Bouillabaisse," Elise said. "It's like fish stew."

Kelsey crinkled her snub nose at the menu. "Yuck."

"Kelsey..." Elise injected a stern note into her voice as she threw Cole a half embarrassed, half amused glance. "Just order something else from the menu, then, and spare us your editorial comments, please."

Kelsey kicked her chair leg while she studied the menu some more. Then she brightened. "I'm gonna have prime rib," she announced, closing her menu.

Elise cleared her throat and Kelsey got a startled look on her face, as if someone had kicked her under the table. Hastily she flipped open the menu and began to peruse it again. "Oh, yeah. I wasn't supposed to order the most expensive thing."

With a groan, Elise buried her face in one hand.

Cole chuckled. "That's okay, Kelsey. You go right ahead and order anything you want tonight."

"Even prime rib?"

"Even prime rib," he assured her.

Elise's cheeks were tinted pink, making her look even prettier in the candlelight. "But that's so much food, Peach."

"We can take what's left home in a doggie bag," Cole pointed out.

"For Bob?" Kelsey asked eagerly.

"Oooh, no." Elise shook her head. "We are absolutely, positively *not* going to feed expensive prime rib to the dog."

"But then why do they call it a doggie bag?"

"Because . . . um . . ." Elise rolled her eyes in exasperation. "Care to field that one, Sheriff?"

"Whoa, not me." Cole held up his hands. "I think the runner scores this time."

"They oughtta call it a *people* bag," Kelsey said.

They were dining at Brennan's, the fanciest restaurant in Tumbleweed. Which might not be saying much compared to big cities like New York or San Francisco, but the food was good, the service excellent and the atmosphere elegant without being stuffy.

Located in a building that had housed a dry goods store back in the old mining days, the restaurant still kept the original brick walls and high, hammered-tin ceiling. Antique wall sconces supplemented the candles burning at each table, and the wooden floorboards squeaked pleasantly each time one of the servers hustled by.

"This place is wonderful," Elise said for about the fifth time that evening.

"How come they put a lemon slice in the water?" Kelsey asked.

"Don't poke at it, please. Just to give it a little extra-special flavor." She gave Cole a flustered smile. "It's awfully generous of you to bring us here. This place is just—just wonderful."

Six times.

"Why, where else would I take my two best girls, except a place that's extraspecial?" Cole winked at Kelsey, who beamed back at him.

Elise seemed a bit jumpy this evening, and Cole figured he knew why. No doubt her tight budget didn't allow for luxuries like dining out, especially not in fancy restaurants like this one. Even though dinner was on him, she wasn't accustomed to blithely ordering a meal that probably cost the equivalent of a couple of new pairs of shoes for her rapidly growing child.

And, unless he missed his guess, the other reason for Elise's edginess had to do with him.

Cole hadn't come right out and asked her, of course, but it seemed pretty likely there hadn't been too many men in her life since her husband had died. And Elise wasn't the type of woman who would casually parade her relationships in front of her child.

No doubt she was finding it a bit awkward to sit at the same table with both her daughter and the man she'd made wild, incredible love with last night.

At least, Cole *hoped* it had been incredible for her. God knows, it had been for him.

He busied himself refilling their wineglasses from the decanter, suddenly uncomfortable for harboring such lusty thoughts about Elise in front of her daughter.

And, hovering behind *that* guilt was an even bigger one. He shouldn't have gone to bed with Elise without being honest with her. Without telling her that he'd basically been spying on her for weeks now.

True, he'd made a couple of feeble attempts to tell her last night, but desire had gotten the best of him. Desire, and the desperate wish not to spoil the magic of the intimate bond that had grown between them.

A bond based on trust, for Elise's part. On lies, for his.

Cole took a deep swallow of wine. Somehow, the taste had turned bitter. He was going to have to confess the truth to Elise. Soon. And just hope it wouldn't destroy the precious, newfound closeness they shared. A closeness he hadn't found with anyone since Laura died.

"Sheriff? Do I get to order dessert, too?"

"Kelsey!" Elise nearly choked on her wine.

Cole rustled her butterscotch hair, which tonight was brushed loose around her shoulders instead of tied in her usual braids or ponytail. "Sure thing, Peach."

The endearment slipped out naturally, surprising him. Kelsey didn't seem to notice. Elise, however, appeared a bit taken aback to hear her own special nickname for Kelsey emerge from someone else's mouth.

Cole tapped his chin. "Let me make a wild guess what you want for dessert."

"'Kay!" Kelsey crossed her arms over the front of her ruffled blue dress and pressed her lips together smugly.

Cole closed his eyes and massaged his temples with his fingertips. "You are going to order…" He snapped his eyes wide open, as if a light bulb had just popped on over his head. "The chocolate fudge cheesecake!"

Kelsey's mouth fell open with astonishment. Elise burst out laughing. And Cole felt a warm glow in the pit of his stomach that had nothing to do with the wine.

"How'd you know, Sheriff?" Kelsey stared at him as if he'd just pulled a rabbit out of the breadbasket.

He huffed on his nails and buffed them modestly on the lapel of his sport coat. "I'm a trained detective, remember? I get paid for figuring things out."

"Wow!" Full-fledged hero worship shone in her adorable green eyes. "I bet you've caught lots of crooks, huh?"

"I guess I've caught my fair share." He winked at her. "How 'bout if you just call me Cole from now on?"

"Sure!" Kelsey's delighted smile tugged at his heart. And right then Cole realized that Elise wasn't the only member of the Grant family who'd come to mean an awful lot to him.

Cole touched Elise's elbow, and even the small contact made her feel all shivery and delicious inside.

"Mind if I take a minute to make a call?" He nodded toward the pay phones on the far side of the theater lobby. "I promised the dispatcher I'd check in—to make sure no one robbed a bank or anything while we were watching the movie."

Elise smiled. "Of course not." People swirled around them, heading for the snack bar or on their way to find seats for the next showing. "We'll wait for you outside," she told Cole, shepherding Kelsey into the flow of people drifting toward the exit.

"I won't be long." He squeezed her arm in farewell, sending her an intimate smile that warmed her all the way to her toes.

The Coronet Theater was a classic, old-fashioned movie house dating from the thirties. Its faded glamour had been lovingly restored with plush red velvet draperies, art deco fixtures and lots of gleaming chrome that sparkled beneath the ornate chandeliers overhead.

Outside, Elise glanced up at the marquee, its outline traced against the night sky by a necklace of dazzling light bulbs. "Did you like the movie?" she asked Kelsey. Silly question. It had action, it had humor, and most important of all, it had animals in it.

It had been Cole's suggestion.

"I *loved* it!" Kelsey replied, hugging herself with enthusiasm.

Elise, too, had enjoyed the evening immensely, even though she'd been nervous at first. Seeing Cole tonight, for the first time since they'd made love, had made her feel as breathless and shy as a teenager on her first date.

Would he act differently toward her now? Did he regret making love to her? Had he been disappointed?

Silly, of course. He'd still been the same old Cole—thoughtful, generous, putting her at ease. And judging by the way he'd casually draped his arm along the back of Kelsey's theater seat so he could reach over and stroke Elise's shoulder, Cole didn't regret last night one bit.

As she and Kelsey moved away from the glass doors of the theater entrance, goose bumps made Elise's skin tingle, even though the star-strewn night was balmy and pleasant. The memory of Cole's hands and mouth caressing her... of his warm breath whispering sweet words in her ear... of his long, hard, naked body fitted perfectly to hers made her heart beat faster with anticipation of nights yet to come.

Maybe even tonight...

"Mom, does the sheriff—I mean, does Cole have any kids?"

Elise guiltily shoved her erotic fantasies aside. Heavens, what if Kelsey had been able to read her mind?

With a pang of sadness, she thought of Cole's unborn child, the child who'd never had a chance to come into the world.

Rather than explain the tragedy to Kelsey, she replied, "No, Peach. He doesn't have any kids."

Kelsey swung herself around one of the iron lampposts that illuminated the quaint downtown streets with reproduction gaslights. "But I think Cole *likes* kids, don't you?"

"Yes, I think so." Elise stepped to the curb next to her daughter. "He certainly likes you."

"He does?" She brightened.

"Of course! Can't you tell?"

Kelsey stopped swinging around the lamppost and rubbed the back of her calf with the opposite shoe. "Do you think Cole would ever like to have a kid like me?"

Elise's heart contracted as if someone had squeezed it with a fist. "Anyone would be incredibly lucky to have a kid like you," she said, stroking Kelsey's long, flowing hair.

Nice dodge, Elise, but it's not enough.

It was as plain as the letters on the movie marquee where Kelsey's thoughts were heading. Where, truth to tell, Elise's own thoughts had ventured a time or two.

Better put a stop to any impossible wishful thinking right now.

"It's been just the two of us for a long time, hasn't it, Peach?"

"Uh-huh."

"Sometimes I think it would be nice if there could be someone else, too."

Kelsey tilted her head to one side. "You mean, like Bob?"

The corners of Elise's mouth twitched. "Well, I was really thinking of another *person.*"

Kelsey's eyes flared open, as if the idea had just occurred to her. "What about Cole?"

Elise sighed. If only real life could turn out as neatly as the movie they'd just seen, instead of being so messy and complicated.

"Kelsey, Cole is our friend. And he's been a very *good* friend to us." Elise braced her hands on her thighs and leaned forward, so she and her daughter were eye to eye. "But it's not a good idea to hope that someday he'll be part of our family." Good advice. Now, if only she could follow it herself.

"But why not?" Kelsey twisted a lock of hair around her finger, managing to look both rebellious and disappointed at the same time.

"Because—because we might have to move again someday."

"But why can't Cole come with us?"

"Peach—" Elise grasped her shoulders "—Cole has a job here. This is his home." Unable to bear the hurt puzzlement in Kelsey's eyes, she let her gaze follow a pair of teenagers strolling down the sidewalk hand in hand. "We can't expect Cole to give up everything just to..."

Elise's voice trailed off. There were quite a few people out tonight, taking a walk after dinner, lingering in front of shop windows, enjoying the warm spring evening. Until now she hadn't been paying them any particular attention, but subconsciously she'd glimpsed something a second ago that disturbed her.

Something... or someone.

She scanned the parade of milling pedestrians again. A middle-aged couple pointing at something in a window. An elderly man with his grandson, eating ice-cream cones as they walked along. Two kids playing tag, darting from lamppost to lamppost...

What was it she could have seen—there!

Elise gasped. Or would have, if she'd been able to draw air into her lungs.

Up the street, peering out from a concealing recess in front of a darkened shop....

Those eyes.

Victor Dominick's eyes.

Icy terror shot through Elise's veins like liquid nitrogen, rocketing her bolt upright. *Run!* screamed every instinct in her body.

In one swift motion, she whirled Kelsey around and propelled her down the sidewalk in the opposite direction.

Kelsey emitted a startled yap of protest. "Mom! Where are we—?"

Elise threw a panicked glance over her shoulder, ready to start screaming bloody murder if she found Dominick bearing down on them. But all that chased them were a few curious stares.

Elise's gaze traveled frantically back up the street.

The eyes had disappeared. No one was watching them. No one was following them.

Her step faltered. Could he have ducked back into—?

Maybe she'd been mistaken.

God knows, over the last two years, there easily had been a dozen occasions when she'd been sure she'd spotted Dominick.

Or imagined she'd spotted him.

She'd never hung around long enough to make sure.

This time, though, Dominick wasn't the only person Elise and Kelsey would be running away from. This time, they both had much more to lose if Elise was wrong.

And this time, they had Cole to protect them.

Elise had only glimpsed those eyes for a second...not long enough to be absolutely certain. She checked behind them one more time.

No sign of him.

She slowed their pace to a fast walk. Blood thundered in her ears.

Kelsey peered up at her uncertainly. "Mom? How come we were running?"

The last thing she wanted was to scare Kelsey unnecessarily. "I...thought we'd play a trick on Cole. Hide around the corner so he can't find us."

Kelsey's worried brow cleared. "Come on! Let's hurry, before he comes out of the movie."

"Peach, I—" Elise splayed a trembling hand over her heart. "I changed my mind. Let's go back." Her chest rose and fell with the remnants of fear and exertion. "Maybe it's kind of a mean trick. Cole might worry about us."

Kelsey studied her as if trying to solve a puzzle. She was far too perceptive not to realize there was something funny going on. But she finally shrugged in agreement.

Elise took firm hold of her hand while they walked back up the block. Just in case.

Cole stepped out from beneath the theater marquee, arching his brows in surprise when he saw them coming down the street. "Where'd you two go off to?"

"Window-shopping," Elise answered promptly. She dredged up a smile, even as her gaze skipped past Cole to alight on each one of the shop fronts farther up the block.

"Yeah? Did you buy any windows?" He chucked Kelsey beneath the chin.

She squealed with laughter and pulled away. "That's not what window-shopping means!"

"No? What is it, then?"

"It's when you just *look* in the windows, but you aren't going to buy anything."

"Ah!" He nodded.

Intent on scanning the immediate vicinity for sinister figures, it took Elise a few moments to realize Cole was watching her curiously.

"Elise, is everything okay?"

She forced herself to meet his eyes. "Just fine."

He turned around to see what she'd been staring at, but Elise knew there was nothing to see now. No trace of Victor Dominick.

She was probably just being paranoid, she told herself. That was all. Her brain had used a trick of light or a deceptive shadow to conjure up the physical image of her worst fears.

She'd just been reminding Kelsey that some day they might have to move on, so it was only logical that their reason for fleeing would have popped up in the back of her mind.

From the dark recesses of her mind—to the dark shadows of a closed building up the street. Not such a long trip. Perfectly understandable how she could have envisioned Dominick when he wasn't really there.

Cole took her arm. "Elise? You sure you're okay? You're white as a sheet."

The warmth of his hand stole through the thin sleeve of her dress, comforting her, soothing away her fears. Now wasn't the time to tell Cole what she *thought* she'd seen. It was embarrassing to admit she was still stalked by these hallucinations, and she didn't want to frighten Kelsey.

Besides, she'd hate to shatter the pleasure of their evening together by bringing up any reminders of why the feelings they shared could lead no further than a dead-end street. She would wait until they were alone, later, to talk to him about it.

"I'm fine," she assured Cole. "Maybe a little light-headed from the wine I had with dinner, that's all."

Doubt crimped the corners of his mouth. Dinner had been hours ago, and she'd barely consumed more than one glass, anyway.

To Elise's relief, Cole chose to let it pass. He squeezed her arm, giving her another one of those meaningful looks that had melted her insides all evening long. Only this one also held a slight promise—he didn't believe she was fine—but he too would wait until later to discover why.

"I'm afraid I'm going to have to escort you two ladies right home," he said regretfully, "instead of going out for ice cream like I promised."

Kelsey pushed out her lower lip. "How come?"

Cole rustled her hair, but it was Elise he looked at while he answered. "Pam, the dispatcher, told me we just got a report of a small plane going down in the Santa Paula Mountains, on the other side of the county. Will you be okay tonight?"

Elise gasped. "Of course. You need to go."

Kelsey's eyes grew wide and somber.

Cole nodded grimly. "They haven't located the wreckage yet, but I've got to head over there as soon as I take you home."

As he ushered them to his car, Elise said, "Maybe I could call and ask Roz for a ride, to save you some time."

"No." Cole's response was surprisingly emphatic. "I'll see you safely home myself."

In her current emotional state, Elise wasn't about to argue.

Victor Dominick clapped his beefy hands together with satisfaction. There had been a few bad moments there, like when the Jordan broad had spotted him.

He'd been so confident she couldn't possibly see through his disguise, especially all the way down the block. But he wouldn't make the mistake of underestimating her again.

At least she hadn't run screaming to her sheriff boyfriend to rescue her. In fact, she must not have told him anything. Because if she had, Mr. Sheriff would have taken her and Little Miss Eyewitness someplace else for safekeeping while he was out scouring the mountains for downed aircraft.

Which meant she probably was planning to take off with the kid as soon as loverboy dropped them off at home.

After the Jordan woman had spotted him peering around the corner, Dominick had hightailed it back to the "borrowed" utility-company truck he'd hot-wired that afternoon. He'd followed the sheriff's car from downtown, figuring that if the jig was up, there still might be a chance to grab his quarry if he could discover where Sheriff Romeo planned to stash them.

Wonder of wonders, the car had proceeded merrily to the Jordans' normal turnoff. Dominick knew from his own careful scouting that Saguaro Road led nowhere, eventually petering out in the middle of the desert. The cop had to be taking them *home*.

Dominick stationed the stolen truck at the turnoff from the highway, knowing the sheriff would have to come back that way, and crossing his fingers that he'd be alone when he did.

It wasn't long before Dominick saw returning headlights. He was strategically parked in concealing darkness, but close enough to the nearest streetlight so he could make out the profile of one solitary occupant as the car passed by.

Now, watching the cop's red taillights vanish down the highway, Dominick felt a rush of exultation. By God, his plan was still going to work! All he had to do was park the utility truck near the Jordan house, hide himself in the shadows near their car and jump the woman and kid when they came out to make a run for it.

He reached into the pocket of his windbreaker, gripping the reassuring bulk of cold, solid steel.

The truck he was driving would blend right into the scenery. None of the neighbors would think it fishy to see a utility-company vehicle parked on the street. And no one would be reporting it stolen until tomorrow, Monday morning, by which time he himself would be winging his way back to Boston, sipping champagne to congratulate himself on a job well done and flirting with the stewardesses in first class.

He started the truck, drove a quarter mile down the road and pulled up in front of the house next door to the Jordans'. He killed the engine and headlights. After ten minutes, long enough to give any nosy neighbors time to drop their curtains back in place and move away from the windows, he stepped out of the truck.

He shut the door as quietly as possible, standing motionless in the dark while the muffled echo gradually faded into the night. Then, he moved through the shadows and crept toward the Jordans' house.

The damn gravel made a scrunching sound as he sidled up the driveway. Hadn't these people ever heard of asphalt? Luckily, he reassured himself, it probably wasn't loud enough for anyone to notice.

He warily approached a tall shrub standing at the corner where the carport met the house—in case it turned out to be some type of cursed cactus.

Perfect. Nothing snagged his clothes or pricked his flesh when he eased himself between the house and the shrubbery. The bush was big enough to conceal him, and close enough to the car, so that with just one long stride he could jam the gun to the woman's temple and grab her car keys as she opened the driver's door.

Once he'd gotten rid of his victims, he would come back for their car, ditch it at the Tucson airport, and make it look as if the Jordans had taken off for parts unknown.

Right now, all he had to do was wait.

Fortunately, he was a patient man. Hadn't he already waited more than two years to put the little blabbermouth and her mother out of the picture once and for all?

Yes. He was very good at waiting.

Especially when he knew it wouldn't be long now.

Chapter 13

Rotating red-and-blue flashers lit up the command-post area like some sort of eerie disco. The jagged outlines of the Santa Paula Mountains loomed overhead, barely visible in the moonless night.

As Cole hung up the cellular phone in his cruiser, he saw Zack Brewster striding toward him, navigating his way through the fleet of law-enforcement and rescue vehicles parked every which way at the base of the mountains.

"Any sign of the wreck?" he asked his deputy.

Zack shook his head as he removed his hat and slicked back sweat-dampened hair. "Nope. *Nada.* We climbed up to the top of the ridge but couldn't see a thing."

"I just got off the phone with the FAA. They're not picking up the emergency beacon that would have started transmitting on impact."

Zack started to unwrap something in his hand.

"What's that?" Cole asked.

The deputy stuffed it in his mouth. "San'wich," he replied in a muffled voice.

"Where'd that come from?"

He pointed with the sandwich. "Fire department guys." He chewed, swallowed, opened his mouth to take another big bite. "They've got more, if you want some."

"Thanks, but I already ate." Dinner seemed a lifetime ago. The cozy atmosphere at Brennan's, the mellow wine, the tasty food.

And, of course, the delightful company.

Cole smiled crookedly, recalling Kelsey's antics, and the warm, tender way Elise had looked at him all during dinner, with candlelight shimmering in her green eyes like sunlight on the sea.

His smile dissolved when he recalled her unsuccessful effort to mask her agitation outside the movie theater. Something had happened to upset her during that brief period while he was making his phone call.

But what?

He felt a little guilty for not immediately pursuing the source of her ill-concealed distress, but duty had called. Somewhere out there in the rugged, coal black mountains, people might be hurt or dying. It was his job to find them, to help them.

He just wished he knew what was troubling Elise.

"Could be a coupla reasons," Zack mused.

Cole glanced at him sharply. Although Zack was a good deputy—thorough, reliable, tenacious as a bulldog behind that easygoing exterior, Cole had never before given him credit for being a mind reader.

"What do you mean?" he asked cautiously.

Zack licked his fingers. "Why they can't detect the emergency beacon from the downed plane." He wadded the sandwich wrapper into a ball, looked around for a trash can, then shrugged and stuffed it into his pocket. "Could be the transmitter batteries are old and corroded, so the thing isn't working like it's supposed to."

"That's a possibility."

"Or, maybe more likely, if the plane went down in a canyon, the signal's being blocked by the surrounding mountains."

"In which case, we might need to request a scout plane or a helicopter to fly over the area and try to pick up the signal from above."

Zack dusted his hands together. "You want me to get on the horn and arrange it?"

Cole stared up at the mountains. It was rough country up there. Easy to get lost in. Not really surprising they hadn't been able to locate the wreck yet.

"Let's give the ground searchers a little more time," he said, deciding to go by the book. And according to the book, you didn't commit a bunch of elaborate, expensive resources to a rescue operation until you were certain someone needed rescuing.

"We haven't had any further verification, have we, of the plane going down?" he asked. Zack had gotten to the scene before Cole did.

"Just that one call."

"What exactly did the guy say?"

Zack fished a toothpick out of his shirt pocket. "Said he was a passing motorist, heard the sound of an engine in trouble, looked out and saw the lights as the plane went down somewhere in the mountains."

Cole leaned against the cruiser and crossed one foot over the other. "How'd he hear the plane engine over the sound of his own car engine, especially if it was off in the distance?"

"Beats me." Zack gnawed on the toothpick. "Driving with his window rolled down? Maybe the plane made a lot of racket."

"Maybe." But little question marks kept buzzing around Cole's head, irritating and persistent as mosquitoes. He leaned into the car and picked up the radio mike. "Pam?" he said when the dispatcher answered. "We get any more reports yet about that plane going down?"

"No. You'll be the first to know, I promise," she replied tartly, justifiably miffed at the implication she might be slacking off at her job.

"Thanks." Cole made a mental note to offer her a proper apology later. "Pam, I need you to play me back the original 911 call that came in about the crash, okay?"

"Certainly." She still sounded peeved. "Hang on for a second."

Static hissed over the radio. The crimson flasher on top of the cruiser pulsated like a strobe light, drenching Cole over and over with the color of blood.

He gazed up at the serrated rampart of mountains, dark, mysterious, forbidding. Somewhere out there...what would they find?

An ominous tingling had begun at the base of his spine. Restlessly, he waited.

Victor Dominick was getting sick and tired of waiting.

How long did it take to dump a few things in a suitcase and hustle the kid out to the car? he wondered.

Maybe the brat had thrown a tantrum and insisted on packing up her doll collection.

Whatever the reason for the delay, it was making him damned uncomfortable. His legs were stiff and cramped from crouching behind the shrubbery, he was getting cold from being motionless for so long, and he was tormented relentlessly by the maddening urge to sneeze. He was probably allergic to the stupid bush.

He hadn't heard any sounds from inside the house for a while. He pressed his ear against the cold stucco. Silence.

Prickling in his sinuses forced him to stifle yet another sneeze. Finally, he couldn't stand it another second. He crept cautiously out from behind the bush, still clinging to the shadows as he moved back for a look at the house.

As dark inside as the ace of spades.

What the devil?

Could they possibly have just ... gone to bed?

Why hadn't the Jordan woman spooked and run? Unless maybe she hadn't spotted him, after all ... ?

The hell with it. He wasn't going to camp out here all night freezing his tail off. He wanted to get this business over with under the concealing cover of darkness. And if the Jordan woman *had* spotted him, or if the sheriff was smarter than Dominick gave him credit for, this might be the last chance to dispose of the kid and her mother once and for all.

Fortunately, Dominick had come prepared with a set of lock-picking tools. The most essential ingredient in every job—careful planning. The second most essential ingredient—a backup plan. He hadn't intended to go inside the house, but now that he had no choice, it was important not to leave behind any evidence of a break-in.

He edged stealthily around to the backyard. He froze, holding his breath, when the gate creaked as he slipped through. But after a few moments ... nothing.

The kitchen door would have been child's play for an ordinary burglar, with the top half consisting of small panes of glass. Piece of cake to knock one out, reach through, unlock the door—and voilà! Open sesame.

Unfortunately, that wasn't an option for him. The sound of shattering glass had a tendency to wake up people and alarm them.

He extracted the case of tools from his jacket pocket, then took a closer look at the lock.

Locks, plural, actually. What did she think this was, Fort Knox?

Damn! His fingers were clumsy as he probed the first one with his picklock. It had been a lot of years since he'd had to do a job like this himself, and he was out of practice. This was going to take time, and time wasn't in unlimited supply.

Presto! One down, two to go. Sweat crawled down his forehead and made his eyes sting. "Easy now," he mumbled under his breath. "Trying to hurry will only make it tougher."

He cracked his knuckles and attacked the next lock.

Cole was listening to the 911 tape for the third time. Call it gut instinct, but there was something just a bit off kilter about the way this guy sounded. Some note that didn't quite ring true.

The 911 operator had just repeated back the information the caller had given her about where he'd seen the plane go down. "All right, sir, may I have your name, please?"

"What the hell do you need that for? A plane just crashed, for God's sake! Get the sheriff out there, and quit worrying about my name."

"Sir, we need to—"

"Look, I've told you all I'm going to. I've done my duty. If those poor people die, it'll be *your* fault for wasting time."

"Sir, I—"

"Get the sheriff out there, *now!*" Click. The caller had hung up.

Cole spoke into the mike. "Okay, Pam. Thanks." He ended the call to the dispatcher and turned to Zack. "What do you make of it?"

Zack shrugged. "Guy sure didn't want to give his name, did he?"

"No."

"'Course, lots of people are reluctant to. Don't want to get involved, or whatever."

"Yeah." Cole grimaced, remembering all the people who hadn't wanted to get involved when they heard Laura being murdered. Maybe *that* was why this guy had set him on edge, why the sound of his arrogant, demanding voice had made his skin crawl.

Get the sheriff out there.

"You know, most people calling in to report an accident sound out of breath. They talk kind of fast. You ever notice that?" he asked Zack.

"Sure. They're kind of panicky, like. Upset."

Upset. The way Elise had looked and sounded earlier this evening.

"This guy didn't sound too panicky, did he?" Cole asked thoughtfully.

"Nah. Then again, he drove a ways before he called in." The call had come from a pay phone in front of the Shop-Rite Supermarket. "Maybe he had time to calm down."

"And that's another thing." Cole wagged his finger. "How come he drove all the way into Tumbleweed before phoning? Why didn't he stop and call from the phone outside that roadhouse halfway between here and town?"

Zack scratched beneath the brim of his hat. "Maybe the phone was out of order."

"He could have gone inside and used the one in there."

"Maybe he wasn't thinking straight. Maybe he was too rattled from seeing the plane go down."

Cole drew his brows into a skeptical furrow. "Did that guy sound rattled to you?"

"Well . . . no."

A plane that had gone down without any distress call. A plane whose flight plan wasn't on file at any nearby airports. A plane whose emergency transmitter signal they couldn't locate.

In fact, the only evidence they had that a plane had crashed in the mountains was one phone call.

A call that might, in fact, be bogus.

What might motivate someone to play such a prank?

Get the sheriff out there.

The sheriff was out here, all right. Along with the majority of the rescue and law-enforcement personnel in Creosote County. If anarchy should break out in Tumbleweed right now, the citizens would have to fend for themselves for a while.

Maybe the call had been a diversion. But for what? For whom?

Get the sheriff out there.

He'd had to take Elise and Kelsey home first. Elise had been disturbed about something. Something she'd seen or heard while he was on the phone.

All at once, a horrifying suspicion crashed into Cole's brain, where it had been knocking progressively louder for attention.

"No. It couldn't be . . . oh, sweet Jesus."

"What is it?" Zack stared at his boss in alarm.

Cole leaped into the cruiser. Ignoring his deputy's open-mouthed expression, he started the car, backed it around and peeled out in a tornado of dust and gravel.

His heart was banging against his ribs like an inmate rattling prison bars. *Dear God, don't let this awful suspicion be correct....*

And if it is, don't let me be too late.

He snatched the radio mike, wrestling the steering wheel with one hand. "Pam? I want you to play that tape again, okay? Only this time for someone who's going to call you as soon as I can get hold of him. Got that?"

The instant he received her affirmative reply, he grabbed his cellular phone and dialed the number of Michael Dunnigan, Boston district attorney, from memory.

As he punched the buttons, his fingers were shaking.

Elise snapped awake from a dream to find herself facing her worst nightmare.

"Good evening, Mrs. Jordan," said the voice in her ear.

She tried to fling herself out of bed, but a heavy weight pinned her down. Terror poured through her, sweeping away the merciful fog of disorientation and confusion. She knew who he was. She knew what he'd come for.

Even if she'd been capable of screaming past the fear clogging her throat, his strong hand over her mouth would have smothered her cries.

"We're going to go for a little ride," he purred quietly. If Elise hadn't already been sick to her stomach with shock and horror, the smell of his breath would have nauseated her. "I realize you may be somewhat—resistant—to the idea, but I think I can persuade you." He shifted his other hand. "Do you recognize what this is?"

She felt the icy, coin-sized ring of metal pressed to her temple. His hand, clamped over the lower half of her face, allowed just enough leeway to nod.

"Good." She sensed him smile in the darkness. "Just remember now, if you don't cooperate with me, you won't be the one I shoot first. Understand?"

Kelsey! she screamed in her mind. *Oh, Peach, wake up! Run! Get away!*

She made a quick, terrified jerk of her head.

"Excellent."

The knowledge that it was Dominick's body pinning her down was so loathsome she was afraid she might retch. *Stay in control,* she warned herself. *Don't panic. It's your only chance to save Kelsey.*

"I'm going to remove my hand from your mouth now." He spoke quietly, calmly, patiently, like a schoolteacher explaining a lesson to a particularly dull student. Her heart was hammering so loudly in her ears, she had to strain to hear him. "There's no point in screaming, because even if one of the neighbors heard you, by the time they got here, your little girl would be dead. Does that make sense to you?"

She nodded.

"Good. No screaming, now." When he lifted his hand, Elise sucked a huge gasp of air into her lungs. The sudden rush of oxygen made her even dizzier.

He climbed off her and stepped back from the bed. "The first thing I want you to do, if you haven't done it already, is pack a suitcase with some clothes."

His words made absolutely no sense to Elise's befuddled brain. She didn't move a muscle.

"Cooperation, Mrs. Jordan," he said in an ominous voice. "That's the key word, remember?"

Somehow, she forced her brain to send the proper signals to her arms and legs. She crawled out of bed, trembling, instinctively trying to shield her thinly clad body with her hands, even though the room was pitch-dark.

"Your suitcase," he said. "Where is it?"

"The—" Her mouth was so dry, she had to swallow several times before she could produce a sound. "The closet."

"Get it."

"I—" She swallowed again. "I can't see."

"Oh, for crying out loud." She heard several thumps from the vicinity of the nightstand, then a click.

The bedside lamp came on, flooding the room with amber light and adding another dimension to Elise's horror. Here she was, face-to-face with the man who'd haunted her nightmares for more than two years.

Victor Dominick had done something to make himself look older, or maybe a life of crime was finally taking its toll on him. But his eyes hadn't changed. They were still the coldest, cruelest, most ruthless eyes she'd ever seen.

She stared at him, paralyzed, like a small animal hypnotized by a cobra. An unmistakable gleam of satisfaction entered those eyes as he visually absorbed her fear.

"I'm surprised you haven't packed already," he said, arching his thick beetle brows. "Surely you noticed me earlier this evening?"

"I—wasn't sure it was you." She had to clench her jaws to keep her teeth from chattering.

"Tsk-tsk. Rather careless of you to take the risk of sticking around." Then his mouth turned hard behind his bushy, salt-and-pepper beard. He used his gun to gesture toward the closet. "Your suitcase, Mrs. Jordan. Get packing."

She crabbed along the wall, keeping as far away from him as possible. Without knowing what she was packing or why, she started yanking items off hangers and throwing them into her suitcase. Her mind kept tripping over itself as it raced along, frantically trying to figure out a way to protect Kelsey.

She heard the familiar jangle of her keys. Then he lobbed her purse at her. "Don't forget to pack this," he said. "Now, get dressed."

"I'm not going to—I mean, I can't..." Elise's weak protest was as much an attempt to stall for time as a result of modesty.

"You can, and you will," he replied with a wolfish leer. "I'm not about to turn my back on you for a second."

Avoiding his eyes, she fumbled for jeans and a sweatshirt, and pulled them on over her nightgown.

"Very good." He brought his other hand over to the one holding the gun and pretended to applaud. "Now, let's go find your charming young daughter."

Oh, God, she had to stop him! She had to throw something through the window to attract attention, or find some weapon she could use against him. But she didn't have a chance because he kept the gun pointed at her every second, and she didn't doubt for a moment that he would use it. And then, what would happen to Kelsey without her?

"Speed it up, Mrs. Jordan." He nudged her in the ribs with the gun. "Remember the key word?"

Cole! she cried inside her head. *Cole, where are you?*

But she knew he wouldn't come, that he couldn't save them.

With Dominick's gun jabbed into the small of her back, her knees knocking together with terror, Elise stumbled into the hallway.

The speedometer crept up near a hundred.

Time, however, had slowed to a crawl. Though it seemed like hours, only five minutes had passed since Cole had awakened Michael Dunnigan and hastily explained his suspicions. Dunnigan had promised to call Pam immediately and listen to the 911 tape.

Cole gripped the steering wheel hard enough to turn his knuckles white, as much to keep his hands from shaking as to keep the car on the road.

Even now, Elise and Kelsey could be in Dominick's clutches. Or... worse.

His gut seized up when he thought about how terrified they would be. "Please, don't let anything happen to them," he muttered through clenched teeth. He didn't think he could stand it if it did.

Somewhere along the way, they'd both become such an important part of Cole's life, he could no longer imagine life without them.

Pain seared through him, like a giant fist had hold of his heart and was trying to rip it right out of his chest.

The phone rang. He grabbed it. Dunnigan.

"Sheriff?"

"Is it Dominick?" Cole's jaw ached from clamping his teeth together.

"I can't be sure. The recording... hearing it over the phone... all I can say is that it *could* be him."

Cole's stomach plummeted through the floorboards. Somehow, not knowing was even worse than having his terrible guess confirmed.

"Hardesty? I don't want you going off half-cocked. If this *isn't* Dominick, I don't want you raising some kind of ruckus that might get back to his spies in Boston and alert him to the fact that we're closing in on him."

Cole's fingers tightened around the phone as if he wanted to throttle it. "Elise's and Kelsey's lives could be in danger."

"Then check it out. It's your job to protect them, remember? But it's also your duty to keep this business under wraps, unless you're absolutely certain Dominick really is down there and poses an immediate threat to them. Got that?''

"Perfectly.'' Cole spat out his reply.

"Keep me posted, all right?''

Cole hung up on him.

He clutched the steering wheel with both hands. Dread poured through him in a sickening torrent when he envisioned the horrible scene that might greet him by the time he reached Elise's house. That might be waiting for him already.

The speedometer needle crept upward again.

Chapter 14

Elise had never felt so helpless, so terrified in her entire life. Victor Dominick, the man they'd been fleeing for two years, the man who intended to kill her child, was standing three feet away from Kelsey.

Ever since he'd forced her into Kelsey's bedroom ahead of him, Elise had done her best to keep her body between Dominick's gun and the sleeping form of her daughter. Obviously, he had some sinister plan up his sleeve and didn't intend to kill them quite yet.

That knowledge, however, was small comfort.

"Okay, wake her up," he ordered.

Elise had just complied with his last order, stuffing clothes from the dresser into Kelsey's suitcase. Even though her brain was numb with fear, at some level it was still functioning well enough to comprehend one important aspect of his plan. With clothes missing and their suitcases gone, anyone who came looking for them was meant to think she and Kelsey had left of their own free will.

Even Cole might very well assume that this sudden departure was just the latest in a long line of middle-of-the-night flights.

Even if he decided to look for them, it would be too late.

Dominick waved his gun impatiently. "Come on, roust the kid. It's time to get moving."

Elise had no choice. Plan or no plan, Dominick would shoot them both if she didn't cooperate.

With the jerky movements of a zombie, she stepped around Bob, who snored undisturbed on the floor beside Kelsey's bed. He certainly hadn't turned out to be the world's greatest watchdog.

In the pale glow of the night-light that was the room's only illumination, Elise observed her daughter's innocent features with a desperate throb of love so intense and overwhelming she thought her heart might explode.

As if through dark mist, she could make out Kelsey's long, silky eyelashes and adorable button nose. Although she was deep in sleep, her mouth twitched at one corner, hinting at a smile.

She was slumbering peacefully in a dream, yet now her mother was about to drag her into a real-life nightmare involving a far worse monster than anything a child's imagination could ever conjure up.

Elise felt metal prod her ribs. "We haven't got all night, Mrs. Jordan."

Forgive me, Peach, she thought. *I couldn't protect you.*

She leaned over and scooped her daughter into her arms. Kelsey's head lolled sleepily against Elise's chest. "Wha—? Mom?"

"Sh," she whispered. "It's all right, honey."

"You're going to have quite a load to carry, what with her and both suitcases," Dominick said sarcastically.

Instantly, Kelsey's eyes flew open. She flung her arms around Elise's neck in a near stranglehold. "Mom!" The word was sucked into her lungs as she drew in a startled breath.

Elise hugged her tightly. "Don't worry, Peach. I'll take care of you." *Nice job you've done so far,* an inner voice taunted.

Kelsey shook sleep-tousled hair out of her eyes and glared bravely at Dominick. "You'll be sorry," she announced. "The sheriff is our friend, and he won't let you get away with this."

Dominick chuckled, and that brief sign of confidence drove another stake of fear through Elise's heart. "I'm afraid the sheriff is busy elsewhere tonight, kid. I took care of that personally."

The plane crash. Elise had nearly forgotten the reason Cole had been called away this evening. Dominick must have fabricated a story about an accident to create a diversion.

Her last fragile, futile seedling of hope withered and died. Cole wouldn't be coming to their rescue.

"Enough chitchat." Dominick waved his gun again. "Put the kid down, and both of you grab a suitcase. You can put some clothes on her in the car." He backed toward the door, and promptly stepped on Bob's tail.

Bob let out a yelp at this rude awakening. His collar jingled as he scrambled to his feet.

"Bob, bite him!" Kelsey cried.

Dominick hastily pointed the gun at the basset hound.

"No!" Kelsey screamed, hurling herself from Elise's arms.

"Kelsey!" Elise seized her and held her back.

Bob cocked his head to one side, so that one long ear touched the floor. His drooping, somber eyes regarded the intruder with curiosity. Then he yawned.

Dominick burst out laughing. "What a useless mutt!" He angled the gun in Elise's direction. She'd pushed Kelsey behind her for safety. "Come on, enough of the comedy routine. Grab the suitcases and let's go."

Elise picked up both suitcases and edged toward the door, shielding Kelsey behind her as much as possible.

"I can carry mine, Mom."

"Never mind, Peach. I've got them." And if, despite overwhelming odds, Elise could create a chance for Kelsey to run for it, even the split second it would take her to drop a suitcase might make all the difference. "Slip on your tennis shoes, okay?" Kelsey could run a lot faster in those than in sandals.

That's good, Elise. Keep thinking ahead. You've got to be able to anticipate your chance if it comes along, because you'll only get one.

As slowly as she dared, she ushered Kelsey down the hall. Now that her brain was beginning to function again, reason cautioned her that the longer she could drag this out, the better.

"Out the back door," Dominick said tersely.

Bob's toenails clicked on the floor as he followed them through the dark kitchen, whining. Apparently, he sensed something wasn't quite as it should be.

Kelsey halted at the back door.

"Open it," Dominick commanded.

She lifted her hand uncertainly to the knob.

"Be quick about it, kid, or Lassie here gets it right between the eyes."

Kelsey whirled around, furious. "Peach!" Elise whispered frantically.

Bob started to growl.

Dominick kicked at him.

"Help!" Kelsey screamed.

With a bloodcurdling howl Elise couldn't believe had come out of the basset hound's throat, Bob lunged for Dominick's leg.

"Oww!" he shouted. "You rotten mutt . . ." He let out a stream of curses as he struggled to extract himself from Bob's jaws.

Elise dropped the suitcases and fumbled with the locks on the back door. In her panic, it took a few seconds to realize they were already unlocked.

She whipped open the door. "Run!" she whispered, practically shoving Kelsey outside.

"Hold it!" Dominick's voice froze both of them in their tracks.

Sick with disappointment, Elise turned slowly around. A glint of metal in the darkness showed her that Dominick had the gun pointed in their direction.

The sound of ripping cloth split the air as he finally tore his leg free from Bob's teeth. Still growling, Bob shook the piece of trouser fabric from side to side as if trying to teach it a lesson.

"Take *that*, you lousy mutt." Dominick launched a vicious kick at Bob's midsection.

The dog let out a yowl of pain. Kelsey shrieked. Elise had to physically restrain her daughter from flinging herself onto the floor next to the injured basset hound.

"That's enough!" Dominick roared. His voice vibrated with fury. "Outside. Now!"

Kelsey sniffled and wiped her eyes. "Mom, he hurt Bob! We can't just leave him here!"

"Bob will be okay, Peach."

"But he's just lying there. He can't get up."

"Move it, you two. Or I'll shoot all three of you right now."

"Kelsey, honey, we have to go." Forcing herself to ignore the hurt and confusion on her daughter's tear-streaked face, Elise hoisted the suitcases and gently nudged Kelsey out the door.

"Keep quiet, now. Either one of you makes a peep, I'll shoot the other one."

Kelsey choked back a sob. Bob's whimpers drifted after them, until Dominick pulled the door shut behind them. After that, they couldn't hear him anymore.

The sheriff's cruiser fishtailed in the gravel as Cole veered off the highway and onto Saguaro Road. He forced himself to slow down as he approached Elise's house. No flashing lights, no sirens, no sound of a speeding vehicle to warn Dominick of his approach. No telling what the guy might do if he panicked.

Cole switched off the engine and headlights and coasted to a stop in front of the house. Complete darkness inside. He fiddled with the overhead light before leaping out of the car, so that it wouldn't switch on and reveal his presence when he opened the door.

Keeping to the shadows, he loped up to the front door, tried the knob. Locked. Probably the back door was, too, but if he had to break in, that would be an easier place to do it.

For a brief moment, while he quickly made his way around to the backyard, it occurred to Cole that this could all be a mistake. Maybe Elise and Kelsey were safely asleep inside and would be frightened out of their wits if they heard him breaking in.

He would take that risk. Gladly.

It looked to him like he wasn't going to have to break in, though. The back door wasn't locked. And right then and there, Cole knew with sickening certainty that he hadn't made a mistake. Something was drastically wrong here.

Cautiously, he eased open the door, straining his ears for the slightest sound from inside.

All at once, a low-slung missile exploded from the kitchen.

Cole had his gun out and adrenaline surging through his veins before he realized what it was. Or *who* it was, rather.

"Bob," he whispered.

The dog was running in frantic circles, nose to the ground, bumping into Cole's legs. His tail whipped back and forth in agitation while he whimpered unhappily.

Cole ducked into the darkened kitchen. Gun raised, he sidled down the hallway, alert to the faintest noise even though he probably wouldn't have heard a marching band parade go by over the loud drumming in his ears.

He sprang into the doorway of Elise's bedroom, gun positioned to fire.

The room was empty.

Down the hall to Kelsey's room. Empty.

Quickly, he searched the rest of the house, flipping on lights as he went. No need for caution now. Only speed.

There was no sign of a struggle. Only a few hangers scattered on the floor of Elise's closet, an open dresser drawer in Kelsey's bedroom. Cole couldn't tell for sure how many of their clothes were missing, but their suitcases were gone.

He forced himself to consider the possibility that Elise had simply decided to leave town. Maybe the reason she'd been upset earlier this evening was because she'd known it was going to be their last one together.

No. Cole shook his head sharply. He couldn't believe that after everything they'd shared, after what they'd come to mean to each other, Elise would just take off.

And it wasn't just his puffed-up male ego talking here. It was conceivable Elise might have left the back door unlocked if she'd decided to walk out of this house forever, but there was absolutely no way on earth she and Kelsey would abandon Bob.

He could more easily believe the sun would rise in the west next morning, than believe Elise would have left Bob alone in the house where he could eventually starve to death.

Dominick had taken them, all right. But where?

Bob began to bark as soon as Cole stepped out the back door. He ran a few steps, stopped to look back, then barked some more.

"You know where they went, fella?" Cole felt a little ridiculous talking to the dog, but it wasn't as if he had a whole lot of other leads to follow.

If Dominick had taken them someplace nearby, maybe Bob *could* lead him there. After all, he was sort of a hound dog, wasn't he?

"Go find 'em, Bob," Cole urged. "Where'd they go? Where's Kelsey?"

Bob's long, drooping ears perked up. With one final bark, he lowered his nose to the dirt and began to snuffle in the direction of the gate.

Cole unhooked the flashlight from his belt and followed the dog around the side of the house, keeping his gun ready, sweeping the light beam from side to side in hopes of spotting some visual clue.

Bob's paws kicked up little spurts of gravel as he sniffed his way down the driveway. For the first time, Cole noticed he was limping.

When they got to the road, Bob unhesitatingly turned left. Once they reached the house next door, however, he halted in his tracks. Nose to gravel, he did some more running in circles. After making a couple of false starts in different directions, he finally just stood there, as if he couldn't make up his mind which way to go.

He looked up at Cole, licked his chops and whined.

Cole knelt down. "Trail ends here, huh?" He scanned the immediate vicinity with the flashlight. Dominick must have forced them into some kind of vehicle he'd parked here.

The flashlight beam picked up a set of tracks that had recently been laid down in the gravel. Wide, heavy tires—probably some kind of truck or van. No way to be sure, of course, that this was the vehicle Dominick had taken them in.

But they were the only recent tracks Cole could see.

He stood up and followed them a ways, expecting them to swing around in a U-turn and head back toward town. Instead, the tracks seemed to continue down Saguaro Road. Out into the desert.

What choice did he have except to follow them? This could very well turn out to be nothing but a wild-goose chase. But these tire tracks were the only lead Cole had, and time was running out. Might already have run out.

He made his decision. "Come on, Bob." He whistled for the dog to follow him back to his cruiser. "You've been a big help so far. Who knows, maybe you can help me again."

He opened the back door for the dog, but by the time he'd sprinted around to the driver's side, Bob had managed to scramble into the front passenger seat.

"Okay, pal. Let's go find them." Cole took a deep breath as he swung out into the road. It was an awfully big desert. And right now, he didn't feel like analyzing too closely how remote the chances were of finding Elise and Kelsey.

He drove a couple of miles, stopping every so often to make sure the distinctive tire marks were still out there. Each time he stopped, Bob started whimpering, as if urging Cole to hurry.

Then, off in the distance, Cole spotted a light. A faint, flickering, moving light. Rising gradually where the road climbed up into a low ridge of hills.

It had to be them. Who else would be driving around out in the middle of the desert at night? The road eventually dead-ended, out near one of the old abandoned silver mines.

Cole thought about calling for backup. To hell with Dunnigan's precious secrecy. Besides, there was no doubt in his mind anymore that this was definitely Dominick they were dealing with.

Only problem was, his potential backup was clear across the county, searching for a downed airplane that didn't exist.

He would have to do this on his own.

Well, except for Bob.

Cole narrowed his eyes at that tiny light still flickering along several miles ahead. "Hang on, pal," he warned the basset hound.

Then he floored it.

Darkness. Pain. Exhaustion. Above all, fear.

Trudging uphill across the rough desert terrain, it seemed to Elise as if the entire universe had been reduced to these four elements. Had *always* consisted of these four elements.

Her arms and shoulders ached from the weight of the suitcases she'd been carrying ever since Dominick had ordered them out of the truck and told them to start walking. He followed close behind, gun in one hand, flashlight in the other. Its wavering beam was like a tiny pinprick against the massive black shroud of night.

Elise had completely lost her sense of direction by now. All she could tell was that they were heading up. And up. And up.

She couldn't imagine where he was taking them. But she could imagine plenty of other things, all of which filled her with a raw, primitive terror that clawed at her insides like a cornered wild animal.

Her need to protect Kelsey was the only barrier that kept her from toppling over the edge of sheer panic.

"How're you doing, Peach?" she asked between searing gasps of air.

"'Kay." Kelsey was huffing and puffing under the rapid pace of their forced march. "Where . . . are we . . . going . . . Mom?"

"I don't know."

"Is he . . . gonna . . . kill us?"

The terrible, innocent simplicity of her question wrenched Elise's heart. And all at once, a new emotion filled her, so pure and sweet it nearly snatched what was left of her breath away.

Fury.

Damn that man for what he'd done to Kelsey! He'd turned her little girl into a child who could sound almost calm when she asked that question.

Is he gonna kill us?

"No, Peach," Elise promised through clenched teeth. "No, that bastard is most definitely *not* going to kill us."

Not both of them, anyway. Because Elise would see Victor Dominick in hell before she would let him harm one precious hair on Kelsey's head.

He might succeed in killing Elise. But, by God, somehow she was going to find a way to take him with her.

"Mom, you used a bad word," Kelsey whispered.

Elise choked back a sound that was half laugh, half sob.

"Here we are," Dominick announced, panting.

Elise stumbled on a rock. "Ow!" She sucked in her breath. Pain shot up from her twisted ankle. Through the ink black night she hadn't noticed even darker shadows looming up ahead of them. Now she could just barely make out the outlines of what appeared to be buildings, shapes that blotted out the sprinkling of stars behind them.

"Keep moving," Dominick said.

Elise hobbled forward, keeping herself as a barricade between him and Kelsey.

"Over there." He pointed with the flashlight beam.

Now that they were passing among the structures, Elise could see they were mostly wooden, and all of them dilapidated. Where on earth—?

Then, it came to her. This was one of the old abandoned mines that still clung to the hillsides outside Tumbleweed.

"Inside." Dominick's flashlight beam illuminated a doorless opening in the side of the closest building. Chunks of decayed wood dangled from above it like rotted teeth. The opening looked like a giant, gaping maw, eager to swallow them up.

Elise hesitated until she felt the persuasive pressure of the gun against her ribs.

"I said, *inside.*"

She drew a deep, quivering breath into her lungs. This was it. However she was going to stop Dominick, it would have to be soon.

"Careful, Peach." Stepping through the opening, she pointed out a sharp, dangerous-looking hunk of rusted debris. Bits of broken glass and shards of metal littered the floor, glittering like deadly diamonds in the flashlight beam.

Elise scanned the darkness as quickly and carefully as she could, searching for something she could use as a weapon.

"Keep moving," Dominick growled.

She edged forward cautiously, keeping Kelsey right beside her.

"Stop."

They were next to some kind of metal framework that rose from the floor up toward what remained of the building's roof.

"First, we get rid of the suitcases."

Elise gasped as one suitcase was torn from her hand and tossed through the framework. For a few seconds, she heard only silence. Then, from somewhere far away—from down *below?*—she heard a series of muffled crashes.

Her brain grappled with this, trying to make sense of it, while at the same time busily struggling for a way to thwart Dominick's murderous intentions.

Then he angled the light so Elise could see the hole they were standing in front of. No, not a hole. More of a vertical tunnel. Like a crude elevator shaft.

Like a *mine* shaft.

All at once, Dominick's plan became horribly, brutally clear. He intended to kill them *and* dispose of their bodies at the same time. By shoving them down the mine shaft.

"You don't have to do this," Elise said in a low voice, before she even realized she was speaking. "We'll go far, far away. We'll never tell anyone anything. Kelsey will never testify against you, I swear it." Her mouth was parched with fear. "We'll leave the country. We'll disappear forever."

Dominick snorted with amusement. "Oh, you're going to disappear forever, all right. In fact, that's *exactly* what I have in mind."

Kelsey clutched Elise. Her entire body trembled like a reed in a windstorm.

"Anyone comes looking for you, they're gonna figure you just took off again. Even your boyfriend the sheriff won't know what happened to you." Behind his beard, Dominick's mouth curled into an evil sneer. "Now, dump the other suitcase down the shaft." He gestured impatiently with his gun. "Come on, hurry it up."

As if in a dream, Elise stared down into that bottomless hole in the ground. She got a good, strong grip on the suitcase, drawing it back as if preparing to toss it down the shaft.

Then, she swung it as hard as she could at Victor Dominick.

In rapid succession, too fast to sort out in her head, she felt a solid *thunk!* heard his roar of anger and saw the gun go flying out of his hand.

She could tell by its beam that the flashlight, too, had landed on the ground.

She shoved Kelsey in the direction of the doorway as hard as she dared. "Run!" she cried. "Run away as fast as you can, and don't stop no matter what!"

"Mom!" Kelsey sobbed.

"*Run*, Peach! *Go!*"

Then she hurled herself at Dominick.

All the fear and fury that had built up inside Elise seemed to explode. She kicked him, punched him, clawed at his face. He was bigger and stronger than she was, and in the end would undoubtedly win, but at least she could give Kelsey a chance to get away. Dominick would have a hard time finding her in the dark.

The gun, she thought suddenly. *If only I could get to the gun before he does ...*

But how could she hope to locate it while locked in this eerie, disorienting, life-or-death struggle? Though the building was nearly devoid of light, it was filled with sounds.

Harsh, rasping breaths, groans of pain and exertion, various thumps and crashes as old mining equipment got knocked aside by their deadly dance.

Elise had only the vaguest idea which direction the gun had flown in. For all she knew, it might have tumbled down the shaft. The same fate, it was becoming obvious, that Dominick still intended for *her*.

Step by step, he was forcing her closer and closer to the mouth of the shaft. Despite the anger and adrenaline pumping through her veins, Elise felt her strength ebbing. Yet every second she could prolong the one-way journey toward her own death would give Kelsey that much extra time to escape.

With a lung-searing gasp, she stole a desperate glance over her shoulder to see how close she was to the gaping hole.

Then she saw the gun.

It lay a short distance off to her left, partially beneath the wreckage of an old table, at just the right angle to reflect a muted glint of light into Elise's field of vision.

She acted on instinct. For no more than half a second, she stopped resisting and let her body go limp, throwing Dominick off balance. He grunted in surprise, briefly loosening his grip on her.

Elise mustered every exhausted remnant of her strength and lunged for the gun.

She didn't quite make it. She sprawled on the ground, oblivious to the miscellaneous debris poking into her body, scrabbling frantically with her outstretched fingertips to capture the gun.

Dominick had landed on top of her, and now he, too, spotted the gun.

In seconds, it was all over. By the time Elise had scrambled to her feet, battered and bruised and gasping for air, Dominick had the gun aimed at her.

His face was filthy. Sweat poured down his forehead, he had a gash over one eye, and he was breathing at least as hard as Elise was.

He also wore a triumphant smile that sent a chill down her spine.

Then the smile faded and his eyes gleamed with that cruel, ruthless intensity she recognized all too well.

"That was a useless move on your part, Mrs. Jordan." He inhaled noisily. "Understandable, maybe, but useless." His gaze slithered toward the doorway. "How long do you think it'll take me to catch up with the kid? Two, maybe three minutes?"

He wiped his dripping brow, grimacing when he noticed the dark stain on his sleeve. "I thought it would be touching if the two of you died together, but it doesn't much matter that I'll have to kill you separately now."

Elise inched up her chin. Her only goal now was to keep him talking, to buy Kelsey every precious second she could. And she sensed that if she showed any weakness, or started begging for her life, Dominick would quickly tire of her.

"You won't get away with this," she said, straining to keep her voice from quavering. "The sheriff won't be fooled into thinking we've gone on the run again. I told him all about you—what happened back in Boston, and why you want to kill us."

"Yes, I know," he replied. "But it doesn't matter. He'll never be able to prove anything. Especially not without any bodies." He leveled the gun at her. "Goodbye, Mrs. Jordan."

Instantly, Elise filled her mind with the cherished images of Kelsey and Cole.

The gun fired.

Every single muscle in her body snapped taut in protest of this final, stunning invasion.

Some tiny, still-functioning fragment of her brain registered surprise that there was no pain. After a second or two, she opened her eyes.

Dominick, too, wore a mask of surprise. His fingers uncurled from the gun, which dropped to the floor in what seemed like slow motion. Then Dominick himself slowly folded in half, swayed and toppled to the ground.

Elise barely had time to wonder at this before she caught a glimpse of motion from the corner of her eye.

Hastily, she dove for the fallen flashlight and aimed it toward the doorway.

Cole stood there. Holstering his gun.

Elise froze, convinced she must be dreaming, that this last-minute rescue was some elaborate trick her dying brain was playing on her.

"Elise," the trick called to her in a low voice that didn't begin to conceal his fear and relief.

With a glad cry, she stumbled forward into his arms.

She clutched the front of his shirt as if it were a lifeline. "I thought you were...that you couldn't...that he was going to..."

"Sh," he whispered between the rough kisses he was stamping on her cheeks, her mouth, her forehead. "It's okay now. Everything's all right."

He stroked her tangled hair over and over again. It was a toss-up which of their hearts was pounding the hardest, but no contest at all when it came to how wonderful Cole's embrace felt. Nothing had ever felt this good to Elise in her whole life.

Except the first time she'd held her baby daughter in her arms.

She jerked back her head, shoving matted, tear-dampened hair from her eyes. "Kelsey," she exclaimed. "Oh, Cole, we've got to find her! She's out there in the desert all alone—''

"Mom?" A wobbly beam of light canted through the doorway. Kelsey followed, carrying a large, cumbersome flashlight with both hands. She nearly tripped over the exuberant basset hound running circles around her. "Cole and Bob found me, and Cole gave me his flashlight and told me to keep Bob quiet and not to come in here until he called me, but then I heard your voice and—and—''

Her enormous, bewildered eyes filled with tears. "Oh, Mom," she squeaked as her face crumpled. "I thought he was going to kill us.''

"Peach..." Elise flung herself forward and grabbed Kelsey in her arms. Silently, she rocked her daughter back and forth, powerless to speak past the lump in her throat, even if she'd been able to find the words to tell Kelsey how much she loved her.

After a few moments, she glanced up at Cole with a trembling, tearful smile, held out her hand and drew him into their embrace.

Chapter 15

"I wish I could stay here with you, Mom."

"I know, Peach." Elise smoothed Kelsey's hair back from her forehead. "But a hospital's no fun to hang around in." She made a face. "Besides, the food's terrible."

Kelsey giggled. And that welcome sound told Elise that her daughter was going to bounce back just fine from the traumatic, violent events of last night.

"You go home with Mrs. Applegate now, and then this afternoon when Roz gets off work, she'll pick you up so you can spend the night at her house."

"Can we come back and visit you?" Kelsey plucked at the plastic ID bracelet they'd snapped around Elise's wrist when she'd been admitted to the emergency room a couple of hours before dawn.

"Of course you can." Elise clasped her hand. "But they're only keeping me in here one night for observation. I'll be home tomorrow morning."

Doris Applegate had been hovering discreetly by the door. Now she approached the hospital bed where, against Elise's protest, Cole and the doctor had insisted she spend the next twenty-four hours.

"Kelsey, dear, I've got all the ingredients for an absolutely scrumptious chocolate cake at home. Would you like to help me bake it?"

Kelsey peered up at her. "Chocolate?"

"It's sort of my specialty, you see. It's quite yummy, if I do say so myself. And, of course, Chester has been looking forward to a visit from you."

"He has?"

"Today's the day I was planning to brush that beautiful long coat of his. But usually he won't sit still for very long. I'll bet he wouldn't squirm nearly so much if you were holding him while I brushed him."

Kelsey nibbled her finger. "Can I try brushing him, too?"

"Of course, dear!" Mrs. Applegate beamed at her, then reached down to pat Elise's hand. "You get some rest now, and don't worry your pretty head for one second. I'll take very good care of Kelsey, I promise."

"I know you will." Elise had to blink back tears of gratitude. Before she'd come to Tumbleweed, it had been a long time since she'd had friends she could count on, friends she could turn to for help. She'd forgotten what a comfort such caring, kind people could be.

Kelsey threw her arms around Elise's neck. Elise's sore shoulder throbbed, but she bit her lip and hugged Kelsey back as hard as her stiff, aching muscles would allow. "You have fun with Mrs. Applegate and Roz today, and I'll see you later," she whispered, afraid her voice would crack if she spoke any louder.

Kelsey unwound her arms. "I love you, Mom," she said solemnly.

"I love you, too." This time, Elise's voice did crack.

Dabbing at her eyes, Mrs. Applegate took Kelsey by the hand. "Come along, dear. I think what your mother needs most right now is a nice long nap."

"Bye, Mom."

"Bye, Peach." Elise waved back as Kelsey carefully shut the door behind them. Her various bumps and bruises caused her far less distress than letting Kelsey out of her sight for even a minute. But how could Kelsey regain any sense of security and self-confidence with her mother clinging to her frantically?

Elise's stomach did an anxious little flip-flop as she settled back against the pillows. It suddenly dawned on her that she was alone for the first time since she'd awakened in her own bed last night to find Victor Dominick's sweaty hand clamped over her face. Now, without the presence of Kelsey or Cole or any of the hospital staff to distract her, the events of the last ten hours were finally free to tumble through her memory in a cascade of terror.

Her teeth began to chatter in delayed reaction. She tugged the blanket over her trembling limbs, all the way up to her neck. Logic told her the hospital must keep the thermostat set at a comfortable level for patients, but all at once Elise was cold . . . so cold. . . .

She couldn't believe Dominick was dead. That he would never threaten them again. That she and Kelsey could actually go back to living normal lives from now on.

No more running. No more lies. No more flinching in fear whenever there was an unexpected knock at the door.

Tap, tap.

The faint sound at the hospital-room door made Elise jump. She grinned sheepishly at herself. Okay, maybe it would take a little more time before her reactions returned to normal.

"Come in," she called.

An enormous bouquet of daffodils and tulips entered her room, followed by Cole.

Elise's heart went wild at the sight of him. And suddenly, she wasn't the least bit cold anymore.

"Hi," he said, balancing the flowers awkwardly, as if he wasn't quite sure what to do with them.

"Hi," she replied softly. A pleasant, tingling pressure had begun to build behind her breastbone, making it difficult to breathe. This wasn't another physical aftereffect of her encounter with Dominick, however.

This was love.

Then again, maybe it *could* be considered one of last night's aftereffects. Because it wasn't until what Elise had thought was going to be the final moment of her life that she'd comprehended how much she loved Cole.

Now, at last, they had a chance together.

"These are for you," he said, holding out the flowers. Immediately, he winced. "Dumb thing to say, huh? Who else would they be for?"

"They're beautiful."

"So are you." He pushed aside the odds and ends littering the bedside table and set down the vase. "You're looking much better than the last time I saw you." He grazed his knuckle tenderly across her cheek and smiled down at her. "The color's come back into your face."

"I look like Frankenstein's monster," she scoffed, pointing at the bandaged stitches in her scalp. "Or maybe a mummy would be more accurate. You should see all the tape they wrapped around my sprained ankle."

"I checked with the doc just now, and he says you're going to be fine. That's all that matters." Cole leaned over and kissed Elise gently on the mouth, as if afraid he might hurt her. He tasted like coffee and jelly doughnut. Strawberry, she thought.

Happiness spread through her like sweet, warm syrup. Cole might have gone home and changed into a crisp, clean uniform, but his expression was still a bit rumpled. "You look tired," she murmured, enjoying the luxury of worrying about *him* for a change. "Have you gotten any sleep?"

Cole had used his cellular phone to summon help to the abandoned mine, and then insisted that both Elise and Kelsey go straight to the hospital emergency room. He had accompanied them there in the ambulance, and hadn't left their sides until Kelsey had been pronounced fit as a fiddle and Elise's superficial injuries had been patched up.

He'd even insisted on keeping Bob at his place while Elise was in the hospital.

Cole pulled up a chair next to the bed, shaking his head in response to her question. "No time for sleep. I've been on the phone to Boston all morning."

Elise rubbed the concern gathering at her temples. "I hope this won't get you in any kind of trouble. Not turning us in to the Boston authorities, I mean."

Discomfort shadowed his features. "No. I mean, I'm not in any trouble, and neither are you. It's all been squared with the Boston D.A.'s office."

She blew a relieved stream of air through her bangs. "I can't believe it's all over."

Cole took her hand. "Elise, there's something I've got to tell you."

He loves me, she thought happily. *The close call last night made him realize it, and now he wants to confess his feelings.*

He turned over her hand and studied her palm. "I—I haven't been honest with you."

Hmm. Not exactly the way *she* would have gone about professing undying love, but still...

"I tried to tell you before we made love the other night, but I... didn't want to spoil things between us."

Dread stirred in the pit of Elise's stomach. Whatever he was about to say, apparently she wasn't going to like it. Maybe he was still in love with Laura's memory.

"The reason why I'm not in any hot water with the Boston authorities is because—" his shoulders heaved in a sigh, then he squeezed her hand and looked her straight in the eye "—is because I *did* contact them earlier. After I found out who you really were, and why you were in hiding."

Elise blinked. "What?" He seemed to be speaking a foreign language. Surely he couldn't possibly mean what it sounded like he was saying.

His mouth tightened into a grim seam. "I called Boston the day you came to my office and asked me not to turn you in."

"You—you did it, anyway?" Her mind simply couldn't bend itself around this concept.

"After you left. I called a friend of mine on the Boston police force, and he put me in touch with the district attorney. Michael Dunnigan."

"Dear God." Elise's skin turned to ice. Hearing that dreaded name from the past finally jolted her into grasping the truth.

Cole had betrayed her.

"Dunnigan asked me not to tell you I'd spoken with him. He asked me to... watch out for you and Kelsey. He was afraid of potential leaks within his office or the police department, and he worried that Dominick might be able to track you down before they were ready to have Kelsey testify."

Cole's expression grew increasingly unhappy while he spoke. But it was nothing compared to the way Elise felt hearing it.

She withdrew her hand from his. "So, you agreed to spy on us."

"I agreed to *protect* you." But there was no mistaking the guilt that lurked in his eyes.

She knotted both hands into fists. "We wouldn't have *needed* protection in the first place, if you hadn't reported us to the Boston cops."

Cole stiffened his spine. "Elise, I'm a law-enforcement officer. It was my job."

"You and your precious job!" Her nails dug angry crescents into her palms. "Can't you forget about your job for two seconds and act like a human being instead of a robot?"

He flinched as if she'd taken a swing at him. "Maybe if I'd done my job properly four years ago," he said in a low voice, "Laura and the baby wouldn't have died."

"That's ridiculous!" Elise cried. "You can't be everywhere at once, protecting people twenty-four hours a day."

"I can do my level best and not shirk my responsibilities."

Pain and outrage welled up inside Elise in equal amounts, along with a healthy portion of humiliation. She'd believed in Cole, trusted him, fallen in love with him. But all she was to him was part of his job.

"You didn't exactly do such a good job of protecting Kelsey and me," she pointed out bitterly. "Dominick never would have found us if you hadn't been so concerned about doing your duty." A little voice inside warned her to stop, but she ignored it. "Thanks to a tip-off from one of the crooked cops on Dominick's payroll, Kelsey and I were nearly killed."

The expression on Cole's face when she hurled the accusation at him almost made Elise wish she could take it back.

Almost, but not quite. She was too hurt. And she wasn't telling Cole anything he hadn't already figured out for himself.

"Elise, believe me," he said quietly. "The last thing I wanted to do was put you and Kelsey in danger."

"But that's exactly what you did, isn't it?" She fed the flames of her own anger because it was easier to deal with the anger than with the agony of a broken heart. "And why should I believe you, anyway? I believed you before, and you betrayed my trust."

Cole jammed his fingers through his hair. "Elise, I never told you I wouldn't contact Boston. I never made any promises."

"No, you just let me go on believing you hadn't. You let me keep deluding myself that the reason you were spending so much time with Kelsey and me was because you *liked* us, and now I find out it was only because you were *spying* on us."

Cole sprang to his feet. "That's absolutely not true!" He paced beside her bed in agitation. "Elise, I *do* like you and Kelsey! It goes way beyond that, in fact, but—"

"Tell me this, Cole." Elise's eyes burned with unshed tears. Now they were getting down to the heart of the matter. "Is that the reason you made love to me, too? Because you were under orders from the Boston D.A. to stay as close to me as possible?"

"No!" He stared at her with what Elise would have sworn was shocked dismay. Except now she realized what a skilled actor Cole was. He moved abruptly toward her, as if he intended to shake some sense into her. Then, apparently recalling her injuries, he backed off.

"Elise, honey, what you and I have between us, what we shared the other night, that has nothing to do with my job or with Dominick or with any orders from the Boston D.A." He spread his hands in a pleading, almost desperate gesture. "Elise, I—I care about both you and Kelsey." He swallowed. "A lot."

How she wanted to accept his words at face value! Her heart practically ached to believe him. But she had believed in him once before, and her trust had nearly gotten Kelsey and herself killed.

She turned her head on the pillow, away from Cole. She couldn't bear to look at him anymore. How could you love someone when you couldn't trust him?

"I think you'd better go," she said, her voice clogged with misery.

"Elise—"

"Please, Cole. Just leave."

She heard his breathing for a minute, and then the muted tread of his shoes moving toward the door. A sob lodged painfully in her throat.

"Before I go, I want to say two things." His voice drifted across the room. "First, I know it was my fault that Dominick found you and that you and Kelsey were nearly killed. I underestimated the danger, and I let him trick me into leaving you unprotected with that phony call he made about the plane crash."

Elise squeezed her eyes shut, wishing she could shut off her hearing as well as her sight.

"I accept full responsibility for the events of last night, and I hope someday you'll forgive me." His voice dropped in volume. "Though I doubt I'll ever be able to forgive myself."

Elise couldn't have replied even if she'd wanted to. The pressure in her chest was too suffocating.

"The second thing I want to say is that I never faked any of my feelings for you, Elise. Or for Kelsey, either. Having the two of you in my life has come to mean a great deal to me." He cleared his throat. "Making love with you was the best thing that's happened to me in a long, long time."

Tears leaked onto the pillow from beneath Elise's eyelids.

After a few beats of silence, she heard him whisper, "Goodbye."

Busy hospital sounds filtered into the room from the corridor, and then the gently closing door cut them off again.

Elise hauled a jagged, splintery breath into her lungs. For a few moments she struggled to shore up her emotional barricade of indignation and anger, but the gaping cavern of loss that had opened up inside her when Cole walked out of the room quickly overwhelmed her defenses.

With a sob of anguish, she rolled onto her back and flung an arm over her swollen eyes. Breathtaking pain crashed through her, making the damage inflicted by Victor Dominick feel like mere pinpricks in comparison.

"Yoo-hoo! Anyone home? Darn, this door is locked."

The muffled voice and brisk rapping at her front door roused Elise from her melancholy thoughts. She was lying on the couch in the living room, sprained ankle propped on a pillow, and had been staring out the window for who knew how long, brooding about Cole.

"Peach, could you let Roz in?" she called. It felt funny to say that, after all the warnings she'd given Kelsey about not answering the door. And she still hadn't gotten used to leaving the door unlocked, even during the day.

Kelsey raced down the hall from her room, with the devoted Bob close behind. "Hi, Roz!" Elise heard her exclaim.

"Hi, yourself, cupcake. Stay down, you goofy-lookin' mutt! This is for Elise and Kelsey, not you."

"Bob's not goofy-looking!" Kelsey protested. "Besides, he saved our lives, didn't you, Bob?" There was a brief burst of sloppy kissing noises, punctuated by the *whap-whap!* of the dog's tail against the floor of the entryway. "Cole said he never could've followed our trail in the dark if Bob hadn't sniffed our tracks."

"Well, mercy me, I take it all back. I had no idea I was insulting a hero when I called you goofy-lookin', you sweet thing." Roz let out a squawk. "No, don't lick my face! You'll ruin my makeup."

Moments later she bustled into the living room, bearing a large covered dish. "Why, la-di-da, look at you lounging there! All you need is a frilly pink negligee and a box of bonbons to complete the picture. Here." She set the dish on the coffee table with a thud. "Just what the doctor ordered."

Elise sniffed cautiously. "Is that Tiny's six-alarm chili I smell?"

"*Seven*-alarm. He made it extra hot, specially for you."

Elise smiled wanly. "Gee, he shouldn't have."

"I tried to tell him." Roz flounced into the nearest chair. "Well, you can probably feed most of it to Cole."

Elise's smile grew even wobblier around the edges, then just up and quit altogether.

Roz slapped her palm on the arm of her chair. "What *is* it with you two? Ever since Kelsey and I came to visit you in the hospital yesterday, whenever Cole's name comes up, you get this funny look on your face like you just swallowed something nasty."

Elise leaned forward, checking that Kelsey wasn't hovering in the doorway.

Roz made a disgusted *tsk*. "Don't worry, she and the dog are in the backyard. I wouldn't dream of pumping you for details about your love life if either one of them could overhear."

Elise settled back with a sigh. "I don't *have* a love life."

Roz uttered a two-syllable reply to express her skepticism about Elise's statement. "Nobody looks as down-in-the-dumps as you do unless their love life is involved. So, out with it. Come on." She scooted forward to the edge of her seat. "Tell Auntie Roz everything."

Elise smiled in spite of herself. "It's really not that interesting, I promise."

"Oh, no?" Roz gave a disbelieving flap of her hand. "Just like the story of your secret identity and hidden past, I guess." She yawned theatrically behind her outstretched fingers. "Dullsville."

Elise plucked at a loose thread on the sofa cushion. "Roz, I—I'm sorry I had to keep all that a secret. You've been a good friend since we moved here, and, well, I feel bad that I couldn't tell you the truth."

"Forget it." She dismissed Elise's apology with a wave. "You did what you had to, to protect Kelsey from that slimeball Dominick."

"I guess the whole town knows all about it by now, huh?"

Roz grinned. "Let's just say you've overthrown the weather as the main topic of conversation for those old codgers who sit all day on the bench outside the post office."

Elise buried her face in her hands and groaned. "Just what I wanted. To be the center of attention."

"Get used to it. This town hasn't seen so much excitement since a tractor-trailer rig jackknifed on the highway ten years back, and the meanest bull in southern Arizona escaped and went on a three-hour rampage before they caught him.

"Now." She wagged a scarlet-painted fingernail at Elise. "You've managed to steer me clear off the subject, which was the trouble between you and the sheriff. I saw him drive past this morning, and his chin was sagging halfway down his chest. So, what gives?"

A painful vise clamped itself around Elise's heart and squeezed. It was a feeling she was starting to get used to, but that didn't ease the hurt any. "I—I thought I could trust Cole, but I was wrong. He turned us in to the Boston authorities, and then agreed to spy on us."

Roz let out a low, shocked whistle. "That doesn't sound like our sheriff."

"He said he had no choice, that it was his duty."

"*That* sounds like our sheriff."

Elise nodded. Her fingers dug into the cushion. "That's why he paid so much attention to Kelsey and me. Why he pretended he...cared about us. Just so it would be easier to keep an eye on us."

"Whoa, there!" Roz held up her hand like a traffic cop. "*That's* the part I don't buy. The sheriff may be a stickler for playing by the rules, but the last thing he is, is dishonest. He wouldn't lie about his feelings, or manipulate you by faking something he didn't feel."

"Maybe not. But how can I ever trust him again?" Elise burst out. "He deceived me by letting me believe something that wasn't true. Not to mention the fact that he almost got Kelsey and me killed."

"Elise, that man cares for both of you. Do you think he would deliberately do something to put either one of you in danger? He thought he was helping to *protect* you, for Pete's sake!"

"All he cares about is doing his job."

"Of course he cares about his job! That's what makes him such a good sheriff. Could you respect a man who *didn't* care about his job?" Roz frowned. "And stop strangling that poor pillow. Your fingers are about to poke right through the fabric."

Elise unclenched her hands. "I just can't forget that he tricked me. That I trusted him, and he violated my trust."

"Don't you think the poor guy feels bad enough about doing what he had to do? I doubt you can punish him any more than he's already punishing himself."

Elise's lips trembled. "I'm not trying to punish him."

"No?" Roz arched one plucked eyebrow and gave her a shrewd glance. "That's what it looks like to me. Cole hurt you, and he made you mad, and by golly, you're going to make him pay by throwing away your chance to be happy together."

Elise's chin seemed permanently stuck at a stubborn angle. "I can't trust him."

"For heaven's sake, can't you find it in your heart to give the man a second chance?"

That was just the trouble, Elise thought unhappily. When she peered into her heart right now, all she found was a confused jumble of anger and hurt and regret.

She'd hoped that her days of running were over. But now she was afraid that, once she sorted out the chaos in her heart, her only choice might be to leave Tumbleweed.

To leave Cole.

Because, what if it simply became too painful to keep on living in the same small town with the man who'd betrayed her and broken her heart?

Chapter 16

Cole couldn't help recalling the very first time he walked up the broad flagstone steps and knocked on Elise's door. His whole life had changed since Elise and Kelsey became part of it.

Just a few short months ago, he'd filled nearly every moment of his waking hours with work. He'd had nothing to look forward to, and no one to share it with. He was just going through the motions.

Then, for a little while, he'd started to pretend he was part of a family.

Unfortunately, that pleasant fantasy had ended. This morning would probably be the last time he ever came up these steps.

He tapped the brass knocker lightly, half hoping Elise wasn't home, so he wouldn't have to face her. Of course, her car was parked beside the house, so it was pretty unlikely his wish would be granted.

He felt like a grade-A skunk, and that was the truth. Not only had he gone behind her back and spied on her, but his deception had nearly cost her and Kelsey their lives.

The irony was, if Cole was dealt the same hand all over again, he would still have no choice but to play his cards the same way.

The door opened without its usual preamble of unlocking snaps and clicks. But Elise kept her hand on the knob when she answered, as if she wanted to be set to slam the door in his face on a moment's notice.

It was a warm morning, and Elise was wearing shorts and a scoop-necked cotton blouse, with her blond hair tied back in a ponytail. Her face was pale, making the hollows under her eyes stand out like bruises.

She didn't seem all that surprised to see him. Probably peeked through the curtains and saw his cruiser in the driveway.

Not unexpectedly, she didn't seem all that *happy* to see him, either.

"Elise." Cole tried on a smile, but it collapsed. "How are you feeling? Your injuries, I mean. How's your ankle?"

She glanced down at her bare foot, which was still bound up with a cloth bandage. "Better, thanks. I can hobble around the house pretty easily now." Her polite answer sounded strained. "The doctor says I can go back to work next week."

"Look, uh..." Cole tapped the manila envelope he'd brought against his palm. "If you need money or anything...I mean, what with having to miss work and all, I'd be more than happy to help out."

She slanted him a shuttered, indecipherable glance. "Thanks, but that isn't necessary."

"We could just make it a loan if you'd feel better about it. Just to tide you over for a while."

To his surprise, the edges of her mouth lifted a little, forming what appeared to be the ghost of a genuine smile. "Now that I'm no longer in hiding, I can liquidate some of my investments," she said. "Money isn't a problem."

"Oh." The way she said it made Cole suspect that might be kind of an understatement. Maybe the joke was on him. Maybe a sheriff's salary seemed like chump change to her. "But you *did* say you were going back to work at the café, didn't you?"

"For the time being." She fiddled with the door latch. "Just until I figure out what I'm going to do." That ghostly smile made a return appearance. "I'm really going to miss working there when I leave. Roz, Tiny, the customers..."

A disturbing possibility poked Cole in the chest like a belligerent drunk. "You're not considering moving away from Tumbleweed, are you?"

Elise's green eyes were cool as polished jade. "I'm considering *all* my options," she replied.

Something akin to despair stirred in Cole's belly. Even though he knew he'd lost Elise, the idea that he would never even get to bump into her occasionally on the street somehow made matters worse.

But he had no right to ask her to stay.

"I brought by the statement you dictated to Zack in the hospital," he said. "About the events of the other night." He slid a report from the manila envelope. "I need you to sign it."

Did he just imagine it, or did a glimmer of disappointment skip across Elise's face when he made it clear he hadn't come for personal reasons?

At any rate, he definitely wasn't imagining the reluctance with which she said, "Guess you'd better come inside."

Cole followed her into the living room. There was the couch where'd they'd sat together so many evenings, sharing coffee and conversation after Kelsey was tucked in bed.

And down that hallway was the bedroom where he and Elise had made love. Where Cole had rediscovered what it felt like to be happy. To be whole again.

Suddenly, the weight of all he had lost felt as heavy and oppressive and unyielding as a ten-foot boulder. He tried his best to push it aside by switching the direction of his thoughts.

"Kelsey in school?" he asked.

Elise glanced up from the pages she was scanning. "Uh-huh. Yesterday was her first day back."

"The other day, when I brought the dog home, she seemed like her usual self. Not like she was traumatized or anything." Cole rubbed the base of his neck. "I'm sure sorry I had to kill someone practically right in front of her."

Elise's lips twisted into a wry curve. "It was a lot less traumatic than the alternative, believe me."

"Yeah." He waited while she finished reading the typed statement. "You know, maybe I never told you this in so many words before. But I think Kelsey's really special. She's a great kid."

Elise's pen hesitated over the bottom of the report. "Thank you," she said softly. Her hand shook a little while she signed her name.

"And it's largely because of you," Cole told her. "Because of the way you've raised her, and taken care of her."

Elise's chin trembled. She had a little trouble sliding the report back into its envelope. "Thank you. That—that's a nice thing for you to say, Cole."

"It's true." He put his hand on the envelope, but didn't take it from her yet. "Maybe this sounds dumb. But a lot of times, when I look at Kelsey, I think about the child Laura and I were going to have."

Elise made a tiny startled sound in the back of her throat.

"I never knew if it was going to be a boy or a girl, but sometimes I imagine it would have been a girl, and that she would have grown up to be a terrific kid like Kelsey."

Tears shimmered in Elise's eyes. "Oh, Cole." She covered her mouth with her fingertips.

"Sometimes, and this is going to sound *really* stupid, I know—" Jiminy Christmas, what the hell was the matter with him? Why was he saying all this stuff he hadn't even realized was true until this very second?

"Sometimes," he went on, "I've even imagined what it would be like if Kelsey *were* my daughter. Yours and mine together, I mean."

Elise didn't say a word, but the astonishment in her eyes told him how surprised she was to hear him say that. A tear trickled down her pale cheek.

Cole took the envelope from her and studied it as if all the secrets of the universe were written on it. "I know you don't believe me, but I have come to care a lot about both you and Kelsey. I don't think I quite realized exactly how much you've both come to mean to me until the other night—" he repressed a shudder "—when I was afraid I was going to be too late. I was afraid that Dominick would kill you before I found you."

"But you found us," she whispered.

"Yeah." He dragged a hand through his hair and forced himself to meet her gaze. There were some things that had to be said eye to eye. "I know you can't forgive me for turning you in to the authorities in Boston. You've said more than once that you think I'm obsessed with my job, that duty is all I care about."

"Cole, please." She shook her head. "It doesn't matter anymore."

"Thing is, maybe you were right. See, after Laura died, I felt so damn guilty." He raised a hand to ward off Elise's protests. "I believed if I'd done my job better, that punk wouldn't have been out on the streets lying in wait for her. It was my job to protect people, and I hadn't even been able to protect someone I loved."

He tossed the envelope onto the coffee table so he could take both Elise's hands in his. "You were the one who helped me see that Laura's death wasn't all my fault. But until I came to realize that, the only way I could handle the guilt was by making sure I did my job *right* from then on. Always play it straight by the book. Never cut corners. Above all, do my duty, no matter how tough it was."

Even though it was a warm day, Elise's hands were freezing.

"That's why I called Boston. That's why I agreed to keep an eye on you for Dunnigan. But there was something else, too. Something in the back of my mind that bothered me about your determination to keep Kelsey from testifying."

Elise's chin shifted a little, just enough to warn Cole he was treading on dangerous ground here.

"It's related to Laura's death, too. To the way she died." Anger awoke inside him. It would probably always be there, but at least now Cole had learned how to keep it in perspective. "No one wanted to get involved when they heard her screams. Even while she lay there dying, it took twenty minutes before anyone bothered to pick up the phone and call for help."

Compassion softened Elise's features.

"That's why it kind of stuck in my craw a little, that you would go to such lengths to keep Kelsey from testifying. I thought it was her duty. That you both had a responsibility to do whatever it took to get a murderer off the streets."

A flush of indignation stained Elise's cheeks. "How can you—"

"Hear me out. Please." Cole gripped her hands tightly. "Then, the other night, when I knew Dominick had you, but I didn't know where—" He expelled a gust of air. "I was terrified. I'd never before felt so helpless, so desperate."

Sympathy pleated her brow as her mouth crimped in understanding.

"When I got to the mine and found Kelsey, I was so relieved—for about half a second. Then she told me Dominick still had you inside the building, and—" Cole swallowed. A sheen of sweat broke out on his forehead. "I ran to the doorway and looked inside." Even now, the memory made his stomach churn. "In my whole life, I'd never known the kind of gut-wrenching fear I felt when I saw him pointing the gun at you, Elise."

"Cole," she said in a choked voice. Her eyes were wet with tears again.

"And at that moment, I understood why a person would do absolutely anything to protect the life of someone he loves."

The word *love* hovered in the air between them, like a puff of breath on a chilly day. But there were too many other words cluttering up the atmosphere. Words like *regret. Lies. Betrayal.*

"Afterward," Cole went on, "it seemed perfectly logical to me. Why you refused to let Kelsey testify. Why you'd gone into hiding, and why you weren't about to let me or anyone else drag her back to Boston."

"I couldn't," she whispered.

"No. I see that now." Reluctantly, Cole released her hands. He still treasured any physical connection between them, but the emotional one meant even more. That was lost now.

"As sheriff, I still believe I did the right thing by contacting the authorities. But if I were a father or husband who found himself in your position—" His mouth hitched into a sad, crooked smile. "Well, I'd've done exactly what you did."

He picked up the envelope from the table. "Even now, I can't say that the choice I made was wrong, Elise. But maybe one of us doesn't *have* to be wrong. Maybe we *both* did the right thing."

Elise wiped her eyes with the back of her wrist. Cole felt her gaze following him as he walked from the room. Beneath the arch leading to the entryway, he paused and turned around. "I guess it's too late to say this now..."

Probably he shouldn't say it at all. But after all the lies he'd handed her, didn't he owe her at least this last portion of honesty?

"Truth is, I...I wish things could have worked out differently between us, Elisc." His shoulders heaved. That massive boulder containing the weight of all he'd lost was nuzzling up next to him again, threatening to roll right over him. "I wish things could have worked out, period."

Elise wrapped her arms around her waist, as if she were hugging herself from cold. Her reply barely carried across the room. "Me, too."

"Tell...tell Kelsey goodbye for me, would you?" The boulder was parked squarely on Cole's chest now. "I—guess maybe it would be better if I don't see her again."

Elise's lips pressed tightly together, so that her chin crumpled. "I'll explain things to her." Her voice wavered.

"Tell her I love—" Cole bit off the end of his sentence. "Tell her I think she's the greatest kid in the world, all right?"

Elise nodded. Her eyes glistened.

No sense putting this off any longer. He was just pro-longing the agony.

For both of them.

Cole took what might be his very last look at the woman who'd brought kindness and decency, joy and laughter, back into his life. Who'd restored meaning to his existence.

Who'd filled his heart with love again.

"Goodbye." He pivoted and strode quickly out of the house, unable to bear hearing her say it, too.

"Bye, Mom."

"See you after school, Peach." Elise waved as her daughter skipped down the sidewalk, her long, plaited hair bouncing up and down her back.

She'd had twenty-four hours already to explain to Kelsey why Cole would no longer be part of their lives. But how could you find words to make a nine-year-old understand why a man she idolized like a father simply wasn't going to be around anymore?

As she drove away from Kelsey's school, however, Elise had to admit that perhaps her search for the right words was just an excuse to postpone a difficult conversation.

Or maybe, deep down inside, Elise didn't really want to have the conversation at all.

For perhaps the hundredth time, she replayed in her mind what Cole had said to her yesterday.

Maybe one of us doesn't have *to be wrong.*

Maybe this wasn't about betrayal. Maybe it was just about having different perspectives.

I understood why a person would do absolutely anything to protect the life of someone he loves.

Did that mean . . . Cole loved her?

Sure sounded like it. He'd as much as said so, hadn't he, even if he'd kept tap-dancing around the actual word? And why would he daydream that Kelsey belonged to both of them, unless he had marriage in mind?

I wish things could have worked out between us, Elise.

She could practically hear Roz yelling inside her head. "Of *course* the man's talking about marriage, you goose!"

Elise's heart began to pound. She was approaching the corner of Saguaro Road. She could continue on home, or...

The imaginary Roz hollered one last piece of advice at her. Elise thumped her hand on the steering wheel. "All right, I'll *do* it!"

As soon as traffic allowed, she made a U-turn across the highway and headed back the way she'd come.

Cole rubbed his eyes and stared at the computer screen again.

It didn't make any difference. The correct information hadn't magically appeared while he wasn't looking. His phone rang. "Mildred, can you come in here for a minute?" he asked, not even waiting to hear what his secretary had buzzed him about. "I still can't get the hang of this darn contraption."

"You've certainly got a mental block about some things," she replied tartly. An exasperated click reverberated in Cole's ear when she hung up.

He swiveled his chair around and hunched over the computer. When he heard the door open, he said, "I just can't figure this out."

"That makes two of us" said a familiar voice. "Maybe we can figure it out together."

Cole spun his chair around so fast he nearly toppled out of it. "Elise!" He scrambled to his feet. "I was expecting...I mean, I *wasn't* expecting..."

"Your secretary was kind enough to loan me a tape measure."

"A tape meas—?" Completely bewildered, he watched Elise stroll briskly across his office. She extended the metal tape measure and held it up to the window. "Elise, uh, what exactly are you doing?"

"Measuring for curtains," she replied, letting the tape rewind with a snap. "This office is positively dreary. I think it's the duty of the sheriff's wife to brighten the place up a bit, don't you?"

Cole's jaw dropped clear to his chest. "What are you—?" He raked a hand through his hair and swallowed. "Elise, are you *proposing* to me?"

She shrugged. "That depends." And though her eyes were twinkling, Cole could read nervousness in them, too. "If I *did* propose, would you accept?"

Happiness crested inside him, like a giant wave about to hit shore. "Well, yes. Now that you mention it, I would."

Her eyes got even more sparkly. "Okay, then. Consider this an official proposal."

The wave of happiness broke over him. He was barely able to stop himself from seizing her and whirling her around in the air. He felt the world's biggest smile about to explode onto his face.

"No offense, Elise, but that was a pretty sorry excuse for a proposal. Here." He took the tape measure from her hand and set it aside. "Let me show you how it's done properly."

Roses bloomed in her cheeks. She didn't appear to be the least put out by his criticism.

Cole clasped her hands in his. "Now, first you say, I love you, darling. Will you marry me?"

Once upon a time, he would have given anything to see Elise smile at him the way she was now. Amazingly, his wish had been granted.

"I love you, darling," she repeated cooperatively. "Will you marry me?"

"Very good." Cole squeezed her hands. "And then, I say—"

"Yes!" they promised in unison.

"Elise." Cole swept her into his embrace at the same instant another crashing wave of happiness practically knocked him off his feet. He buried his face in her hair, breathing in that precious, tantalizing fragrance of wildflowers. She felt so warm, so wonderful, so completely right in his arms.

She made him feel whole.

When Cole drew back and kissed her, the joy bubbling through Elise filled her with such lightness, she thought she might float right up to the ceiling. She tightened her arms around his waist and held on for dear life.

It felt like she'd finally come home. As if, during those years in hiding, she hadn't just been running away from someone. She'd been running *to* someone.

Against all the odds, she'd found him.

Time lost all meaning for a while, so that when their lips reluctantly parted at last, Elise had no idea how long they'd been standing there kissing.

No matter. They had all the time in the world now.

Cole bent his head and brushed the tip of his nose against hers. "I can't believe how incredibly lucky I am, getting not one, but two wonderful women in one fell swoop."

"Not to mention a wonderful basset hound," she pointed out teasingly.

"My cup runneth over," he said with a grin. Then his blue eyes turned sober. "Elise, what made you change your mind? Why did you decide to forgive me?"

"Actually, I decided there was nothing to forgive," she replied, playing with one of his shirt buttons. "I realized that one of the reasons I love you is because things like duty and responsibility are important to you. What could be a more important quality for a husband and father?''

Cole brought his hand to her cheek. ''You and Kelsey mean everything in the world to me, Elise.''

Tears prickled her eyelids. ''I felt betrayed when you acted like a sheriff. But then I realized that being sheriff is part of who you are. And loving you means loving *all* of you, even the parts I'm sometimes at cross-purposes with.''

Cole touched his lips to hers, tenderly using his thumb to whisk a tear from the corner of her eye. ''The last thing I ever wanted was to put you and Kelsey in danger.''

''I know that.'' Elise took a deep breath and smiled at him. ''But it actually turned out for the best, didn't it? If you hadn't contacted the Boston authorities, Dominick would still be after us. And the three of us would never have had a chance to become a family.''

Cole hugged her. ''I love you, Elise.''

''I love you, too. And so does Kelsey.''

He loosened his arms and linked them around her waist. ''Think she'll want to take part in the wedding?''

''Kelsey? Heavens, she'll insist on it.'' Elise pressed a fingertip to her chin and sighed. ''That does pose a slight problem, though.''

He donned a worried frown. ''What?''

''Er...how would you feel about having a basset hound as best man?''

Cole hoisted his gaze toward the ceiling. ''Arf,'' he said.

*   *   *   *   *

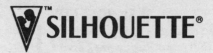

™SILHOUETTE®

Tempting... Tantalising... Terrifying!

Strangers
in the night

Three spooky love stories in one compelling
volume by three masters of the genre:

Dark Journey by Anne Stuart
Catching Dreams by Chelsea Quinn Yarbro
Beyond Twilight by Maggie Shayne

Available: July 1997   Price: £4.99

SILHOUETTE Sensation®

COMING NEXT MONTH

AT THE MIDNIGHT HOUR Alicia Scott

The Guiness Family

Elizabeth Guiness was hell-bent on reuniting the fractured family for whom she was working, but Richard Keaton, her darkly handsome boss, seemed incapable of love—especially after the murder, where he was the prime suspect... Liz couldn't resist getting involved. But it just might get her killed...

MUMMY'S HERO Audra Adams

Evan Forrester had no use for people cluttering up his life. Yet suddenly his house was overrun with females! His new neighbour's irresistible twin daughters were invading his home, corrupting his dog and demanding his attention, while their mother... Their mother made him long for so much more...

MAN WITHOUT A MEMORY Maura Seger

Heartbreakers

His past had been erased by an assassin's bullet. Lauren Walters helped the man with no name flee from his enemies because, despite all the evidence, she felt he was a man she could trust. She tried *not* to be influenced by a breathtaking desire for a man who was a stranger even to himself.

MEGAN'S MATE Nora Roberts

The Calhoun Saga

Megan O'Riley stood on the brink of a new life. She buried her passions and vowed never, ever to let her heart lead her astray again. But rugged Nathaniel Fury set his mind on Megan the day they first met and all her resistance would not divert him. How would this passionate man sway this practical woman?

COMING NEXT MONTH FROM
▼™SILHOUETTE®

Intrigue
Danger, deception and desire

GUARDED MOMENTS Cassie Miles
BULLETPROOF HEART Sheryl Lynn
EDGE OF ETERNITY Jasmine Cresswell
NO WAY OUT Tina Vasilos

Special Edition
Satisfying romances packed with emotion

MUM FOR HIRE Victoria Pade
THE FATHER NEXT DOOR Gina Wilkins
A RANCH FOR SARA Sherryl Woods
RUGRATS AND RAWHIDE Peggy Moreland
A FAMILY WEDDING Angela Benson
THE WEDDING GAMBLE Muriel Jensen

Desire
Provocative, sensual love stories for the woman of today

TALLCHIEF'S BRIDE Cait London
A BRIDE FOR ABEL GREENE Cindy Gerard
LOVERS ONLY Christine Pacheco
ROXY AND THE RICH MAN Elizabeth Bevarly
CITY GIRLS NEED NOT APPLY Rita Rainville
REBEL'S SPIRIT Susan Connell

Barbara

DELINSKY

THROUGH MY EYES

A Friend in Need...
is a whole lot of trouble!

Jill Moncrief had to face painful memories to
help a friend in trouble. Hot-shot attorney Peter
Hathaway was just the man she needed—but
the last man on earth she should want...

**AVAILABLE IN PAPERBACK
FROM JULY 1997**

ERICA SPINDLER

Bestselling Author of *Forbidden Fruit*

FORTUNE

BE CAREFUL WHAT YOU WISH FOR... IT JUST MIGHT COME TRUE

Skye Dearborn's wishes seem to be coming true, but will Skye's new life prove to be all she's dreamed of—or a nightmare she can't escape?

"A high adventure of love's triumph over twisted obsession."

—*Publishers Weekly*

"Give yourself plenty of time, and enjoy!"

—*Romantic Times*

AVAILABLE IN PAPERBACK FROM JULY 1997

JASMINE CRESSWELL

Internationally-acclaimed Bestselling Author

SECRET SINS

The rich are different—they're deadly!

Judge Victor Rodier is a powerful and dangerous man. At the age of twenty-seven, Jessica Marie Pazmany is confronted with terrifying evidence that her real name is Liliana Rodier. A threat on her life prompts Jessica to seek an appointment with her father—a meeting she may live to regret.

MIRA®

**AVAILABLE IN PAPERBACK
FROM JULY 1997**

Bureau de Change

How would you like to win a year's supply of Silhouette® books? Well you can and they're FREE! Simply complete the competition below and send it to us by 31st January 1998. The first five correct entries picked after the closing date will each win a year's subscription to the Silhouette series of their choice. What could be easier?

1.	Lira	Sweden	____
2.	Franc	U.S.A.	____
3.	Krona	Sth. Africa	____
4.	Escudo	Spain	____
5.	Deutschmark	Austria	____
6.	Schilling	Greece	____
7.	Drachma	Japan	____
8.	Dollar	India	____
9.	Rand	Portugal	4
10.	Peseta	Germany	____
11.	Yen	France	____
12.	Rupee	Italy	____

C7G

Please turn over for details of how to enter...

How to enter...

It's that time of year again when most people like to pack their suitcases and head off on holiday to relax. That usually means a visit to the Bureau de Change... Overleaf there are twelve foreign countries and twelve currencies which belong to them but unfortunately they're all in a muddle! All you have to do is match each currency to its country by putting the number of the currency on the line beside the correct country. One of them is done for you! Don't forget to fill in your name and address in the space provided below and pop this page in a envelope (you don't even need a stamp) and post it today. Hurry competition ends 31st January 1998.

Silhouette Bureau de Change Competition
FREEPOST, Croydon, Surrey, CR9 3WZ

EIRE readers send competition to PO Box 4546, Dublin 24.

Please tick the series you would like to receive if you are a winner

Sensation™ ❑ Intrigue™ ❑ Desire™ ❑ Special Edition™ ❑

Are you a Reader Service™ Subscriber?   Yes ❑   No ❑

Ms/Mrs/Miss/Mr_____

(BLOCK CAPS PLEASE)

Address_____

_____

_____ Postcode_____

(I am over 18 years of age)